A SEA OF SHIELDS

(BOOK #10 IN THE SORCERER'S RING)

MORGAN RICE

ISBN: **978-1-939416-67-4**

Books by Morgan Rice

THE SORCERER'S RING
A QUEST OF HEROES (BOOK #1)
A MARCH OF KINGS (BOOK #2)
A FEAST OF DRAGONS (BOOK #3)
A CLASH OF HONOR (BOOK #4)
A VOW OF GLORY (BOOK #5)
A CHARGE OF VALOR (BOOK #6)
A RITE OF SWORDS (BOOK #7)
A GRANT OF ARMS (BOOK #8)
A SKY OF SPELLS (BOOK #9)
A SEA OF SHIELDS (BOOK #10)
A REIGN OF STEEL (BOOK #11)

THE SURVIVAL TRILOGY
ARENA ONE (Book #1)
ARENA TWO (Book #2)

the Vampire Journals
turned (book #1)
loved (book #2)
betrayed (book #3)
destined (book #4)
desired (book #5)
betrothed (book #6)
vowed (book #7)
found (book #8)
resurrected (book #9)
craved (book #10)

Earl: "O that we now had here
But one ten thousand of those men in England…"

Henry V: "No, my fair cousin…
The fewer men, the greater share of honour.
God's will! I pray thee, wish not one man more."

--William Shakespeare
Henry V

CHAPTER ONE

Gwendolyn screamed and screamed as the pain tore her apart.

She lay on her back in the field of wildflowers, her stomach hurting her more than she imagined possible, thrashing, pushing, trying to get the baby out. A part of her wished it would all stop, that she could just reach safety before the baby came. But a bigger part of her knew the baby was coming now, whether she liked it or not.

Please, God, not now, she prayed. *Just another few hours. Just let us reach safety first.*

But it was not meant to be. Gwendolyn felt another tremendous pain rip through her body, and she leaned back and shrieked as she felt the baby turning inside her, closer to emerging. She knew there was no way she could stop it.

Instead, Gwen resorted to pushing, forcing herself to breathe as the nurses had taught her, trying to help it come out. It didn't seem to be working, though, and she moaned in agony.

Gwen sat up once again and looked around for any sign of humanity.

"HELP!" she screamed at the top of her lungs.

No answer came. Gwen was in the midst of summer fields, far away from a soul, and her scream was absorbed by the trees and the wind.

Gwen always tried to be strong, but she had to admit she was terrified. Less for herself, and more so for the baby. What if no one found them? Even if she could deliver on her own, how would she ever be able to walk out of this place with the baby? She had a sinking feeling that she and the baby would both die here.

Gwen thought back to the Netherworld, to that fateful moment with Argon when she had freed him, the choice she'd had to make. The sacrifice. The unbearable choice that had been forced upon her, having to choose between her baby and her husband. She wept now, recalling the decision she'd made. Why did life always demanded sacrifices?

Gwendolyn held her breath as the baby suddenly shifted inside her, a pain so severe it reverberated from the top of her skull down to her toes. She felt as if she were an oak tree being split in two from the inside out.

Gwendolyn arched back and groaned as she looked up to the skies, trying to imagine herself anywhere but here. She tried to hold onto something in her mind, something that would give her a sense of peace.

She thought of Thor. She saw the two of them together, when they had first met, walking through these same fields, holding hands, Krohn jumping at their feet. She tried to bring the picture to life in her mind, tried to focus on the details.

But it wasn't working. She opened her eyes with a start, the pain jolting her back to reality. She wondered how she had ever ended up here, in this place, all alone—then remembered Aberthol, telling her about her dying mother, her rushing out to see her. Was her mother dying too at this moment?

Suddenly, Gwen cried out, feeling as if she were dying, and she looked down and saw the crown of the baby's head emerging. She leaned back and shrieked as she pushed and pushed, sweating, her face bright red.

There came one final push, and suddenly, a cry pierced the air.

A baby's cry.

Suddenly, the sky blackened. Gwen looked up and watched in fear as the perfect summer day, without warning, turned to night. She watched as the two suns were suddenly eclipsed by the two moons.

A total eclipse of both suns. Gwen could hardly believe it: it only happened, she knew, once every ten thousand years.

Gwen watched in terror as she was immersed in the darkness. Suddenly, the sky filled with lightning, streaks flashing down, and Gwen felt herself pelted by small pellets of ice. She could not understand what was happening, until she finally realized it was hailing.

All of this, she knew, was a profound omen, all occurring at the precise moment of her baby's birth. She looked down at the child and knew immediately that he was more powerful than she could fathom. That he was of another realm.

As he emerged, crying, Gwen instinctively reached down and grabbed him, pulling him to her chest before he could slip into the grass and the mud, sheltering him from the hail as she wrapped her arms around him.

He wailed, and as he did, the earth began to quake. She felt the ground tremble, and in the distance, she saw boulders rolling down hillsides. She could feel the power of this child coursing through her, affecting the entire universe.

As Gwen clutched him tight, she felt weaker by the moment; she felt herself losing too much blood. She grew light-headed, too weak to move, barely strong enough to hold her baby, who would not stop wailing on her chest. She could barely feel her own legs.

Gwen had a sinking premonition that she would die here, on these fields, with this baby. She no longer cared about herself—but she could not imagine the idea of her baby dying.

"NO!" Gwen shrieked, summoning every last bit of strength she had to shout her protest up to the heavens.

As Gwen dropped her head back, lying flat on the ground, a shriek came in response. It was not a human shriek. It was that of an ancient creature.

Gwen began to lose consciousness. She looked up, her eyes closing on her, and saw what appeared to be an apparition from the skies. It was a massive beast, swooping down for her, and she realized dimly that it was a creature she loved.

Ralibar.

The last thing Gwen saw, before her eyes shut for good, was Ralibar swooping down, with his huge, glowing green eyes and his ancient red scales, his claws extended, and aiming right for her.

CHAPTER TWO

Luanda stood frozen in shock, staring down at Koovia's corpse, still holding the bloody dagger in her hand, hardly believing what she had just done.

The entire feasting hall fell silent and stared at her, amazed, no one moving an inch. They all stared at Koovia's corpse at her feet, the untouchable Koovia, the great warrior of the McCloud kingdom, second only in prowess to King McCloud, and the tension was so thick in the room it could be cut with a knife.

Luanda was the most shocked of all. She felt her palm burning, the dagger still in it, felt a heat rush over her, exhilarated and terrified at having just killed a man. She was most of all proud that she had done it, proud that she had stopped this monster before he could lay hands on her husband or on the bride. He got what he deserved. All of these McClouds were savages.

There came a sudden shout, and Luanda looked up to see Koovia's lead warrior, just a few feet away, suddenly burst into action, vengeance in his eyes, and rush for her. He raised his sword high and aimed for her chest.

Luanda was still too numb to react, and this warrior moved quickly. She braced herself, knowing that in just a moment, she would feel the cold steel pierce through her heart. But Luanda did not care. Whatever happened to her now no longer mattered, now that she had killed that man.

Luanda shut her eyes as the steel came down, ready for death—and was surprised instead to hear a sudden clang of metal.

She opened her eyes and saw Bronson stepping forward, raising his sword and blocking the warrior's blow. It surprised her; she did not think he had it in him, or that he, with his one good hand, could stop such a mighty blow. Most of all, she was touched to realize that he cared for her that much, enough to risk his own life.

Bronson deftly swung his sword around, and even with just one, he had such skill and might that he managed to stab the warrior through the heart, killing him on the spot.

Luanda could hardly believe it. Bronson had, once again, saved her life. She felt deeply indebted to him, and a fresh rush of love for him. Perhaps he was stronger than she had imagined.

Shouts erupted on both sides of the feasting hall as the McClouds and MacGils rushed for each other, anxious to see who could kill the other first. All pretenses of civility that had occurred throughout the day's wedding and the night's feast were gone. Now it was war: warrior against warrior, all heated by drink, fueled by rage, by the indignity that the McClouds had tried to perpetrate in trying to violate their bride.

Men leapt over the thick wooden table, anxious to kill each other, stabbing each other, grabbing at each other's faces, wrestling each other down to the table, knocking over food and wine. The room was so tight, packed with so many people, that it was shoulder to shoulder, with barely any room to maneuver, men grunting and stabbing and screaming and crying as the scene fell into complete, bloody chaos.

Luanda tried to collect herself. The fighting was so quick and so intense, the men filled with such bloodlust, so focused on killing each other, that no one but she took a moment to look around and observe the periphery of the room. Luanda observed it all, and she took it all in with a greater perspective. She was the only one who observed the McClouds slithering around the edges of the room, slowly barring the doors, one at a time, and then slinking out as they did.

The hairs rose on the back of her neck as Luanda suddenly realized what was happening. The McClouds were locking everyone in the room—and fleeing for a reason. She watched them grab torches off the wall, and her eyes opened wide in panic. She realized with horror that the McClouds were going to burn down the hall with everyone trapped inside—even their own clansmen.

Luanda should have known better. The McClouds were ruthless, and they would do anything in order to win.

Luanda looked about, watching it all as it was unfolding before her, and she saw one door still left unbarred.

Luanda turned, broke away from the melee, and sprinted for the remaining door, elbowing and shoving men out of her way. She saw a McCloud, too, sprinting for that door on the far side of the room, and she ran faster, lungs bursting, determined to beat him to it.

The McCloud did not see Luanda coming as he reached the door, grabbed a thick, wooden beam, and prepared to bar it. Luanda charged him from the side, raising her dagger and stabbing him in the back.

The McCloud cried out, arched his back, and dropped to the ground.

Luanda grabbed the beam, yanked it off the door, threw it open, and ran outside.

Outside, eyes adjusting to the dark, Luanda looked left and right and saw McClouds, all lining up outside the hall, all bearing torches, preparing to set it on fire. Luanda flooded with panic. She could not let it happen.

Luanda turned, sprinted back into the hall, grabbed Bronson, and yanked him away from the skirmish.

"The McClouds!" she yelled urgently. "They are preparing to burn down the hall! Help me! Get everyone out! NOW!"

Bronson, understanding, opened his eyes wide in fear, and to his credit, without hesitating, he turned, rushed to the MacGil leaders, yanked them from the fight, and yelling at them, gesticulated toward the open door. They all turned and realized, then yelled orders to their men.

To Luanda's satisfaction, she watched as the MacGil men suddenly broke away from the fight, turned, and ran for the one open door which she had saved.

While they were organizing, Luanda and Bronson wasted no time. They sprinted for the door, and she was horrified to watch another McCloud race for it, pick up the beam, and try to bar it. She did not think they could beat him to it this time.

This time, Bronson reacted; he raised his sword high overhead, leaned forward, and threw it.

It flew through the air, end over end, until finally it impaled itself in the McCloud's back.

The warrior screamed and collapsed to the ground, and Bronson rushed to the door and threw it wide open just in time.

Dozens of MacGils stormed through the open door, and Luanda and Bronson joined them. Slowly, the hall emptied of all the MacGils, the McClouds left to watch in wonder as to why their enemies were retreating.

Once all of them were outside, Luanda slammed the door, picked up the beam with several others, and barred the door from the outside, so that no McClouds could follow.

The McClouds outside began to notice, and they started to drop their torches and draw their swords instead to charge.

But Bronson and the others gave them no time. They charged the McCloud soldiers all around the structure, stabbing and killing them as they lowered their torches and fumbled with their arms. Most of the McClouds were still inside, and the few dozen outside could not stand up to the rush of the enraged MacGils, who, blood in their eyes, killed them all quickly.

Luanda stood there, Bronson by her side, beside the MacGil clansmen, all of them breathing hard, thrilled to be alive. They all looked to Luanda with respect, knowing they owed her their lives.

As they stood there, they began to hear the banging of the McClouds inside, trying to get out. The MacGils slowly turned and, unsure what to do, looked to Bronson for leadership.

"You must put down the rebellion," Luanda said forcefully. "You must treat them with the same brutality with which they intended to treat you."

Bronson looked at her, wavering, and she could see the hesitation in his eyes.

"Their plan did not work," he said. "They are trapped in there. Prisoners. We will put them under arrest."

Luanda shook her head fiercely.

"NO!" she screamed. "These men look to you for leadership. This is a brutal part of the world. We are not in King's Court. Brutality reigns here. Brutality demands respect. Those men inside cannot be left to live. An example must be set!"

Bronson bristled, horrified.

"What are you saying?" he asked. "That we shall burn them alive? That we treat them with the same butchery with which they treated us?"

Luanda locked her jaw.

"If you do not, mark my words: surely one day they will murder you."

The MacGil clansmen all gathered around, witnessing their argument, and Luanda stood there, fuming in frustration. She loved Bronson—after all, he had saved her life. And yet she hated how weak, how naïve, he could be.

Luanda had enough of men ruling, of men making bad decisions. She ached to rule herself; she knew she would be better than any of them. Sometimes, she knew, it took a woman to rule in a man's world.

Luanda, banished and marginalized her entire life, felt she could no longer sit on the sidelines. After all, it was thanks to her that all these men were alive right now. And she was a King's daughter—and firstborn, no less.

Bronson stood there, staring back, wavering, and Luanda could see he would take no action.

She could stand it no further. Luanda screamed out in frustration, rushed forward, snatched a torch from an attendant's hand, and as all the men watched her in stunned silence, she rushed before them, held the torch high, and threw it.

The torch lit up the night, flying high through the air, end over end, and landing on the peak of the thatched roof of the feasting hall.

Luanda watched with satisfaction as the flames began to spread.

The MacGils all around her let out a shout, and all of them followed her example. They each picked up a torch and threw it, and soon the flames rose up and the heat grew stronger, singeing her face, lighting up the night. Soon, the hall was alight in a great conflagration.

The screams of the McClouds trapped inside ripped through the night, and while Bronson flinched, Luanda stood there, cold, hard, merciless, hands on her hips, and took satisfaction from each one.

She turned to Bronson, who stood there, mouth open in shock.

"That," she said, defiant, "is what it means to rule."

CHAPTER THREE

Reece walked with Stara, shoulder to shoulder, their hands swaying and brushing each other, yet not holding hands. They walked through endless fields of flowers high up on the mountain range, bursting with color, with a commanding view of the Upper Isles. They walked in silence, Reece overwhelmed with conflicting emotions; he hardly knew what to say.

Reece thought back to that fateful moment when he had locked eyes with Stara at the mountain lake. He had sent his entourage away, needing time alone with her. They had been reluctant to leave the two of them alone—especially Matus, who knew too well their history—but Reece had insisted. Stara was like a magnet, pulling Reece in, and he wanted no one else around them. He needed time to catch up with her, to talk to her, to understand why she looked at him with the same look of love that he was feeling for her. To understand if all of this was real, and what was happening to them.

Reece's heart pounded as he walked, unsure where to begin, what to do next. His rational mind screamed at him to turn around and run, to get as far away from Stara as possible, to take the next ship back to the mainland and never think of her again. To go back home to the wife-to-be who was loyally waiting for him. After all, Selese loved him, and he loved Selese. And their marriage was but days away.

Reece knew it was the wise thing to do. The *right* thing to do.

But the logical part of himself was being overwhelmed by his emotions, by passions he could not control, that refused to be subservient to his rational mind. They were passions that forced him to stay here by Stara's side, to walk and walk with her through these fields. It was the uncontrollable part of himself that he had never understood, that had driven him, his entire life, to do impulsive things, to follow his heart. It had not always led him to the best decisions. But a strong, passionate streak ran through Reece, and he was not always able to control it.

As Reece walked beside Stara, he wondered if she was feeling the same way he was. The back of her hand brushed against his as she walked, and he thought he could detect a slight smile at the corner of her lips. But she was hard to read—she always had been. The very first time he'd met her, as young children, he remembered being struck, unable to move, unable to think of anything else but her for days on end. There was something about her translucent eyes, something about the way she held herself, so proud and noble, like a wolf staring back at him, that was mesmerizing.

As children, they knew that a relationship between cousins was forbidden. But it never seemed to faze them. Something existed between them, something so strong, too strong, pulling them toward each other despite whatever the world thought. They played together as children, instant best friends, choosing each other's company immediately over any of their other cousins or friends. When they visited the Upper Isles, Reece found himself spending every waking moment with her; she had reciprocated, rushing to his side, waiting by the shore for days on end until his boat arrived.

At first, they had just been best friends. But then they grew older, and one fateful night beneath the stars, it had all changed. Despite being forbidden, their friendship turned to something stronger, bigger than both of them, and neither was able to resist.

Reece would leave the Isles dreaming of her, distracted to the point of depression, facing sleepless nights for months. He would see her face every night in bed, and would wish an ocean, and a family law, did not lie between them.

Reece knew she felt the same; he had received countless letters from her, borne on the wings of an army of falcons, expressing her love for him. He had written back, though not as eloquently as she.

The day the two MacGil families had a falling out was one of the worst days of Reece's life. It was the day that Tirus's eldest son died, poisoned by the very same poison Tirus had planned for Reece's father. Nonetheless, Tirus blamed King MacGil. The rift began, and it was the day that Reece's heart—and Stara's—had died inside. His father was all-powerful, as was Stara's, and they had both been forbidden to communicate with any of the other MacGils. They never traveled back there again, and Reece had stayed up nights in anguish, wondering, dreaming, how he could see Stara again. He knew from her letters that she had felt the same.

One day her letters stopped. Reece suspected they were intercepted somehow, but he never knew for certain. He suspected his no longer reached her, either. Over time, Reece, unable to go on, had to make the painful decision to force thoughts of her from his heart, had had to learn to push them from his mind. At the oddest times Stara's face would come back to him, and he never stopped wondering what had become of her. Did she still think of him, too? Had she married someone else?

Now, this day, seeing her again brought it all back. Reece realized how fresh it all still burned in his heart, as if he'd never left her side. She was now an older, fuller, even more beautiful version of herself, if possible. She was a woman. And her gaze was even more transfixing than it had ever been. In that gaze Reece detected love, and he felt restored to see that she still held the same love for him that he had for her.

Reece wanted to think of Selese. He owed that to her. But try as he did, it was impossible.

Reece walked with Stara along the ridge of the mountain, both silent, neither quite knowing what to say. Where could one begin to fill in the space of all those lost years?

"I hear you shall marry soon," Stara said finally, breaking the silence.

Reece felt a pit in his stomach. Thinking of marrying Selese had always brought him a rush of love and excitement; but now, coming from Stara, it made him feel devastated, as if he had betrayed her.

"I'm sorry," Reece replied.

He did not know what else to say. He wanted to say: *I don't love her. I see now that it was a mistake. I want to change everything. I want to marry you instead.*

But he *did* love Selese. He had to admit that to himself. It was a different kind of love, perhaps not as intense as his love for Stara. Reece was confused. He did not know what he was thinking or feeling. Which love was stronger? Was there even such a thing as degree when it came to love? When you loved someone, didn't that mean you loved them, no matter what? How could one love be stronger?

"Do you love her?" Stara asked.

Reece breathed deep, feeling caught in an emotional storm, hardly knowing how to reply. They walked for a while, he gathering his thoughts, until he was finally able to respond.

"I do," he replied, anguished. "I cannot lie."

Reece stopped and took Stara's hand for the first time.

She stopped and turned to face him.

"But I love you, too," he added.

He saw her eyes fill with hope.

"Do you love me more?" she asked softly, hopeful.

Reece thought hard.

"I've loved you my entire life," he said, finally. "You're the only face of love I'd ever known. You are what love means to me. I love Selese. But with you...it is like you are a part of me. Like my very own self. Like something I cannot be without."

Stara smiled. She took his hand and they continued walking side by side, she swinging their slightly, a smile on her face.

"You do not know how many nights I spent missing you," she admitted, looking away. "My words were born on so many falcons' wings—only to have them removed from my father. After the rift, I could not reach you. I even tried once or twice to sneak on a ship for the mainland—and I was caught."

Reece felt overwhelmed to hear all this. He'd had no idea. He'd always wondered how Stara had felt about him after the rift. Hearing this, he felt a stronger attachment to her than ever. He knew now that it was not just he that had felt that way. He did not feel as crazy. What they had was, indeed, real.

"And I never stopped dreaming of you," Reece replied.

They finally reached the very peak of the mountain ridge, and they stopped and stood there side by side, looking out together over the Upper Isles. From this vantage point they could see forever, across the island chain to the ocean, the mist above it, the waves crashing below, Gwendolyn's hundreds of ships lined up along the rocky shores.

They stood there in silence for a very long time, holding hands, savoring the moment. Savoring being together, finally, after all these years and all these people and life events striving to keep them apart.

"Finally, we are here, together—and yet ironically, it is now that you are most bound, with your wedding days away. It seems as if there is always something destined to come between us."

"And yet I am here today," Reece replied. "Perhaps destiny is telling us something else?"

She squeezed his hand tight, and Reece squeezed hers back. As they looked out, Reece's heart pounded, and he felt more confused than he ever had in his life. Was all this meant to be? Was he meant to run into Stara here, to see her before his wedding, to prevent him from making a mistake and marrying someone else? Was destiny, after all these years, trying to bring them together after all?

Reece could not help but feel that it was so. He felt that he had run into her by some stroke of fate, perhaps to give him one last chance before his wedding.

"What the fates bring together, no man can tear apart," Stara said.

Her words sank into Reece as she looked into his eyes, mesmerizing him.

"So many events in our lifetime have tried to keep us apart from each other," Stara said. "Our clans. Our homelands. An ocean. Time…. Yet nothing has been able to keep us from each other. So many years have passed, and our love remains as strong. Is it a coincidence that you should see me before you are to marry? Fate is telling us something. It is not too late."

Reece looked at her, his heart pounding. She looked at him, her translucent eyes reflecting the sky above and the ocean below, holding so much love for him. He felt more confused than ever, and unable to think clearly.

"Perhaps I should call the wedding off," he said.

"It is not for me to tell you," she replied. "You must search your own heart."

"Right now," he said, "my heart tells me *you* are the one I love. You are the one I've always loved."

She looked back at him earnestly.

"I have never loved another," she said.

Reece could not help himself. He leaned in, and his lips met hers. He felt the world melting all around him, felt immersed in love as she kissed him back.

They held the kiss until they could no longer breathe, until Reece realized, despite everything within him protesting otherwise, that he could never wed any other but Stara.

CHAPTER FOUR

Gwendolyn stood on a golden bridge. Clutching its rail, she looked down over the edge and saw a raging river beneath her. The rapids roared with fury, rising ever higher as she watched. She could feel their spray even from here.

"Gwendolyn, my love."

Gwen turned to see Thorgrin standing on the far shore, perhaps twenty feet away, smiling, holding out a hand.

"Come to me," he pleaded. "Cross the river."

Relieved to see him, Gwen began to walk toward him—until another voice stopped her in her tracks.

"Mother," came a soft-spoken voice.

Gwen spun to see a boy standing on the opposite shore. Perhaps ten, he was tall, proud, broad-shouldered, with a noble chin, a strong jaw, and glistening gray eyes. Like his father. He wore a beautiful, shining armor, of a material she did not recognize, and had warrior's weapons around his belt. She could sense his power even from here. An unstoppable power.

"Mother, I need you," he said.

The boy reached out a hand, and Gwen started toward him.

Gwen stopped and looked back and forth between Thor and her son, each extending a hand, and she felt torn, conflicted. She did not know which way to go.

Suddenly, as she stood there, the bridge collapsed beneath her.

Gwendolyn screamed as she felt herself plunging into the rapids below.

Gwen fell into the icy water with a shock and tumbled and turned through the raging waters. She bobbed up, gasping for air, and looked back to see her son and her husband, standing on opposite shores, each holding out their hands, each needing her.

"Thorgrin!" she yelled out. Then: "My son!"

Gwen reached for them both, screaming—but she soon felt herself plummeting over the edge of a waterfall.

Gwen shrieked as she lost sight of them and dropped hundreds of feet toward sharp rocks below.

Gwendolyn woke screaming.

She looked all around, covered in a cold sweat, confused, wondering where she was.

She slowly realized she lay in a bed, in a dim castle chamber, torches flickering along the walls. She blinked several times, trying to understand what had happened, still breathing hard. Slowly, she realized it was all just a dream. A horrible dream.

Gwen's eyes adjusted, and she spotted several attendants standing about the room. She noticed Illepra and Selese standing on either side of her, running cold compresses along her arms and legs. Selese wiped her forehead gently.

"Shhh," Selese comforted. "It was just a dream, my lady."

Gwendolyn felt a hand squeeze hers, and she looked over and her heart lifted to see Thorgrin. He knelt by her bedside, holding her hand, his eyes alight with joy to see her awake.

"My love," he said. "You are okay."

Gwendolyn blinked, trying to figure out where she was, why she was in bed, what all these people were doing here. Then suddenly, as she tried to move, she felt an awful pain in her stomach—and she remembered.

"My baby!" she called out, suddenly frantic. "Where is he? Does the boy live?"

Gwen, desperate, studied the faces around her. Thor clasped her hand firmly and smiled wide, and she knew all was okay. She felt her entire life reassured by that smile.

"He lives, indeed," Thor replied. "Thanks to god. And to Ralibar. Ralibar flew you both here, just in time."

"He is perfectly healthy," Selese added.

Suddenly, a cry tore through the air, and Gwendolyn looked over to see Illepra step forward, holding the crying baby bundled in a blanket in her arms.

Gwendolyn's heart flooded with relief, and she burst into tears. She started crying hysterically, weeping at the sight of him. She was so relieved, tears of joy washed over her. The baby was alive. She was alive. They had survived. Somehow, they had made it through this terrible nightmare.

She had never felt more grateful in her life.

Illepra leaned forward and placed the baby on Gwen's chest.

Gwendolyn sat up and looked down, examining him. She felt reborn at the touch of him, the weight of him in her arms, his smell, the way he looked. She rocked him and held him tight, all swaddled up in blankets. Gwendolyn felt herself filled with waves of love for him, with gratitude. She could hardly believe it; she had a baby.

As he was placed her arms, the baby suddenly stopped crying. He became very still, and he turned, opened his eyes, and looked right at her.

Gwen felt a jolt of shock race through her body as their eyes locked. The baby had Thor's eyes—gray, sparkling eyes that seemed to come from another dimension. They stared right through her. As she stared back, Gwendolyn felt as if she had known him from another time. For all time.

In that instant, Gwen felt a stronger bond to him than she had to anyone or anything in her life. She clasped him tight, and vowed to never let him go. She would walk through fire for him.

"He has your features, my lady," Thor said to her, smiling as he leaned over and looked with her.

Gwen smiled back, crying, overwhelmed with emotion. She had never been so happy in her life. This was all she ever wanted, to be here with Thorgrin and their child.

"He has your eyes," Gwen replied.

"All that he doesn't yet have is a name," Thor said.

"Perhaps we should name him after you," Gwendolyn said to Thor.

Thor shook his head, adamant.

"No. He is his mother's child. He bears your features. A true warrior should carry the spirit of his mother, and the skills of his father. He needs both to serve him well. He will have my skills. And he should be named after you."

"Then what do you propose?" she asked.

Thor thought.

"His name should sound like yours. The son of Gwendolyn should be named...Guwayne."

Gwen smiled. She instantly loved the ring of it.

"Guwayne," she said. "I like that."

Gwen smiled wide as she held the baby tight.

"Guwayne," she said down to the child.

Guwayne turned and opened his eyes again, and as he looked right through her, she could have sworn she saw him smile. She knew he was too young for that, but she did see a flicker of something, and she felt certain that he approved of the name.

Selese leaned forward and applied a salve to Gwen's lips, and gave her something to drink, a thick, dark liquid. Gwen immediately perked up. She felt she was slowly coming back to herself.

"How long have I been here?" Gwen asked.

"You have been asleep for nearly two days, my lady," Illepra said. "Ever since the great eclipse."

Gwen closed her eyes, and she remembered. It all came rushing back to her. She remembered the eclipse, the hail, the earthquake. . . She had never seen anything like it.

"Our baby portends great omens," Thor said. "The entire kingdom witnessed the events. His birth is already spoken of, far and wide."

As Gwen clutched the boy tight, she felt a warmth spread through her, and she sensed herself how special he was. Her entire body tingled as she held him, and she knew this was no ordinary child. She wondered what sort of powers ran in his blood.

She looked over at Thor, wondering. Was this boy a druid, too?

"Have you been here all this time?" she asked Thor, realizing he had been by her side all this time and overwhelmed with gratitude toward him.

"I have, my lady. I came as soon as I heard. Aside from last night. I spent the night at the Lake of Sorrows. Praying for your recovery."

Gwen burst into tears again, unable to control her emotions. She had never felt more content in her life; holding this child made her feel complete in a way she had not thought possible.

Despite herself, Gwen flashed back to that fateful moment in the Netherworld, to the choice she had been forced to make. She squeezed Thor's hand and held the baby tight, wanting both of them close to her, wanting both of them to be with her forever.

Yet she knew that one of them would have to die. She cried and cried.

"What is wrong, my love?" Thor finally asked.

Gwen shook her head, unable to tell him.

"Do not worry," he said. "Your mother still lives. If that's why you are crying."

Gwen suddenly remembered.

"She is gravely ill," Thor added. "But there is still time yet to see her."

Gwen knew that she had to.

"I must see her," she said. "Take me to her now."

"Are you sure, my lady?" Selese asked.

"In your condition, you should not be moved," Illepra added. "Your delivery was most abnormal, and you must recover. You are lucky to be alive."

Gwen shook her head, adamant.

"I will see my mother before she dies. Take me to her. Now."

CHAPTER FIVE

Godfrey sat in the center of the long wooden table in the drinking hall, a mug of ale in each fist, singing with the large group of MacGils and McClouds, slamming his mugs on the table with the rest of them. They were all swaying back and forth, slamming their mugs to punctuate each phrase, ale spilling over the back of their hands and onto the table. But Godfrey did not care. He was deep into drink, as he had been every night this week, and he was feeling good.

On either side of him sat Akorth and Fulton, and as he looked side to side, he took satisfaction in seeing dozens of MacGils and McClouds around the table, former enemies all assembling for this drinking event he had put together. It had taken Godfrey several days of combing the Highlands to reach this point. At first, the men had been wary; but when Godfrey had rolled out the casks of ale, then the women, they started coming.

It had begun with just a few men, wary of each other, keeping to their own sides of the hall. But as Godfrey managed to pack the drinking hall, perched here on this peak of the Highlands, men began to loosen up, to interact. There was nothing, Godfrey knew, like the lure of free ale to bring men together.

What had pushed them over the edge, had made them like brothers, was when Godfrey had introduced the women. Godfrey had called upon all of his connections on both sides of the Highlands to clear out the brothels, and had paid all the women liberally. They now packed the hall with the soldiers, most sitting on a soldier's lap, and all the men were content. The well-paid women were happy, the men were happy, and the

30

entire hall rang with joy and cheer as the men stopped focusing on each other and instead focused on the drink and the women.

As the night went on, Godfrey began to overhear talk between certain MacGils and McClouds of their becoming friends, making plans to go on patrol together. It was exactly the sort of bonding that his sister had sent him here to achieve, and Godfrey felt proud of himself that he had done it. He had also enjoyed himself along the way, his cheeks rosy with too much ale. There was something, he realized, to this McCloud ale; it was stronger on this side of the Highlands, and went straight to one's head.

Godfrey knew there were many ways to strengthen an army, to bring people together, and to govern. Politics were one; government was another; enforcement of law was another. But none of these reached men's hearts. Godfrey, for all his faults, knew how to reach the common man. He *was* the common man. While he might have the nobility of the royal family, his heart had always been with the masses. He had a certain wisdom, born of the streets, that all of those knights in shining silver would never have. They were above it all. And Godfrey admired them for that. But, Godfrey realized, there was a certain advantage to being below it all, too. It gave him a different perspective on humanity—and sometimes one needed both perspectives to fully understand the people. After all, the greatest mistakes the Kings had made had always come from their being out of touch with the people.

"These McClouds know how to drink," Akorth said.

"They do not disappoint," Fulton added, as two more mugs were slid down the table before them.

"This drink is too strong," Akorth said, letting out a large belch.

"I don't miss our hometown at all," Fulton added.

31

Godfrey got shoved in the ribs, and he looked over and saw some McCloud men, swaying too hard, laughing too loud, drunk as they coddled women. These McClouds, Godfrey realized, were rougher around the edges than the MacGils. The MacGils were tough, but the McClouds—there was something to them, something a bit uncivilized. As he surveyed the room with his expert eye, Godfrey saw the McClouds holding their women a bit too tight, slamming their mugs a bit too hard, elbowing each other roughly. There was something about these men that kept Godfrey on edge, despite all the days he had spent with them. Somehow, he did not fully trust these people. And the more time he spent with them, the more he was beginning to understand why the two clans were apart. He wondered if they could ever truly be one.

The drinking reached its peak, and more mugs were being passed around, twice as many as before, and the McClouds were not slowing, as soldiers usually did at this point. Instead, they were drinking even more, way too much. Godfrey, despite himself, began to feel a bit nervous.

"Do you think men can ever drink too much?" Godfrey asked Akorth.

Akorth scoffed.

"A sacrilegious question!" he blurted.

"What's gotten into you?" Fulton asked.

But Godfrey watched closely as a McCloud, so drunk he could barely see, stumbled into a group of fellow soldiers, knocking them down with a crash.

For a second there was a pause, as the room turned to look at the group of soldiers on the floor.

But then the soldiers bounced back up, screaming and laughing and cheering, and to Godfrey's relief, the festivities continued.

"Would you say they've had enough?" Godfrey asked, beginning to wonder if this was all a bad idea.

Akorth looked at him blankly.

"Enough?" he asked. "Is there such a thing?"

Godfrey noticed that he himself was slurring his words, and his mind was not as sharp as he would have liked. Still, he was beginning to sense something turn in the room, as if something was not quite as it should be. It was all a bit too much, as if the room had lost all sense of self-restraint.

"Don't touch her!" someone suddenly screamed out. "She's mine!"

The tone of the voice was dark, dangerous, cutting through the air and making Godfrey turn.

On the far side of the hall a MacGil soldier stood, chest out, arguing with a McCloud; the McCloud reached out and snatched a woman off of the MacGil's lap, wrapping one arm around her waist and yanking her backwards.

"She *was* yours. She's mine now! Go find another!"

The MacGil's expression darkened, and he drew his sword. The distinctive sound cut through the room, making every head turn.

"I said she's *mine!*" he screamed.

His face was bright red, hair matted with sweat, and the entire room watched, riveted by the deadly tone.

Everything stopped abruptly and the room grew quiet, as both sides of the room watched, frozen. The McCloud, a large, beefy man, grimaced, took the woman, and threw her roughly to the side. She went flying into the crowd, stumbling and falling.

The McCloud clearly didn't care about the woman; it was now obvious to all that bloodshed was what he really wanted, not the woman.

The McCloud drew his own sword, and faced off.

"It will be your life for hers!" the McCloud said.

Soldiers backed away on all sides, allowing a small clearing for them to fight, and Godfrey saw everyone tensing up. He knew he had to stop this before it turned into a full-fledged war.

Godfrey jumped over the table, slipping on mugs of beer, scurried across the hall, and ran into the midst of the clearing, between the two men, holding out his palms to keep them at bay.

"Men!" he cried, slurring his words. He tried to stay focused, to make his mind think clearly, and he sincerely regretted having drunk as much as he had now.

"We're all men here!" he shouted. "We are all one people! One army! There's no need for a fight! There are plenty of women to go around! Neither of you meant it!"

Godfrey turned to MacGil, and MacGil stood there, frowning, holding his sword.

"If he apologizes, I will accept it," MacGil said.

The McCloud stood there, confused, then suddenly his expression softened, and he broke into a smile.

"Then I apologize!" the McCloud called out, holding out his left hand.

Godfrey stepped aside, and the MacGil took it warily, the two of them shaking hands.

As they did, though, suddenly the McCloud clasped the MacGil's hand, yanked him in close, raised his sword, and stabbed him right in the chest.

"I apologize," he added, "for not killing you sooner! MacGil scum!"

The MacGil fell to the ground, limp, blood pouring onto the floor.

Dead.

Godfrey stood there in shock. He was just a foot away from the soldiers, and he could not help but feel as if somehow this were all his fault. He had encouraged the MacGil to drop his guard; he was the one who had tried to broker the truce. He had been betrayed by this McCloud, made a fool of in front of all his men.

Godfrey was not thinking clearly, and fueled by drink, something inside him snapped.

In one quick motion, Godfrey bent down, snatched the dead MacGil's sword, stepped up, and stabbed the McCloud through the heart.

The McCloud stared back, eyes wide in shock, then slumped down to the ground, dead, the sword still embedded in his chest.

Godfrey looked down at his own bloody hand, and he could not believe what he had just done. It was the first time he had ever killed a man hand to hand. He never knew he had it in him.

Godfrey had not been planning to kill him; he had not even thought it through carefully. It was some deep part of himself that overcame him, some part that demanded vengeance for the injustice.

The room suddenly broke into chaos. From all sides, men screamed and attacked each other, enraged. Sounds of swords being drawn filled the room, and Godfrey felt himself shoved hard out of the way by Akorth, right before a sword just missed his head.

Another soldier—Godfrey could not remember who or why—grabbed him and threw him across the beer-lined table, and the last thing Godfrey remembered was sliding down the wooden table, his head smashing into every mug of ale, until finally he landed on the floor, banging his head, and wishing he were anywhere but here.

CHAPTER SIX

Gwendolyn, in the wheelchair, Guwayne in her arms, braced herself as the attendants opened the doors and Thor rolled her in to her mother's sick chamber. The Queen's guard bowed their heads and stepped aside, Gwen clutching the baby tighter as they entered the darkened chamber. The room was silent, stifling, airless. Torches flickered dimly on either wall. She could sense death in the air.

Guwayne, she thought. *Guwayne. Guwayne.*

She said the name silently in her head, over and over to herself, trying to focus on anything but her dying mother. As she thought it, the name brought her comfort, filled her with warmth. *Guwayne*. The miracle child. She loved this baby more than she could say.

Gwen wanted her mother to see him before she died. She wanted her mother to be proud of her, and she wanted her mother's blessing. She had to admit it. Despite their troubled past, Gwen wanted peace and resolution in their relationship before she died. She was in a fragile state right now, and the fact that she had become closer to her mother these past moons only made Gwen feel even more distraught.

Gwen felt her heart clench as the doors closed behind her. She looked about the room and saw a dozen attendants standing near her mother, people from the old guard whom she recognized, who used to watch over her father. The room was filled with people. It was a deathwatch. At her mother's side, of course, was Hafold, her dutiful servant to the end, standing guard over her, not letting anyone close, as she had all throughout her life.

As Thor wheeled Gwendolyn close to her mother's bedside, Gwen wanted to get up, to lean over her mother, to give her a hug. But her body still ached with pain, and in her condition, she was unable.

Instead, she reached out with one hand and held her mother's wrist. It was cold to the touch.

As she did, her mother, lying there unconscious, slowly opened one eye. Her mother looked surprised and pleased at the sight of Gwen, and she slowly opened both eyes, and opened her mouth to speak.

She mouthed words, but they came out as a gasp. Gwen could not understand her.

Her mother cleared her throat and waved her hand for Hafold.

Hafold immediately bent over, leaning her ear close to the Queen's mouth.

"Yes, my lady?" Hafold asked.

"Send everyone out. I want to be alone with my daughter and Thorgrin."

Hafold looked briefly at Gwen, resentfully, then replied, "As you wish, my lady."

Hafold immediately rounded everyone up and ushered them out the door; then she came back and took her position again at the Queen's side.

"Alone," the Queen repeated to Hafold, with a knowing look.

Hafold looked down, surprised, then gave Gwen a jealous look and stormed out of the room, closing the door firmly behind her.

Gwen sat there with Thor, relieved they were all gone. A heavy blanket of death hung in the air. Gwendolyn felt it—her mother would not be with her much longer.

Her mother clasped Gwen's hand, and Gwen squeezed hers. Her mother smiled, and a tear rolled down her cheek.

"I am pleased to see you," her mother said. It came out as a whisper, just audible.

Gwen felt like crying again, and she tried her hardest to be strong, to hold back her tears for her mother's sake. Yet she could not help herself; tears suddenly came pouring out, and she cried and cried.

"Mother," she said. "I'm sorry. I'm so, so sorry. For everything."

Gwen felt overcome with sorrow that they had not been closer in life. The two of them had never fully understood each other. Their personalities had always clashed, and they could never see things the same way. Gwen was sorry for their relationship, even if she was not to blame. She wished, looking back, that there was something she could have said or done to make it different. But they had just been on two sides of the spectrum with everything in their lives. And it seemed that no effort on either of their part could ever change that. They were just two very different human beings, stuck in the same family, stuck in a mother-daughter relationship. Gwen was never the daughter she'd wanted, and the Queen was never the mother Gwen had wanted. Gwen wondered why they had been meant to be together.

The Queen nodded, and Gwen could see that she understood.

"It is I who am sorry," she replied. "You are an exceptional daughter. And an exceptional Queen. A far greater Queen than I ever was. And a far greater ruler than even your father was. He would be proud. You deserved a better mother than I."

Gwen brushed back tears.

"You were a fine mother."

Her mother shook her head.

"I was a good Queen. And a devoted wife. But I was not a good mother. Not to you, at least. I think I saw too much of myself in you. And that scared me."

Gwen squeezed her hand, crying, wishing they could have more time together, wishing they could have talked like this earlier in their lives. Now that she was Queen, now that they were both older, and now that she had a child, Gwen wanted her mother here. She wanted to be able to turn to her as her advisor. Yet ironically, the time she wanted her around the most was the one time she could not have her.

"Mother, I want you to meet my child. My son. Guwayne."

The Queen's eyes opened wide in surprise, and she lifted her head on her pillows and looked down and saw, for the first time, Gwen holding Guwayne in her arms.

The Queen gasped, and she sat up more, then burst out sobbing.

"Oh, Gwendolyn," her mother said. "He is the most beautiful baby I have ever seen."

She reached out and touched Guwayne, laying her fingertips on his forehead, and as she did, she cried harder.

Her mother slowly turned and looked over at Thor.

"You will be a fine father," she said. "My former husband loved you. I have come to understand why. I was wrong about you. Forgive me. I am glad you're with Gwendolyn."

Thor nodded solemnly, reached over, and clasped the Queen's shoulder as she reached out for him.

"There is nothing to forgive," he said.

The Queen turned and looked at Gwendolyn, and her eyes hardened; Gwen saw something inside them shifting, saw the former hard Queen coming back to life.

"You face many trials now," her mother said. "I've been keeping track of all of them. I still have my people everywhere too. I fear for you."

Gwendolyn patted her hand.

"Mother, do not trouble yourself with this now. This is no time for affairs of state."

Her mother shook her head.

"It is *always* time for affairs of state. And now most of all. Funerals, do not forget, are affairs of state. They are not family events; they are political ones."

Her mother coughed for a long time, then breathed deep.

"I haven't much time, so listen to my words," she said, her voice weaker. "Take them to heart. Even if you do not wish to hear them."

Gwen leaned in closer and nodded solemnly.

"Anything, Mother."

"Do not trust Tirus. He will betray you. Do not trust his people. Those MacGils, they are not us. They are us in name only. Do not forget this."

Her mother wheezed, trying to catch her breath.

"Do not trust the McClouds, either. Do not imagine you can make peace."

Her mother wheezed, and Gwen thought about that, trying to grasp its deeper meaning.

"Keep your army strong and your defenses stronger. The more you realize that peace is an illusion, the more peace you will secure."

Her mother wheezed again, for a long time, closing her eyes, and it broke Gwen's heart to see what an effort this was for her.

On the one hand, Gwen thought that perhaps these were just the words of a dying Queen who had been jaded too long; yet on the other hand, she could not help but admit that there was some wisdom in them, perhaps wisdom that she herself did not want to acknowledge.

Her mother opened her eyes again.

"Your sister, Luanda," she whispered. "I want her at my funeral. She is my daughter. My firstborn."

Gwendolyn breathed, surprised.

"She has done terrible things, deserving of exile. But allow her this grace, just once. When they put me in the earth, I want her there. Do not refuse the request of a dying mother."

Gwendolyn sighed, torn. She wanted to please her mother. Yet she did not want to allow Luanda back, not after what she had done.

"Promise me," her mother said, clutching Gwen's hand firmly. "*Promise me.*"

Finally, Gwendolyn nodded, realizing she could not say no.

"I promise you, Mother."

Her mother sighed and nodded, satisfied, then leaned back in her pillow.

"Mother," Gwen said, clearing her throat. "I want you to give my child a blessing."

Her mother opened her eyes weakly and looked at her, then closed them and slowly shook her head.

"That baby already has every blessing a child could want. He has my blessing—but he does not need it. You will come to see, my daughter, that your child is far more powerful than you or Thorgrin or anyone who has come before, or will come since. It was all prophesied, years ago."

Her mother wheezed for a long time, and just when Gwen thought she was done, just when she was preparing to leave, her mother opened her eyes one last time.

"Do not forget what your father taught you," she said, her voice so weak she could barely talk. "Sometimes a kingdom is most at peace when it is at war."

41

CHAPTER SEVEN

Steffen galloped down the dusty road, heading east from King's Court, as he had been for days, trailed by a dozen members of the Queen's guard. Honored that the Queen had endowed him with this mission and determined to fulfill it, Steffen had been riding from town to town, accompanied by a caravan of royal carriages, each laden with gold and silver, royal coin, building supplies, corn, grain, wheat, and various provisions and building materials of every sort. The Queen was determined to bring aid to all the small villages of the Ring, to help them rebuild, too, and in Steffen, she had found a determined missionary.

Steffen had already visited many villages, had dispersed wagons full of supplies on the Queen's behalf, carefully and precisely allocating them to the villages and families most in need. He had taken pride in seeing the joy in their faces as he'd doled out supplies and allocated manpower to help rebuild the villages outlying King's Court. One village at a time, on Gwendolyn's behalf, Steffen was helping to restore faith in the power of the Queen, the power of the rebuilding of the Ring. For the first time in his life, people looked past his appearance, people treated him with respect, like a regular person. He loved the feeling. The people were starting to realize that they, too, were not forgotten under this Queen, and Steffen was thrilled to be a part of helping to spread their love and devotion to her. There was nothing he wanted more.

As fate would have it, the route the Queen had set him on was leading Steffen, after many villages, to his very own village, to the place he was raised. Steffen felt a sense of dread, a pit in his stomach, as he realized his own village was next on the list. He wanted to turn away, to do anything to avoid it.

But he knew he could not. He had vowed to Gwendolyn to fulfill his duty, and his honor was at stake—even if it entailed his going back to the very same place that occupied his nightmares. It was the place holding all the people he had known while he was raised, the people who had taken great pleasure in tormenting him, in mocking the way he was shaped. The people who had made him feel deeply ashamed of himself. Once he'd left, he'd vowed to never return, to never set eyes on his family again. Now, ironically, his mission led him here, requiring him to allocate for them whatever resources they might need on behalf of the Queen. The fates had been too cruel.

Steffen crested a hill and caught his first glimpse of his town. His stomach dropped. Just seeing it, he already thought less of himself. He was beginning to diminish, to crawl up inside, and it was a feeling he hated. He had been feeling so good, better than he ever had in his life, especially given his new position, his entourage, his answering to the Queen herself. But now, seeing this place, there came rushing back the way people used to perceive him. He hated the feeling.

Were these people still here? he wondered. Were they as cruel as they had always been? He hoped not.

If Steffen ran into his family here, what would he say to them? What would they say to him? When they saw the station he had achieved, would they be proud? He had achieved a station and rank higher than anyone in his family, or village, had ever achieved. He was one of the Queen's highest advisors, a member of the inner royal council. They would be flabbergasted to hear what he had achieved. Finally, they would have to admit they had been wrong all along about him. That he was not worthless after all.

Steffen hoped that maybe, that was how this would go. Maybe, finally, his family would admire him, and he would achieve some vindication amongst his people.

Steffen and his royal caravan pulled up to the gates to the small town, and Steffen directed them all to come to a stop.

Steffen turned and faced his men, a dozen of the Queen's royals guards, who all looked to him for direction.

"You will await me here," Steffen called out. "Outside the town gates. I don't want my people to see you yet. I want to face them alone."

"Yes, our Commander," they replied.

Steffen dismounted, wanting to walk the rest of the way, to enter the town on foot. He did not want his family to see his royal horse, or any of his royal entourage. He wanted to see how they'd react to him as he was, without seeing his station or rank. He even took off the royal markings on his new clothing, stripping them and leaving them in the saddle.

Steffen walked past the gates and into the small, ugly village he remembered, smelling of wild dogs, chickens running loose in the streets, old ladies and children chasing them. He walked past rows and rows of cottages, a few made of stone but most made of straw. The streets here were in poor shape, littered with holes and animal waste.

Nothing had changed. After all these years, nothing had changed at all.

Steffen finally reached the end of the street, turned left, and his stomach clenched as he saw his father's house. It looked the same as it always had, a small wood cottage with a sloped roof and a crooked door. The shed in the back was where Steffen had been made to sleep. The sight of it made him want to raze it.

Steffen walked up to the front door, which was open, stood at the entrance, and looked inside.

His breath was taken away as he saw his whole family there: his father and mother, all of his brothers and sisters, all of them crammed into that small cottage, as they had always been. All of them gathered around the table, as always, fighting over scraps, laughing with each other. They had never laughed with Steffen, though. Only *at* him.

They all looked older, but otherwise, just the same. He watched them all in wonder. Had he really hailed from these people?

Steffen's mother was the first to spot him. She turned, and at the sight of him she gasped, dropped her plate, smashing it on the floor.

His father turned next, then all the others, all staring back, in shock to see him again. They each wore an unpleasant expression, as if an unwelcome guest had arrived.

"So," his father said slowly, scowling, coming around the table toward him, wiping grease from his hands with a napkin in a threatening way, "you have returned after all."

Steffen remembered his father used to tie that napkin of his into a knot, wet it, and whip him with it.

"What's the matter?" his father added, a sinister smile on his face. "You couldn't make it in the big city?"

"He thought he was too good for us. And now he has to come running back to his home like a dog!" one of his brothers yelled out.

"Like a dog!" echoed one of his sisters.

Steffen was seething, breathing hard—but he forced himself to hold his tongue, to not stoop to their level. After all, these people were provincial, riddled with prejudice, the result of a life spent locked in a small town; he, though, had seen the world, and had come to know better.

His siblings—indeed, everyone in the room—laughed at him in the small cottage.

The only one not laughing, staring at him, wide-eyed, was his mother. He wondered if maybe she was the only redeemable one. He wondered if perhaps she would be happy to see him.

But she just slowly shook her head.

"Oh, Steffen," she said, "you should not have come back here. You are not a part of this family."

Her words, delivered so calmly, without malice, hurt Steffen most of all.

"He never was," his father said. "He's a beast. What are you doing here, boy? Come back for more scraps?"

Steffen did not answer. He did not have the gift of speech, of witty, quick-thinking retorts, and certainly not in an emotional situation like this. He was so flustered, he could hardly form words. There were so many things he wished to say to them all. But no words came to him.

So instead he just stood there, seething, silent.

"Cat got your tongue?" his father mocked. "Then out of my way. You're wasting my time. This is our big day, and you're not going to ruin it for us."

His father shoved Steffen out of the way as he rushed past him, stepping outside the doorway, looking both ways. The whole family waited and watched, until his father came back in, grunting, disappointed.

"Did they come yet?" his mother asked hopefully.

He shook his head.

"Don't know where they could be," his father said.

Then he turned to Steffen, angry, turning bright red.

"You get out of the door," he barked. "We're waiting for a very important man, and you're blocking the way. You're going to ruin it, aren't you, as you always ruined everything? What timing you have, to show up at a moment like this. The Queen's own commander will be arriving here any moment, to distribute food and supplies to our village. This is our moment to petition him. And look at you," his father sneered, "standing there, blocking our door. One sight of you, and he will pass our house over. He'd think we're a house of freaks."

His brothers and sisters broke into laughter.

"A house of freaks!" one of them echoed.

Steffen stood there, turning bright red himself, staring back at his father, who faced him, scowling.

Steffen, too flustered to reply, slowly turned his back, shook his head, and walked out the door.

Steffen walked out into the street, and as he did, he signaled for his men.

Suddenly, dozens of gleaming royal carriages appeared, racing through the village.

"They're coming!" screamed Steffen's father.

Steffen's entire family rushed out, running past Steffen, standing there, lining up, gaping at the wagons, at the royal guard.

The royal guard all turned and looked to Steffen.

"My lord," one of them said, "shall we distribute here or shall we carry on?"

Steffen stood there, hands on his hips, and stared back at his family.

As one, his entire family turned and, shocked beyond words, stared at Steffen. They kept looking back and forth between Steffen and the royal guard, completely flabbergasted, as if unable to comprehend what they were seeing.

Steffen walked slowly, mounted his royal horse, and sat before all the others, sitting in his gold and silver saddle, looking down on his family

"*My lord?*" his father echoed. "Is this some sort of sick joke? *You?* The royal commander?"

Steffen merely sat there, looking down his father, and shook his head.

"That is right, Father," Steffen replied. "I am the royal commander."

"It can't be," his father said. "It can't be. How could a beast be chosen to the Queen's guard?"

Suddenly, two royal guardsmen dismounted, drew their swords, and rushed for his father. They held the tips of their swords at his throat firmly, pressing hard enough that his father opened his eyes wide in fear.

"To insult the Queen's man is to insult the Queen herself," one of the men snarled at Steffen's father.

His father gulped, terrified.

"My lord, shall we have this man imprisoned?" the other asked Steffen.

Steffen surveyed his family, saw the shock in all their faces, and debated.

"Steffen!" His mom came rushing forward, clasping his legs, pleading. "Please! Do not imprison your father! And please—give us provisions. We need them!"

"You owe us!" his father snapped. "For all that I gave you, your whole life. You owe us."

"Please!" his mom pleaded. "We had no idea. We had no idea who you had become! Please don't harm your father!"

She dropped to her knees and started to weep.

Steffen merely shook his head down at these lying, deceitful, honorless people, people who had been nothing but cruel to him his entire life. Now that they realized he was somebody, they wanted something from him.

Steffen decided they did not even deserve a response from him.

He realized something else, too: his whole life he had held his family up on a pedestal. As if they were the great ones, they were the perfect ones, the successful ones, the ones he wanted to become. But now he realized the opposite was true. It had all, his entire upbringing, been a grand delusion. These were just pathetic people. Despite his shape, he was above them all. For the first time, he realized that.

He looked down at his father, at sword-point, and a part of him wanted to hurt him. But another part of him realized one final thing: they did not deserve his vengeance, either. They would have to be somebody to deserve that. And they were nobody.

He turned to his men.

"I think this village will do just fine on their own," he said.

He kicked his horse, and in a great cloud of dust they all rode out of town, Steffen determined to never return to this place again.

CHAPTER EIGHT

The attendants threw open the ancient oak doors, and Reece hurried out of the nasty weather, wet from the driving wind and rain of the Upper Isles, and into the dry refuge of Srog's fort. He was immediately relieved to be dry as the doors slammed behind him, wiping water from his hair and face, and he looked up to see Srog hurrying over to give him a hug.

Reece embraced him back. He had always had a warm spot for this great warrior and leader, this man who had led Silesia so well, who had been loyal to Reece's father, and even more loyal to his sister. Seeing Srog, with his stiff beard, broad shoulders, and friendly smile, brought back memories of his father, of the old guard.

Srog leaned back and clasped a beefy hand on Reece's shoulder.

"You resemble your father too much as you grow older," he said warmly.

Reece smiled.

"I hope that's a good thing."

"It is indeed," Srog replied. "There was no finer man. I would have walked through fire for him."

Srog turned and led Reece through the hall, all of his men falling in behind them as they wound their way through the fort.

"You are a most welcome face to see here in this miserable place," Srog said. "I am grateful to your sister for sending you."

"It seems I have chosen a bad day to visit," Reece said as they passed an open-air window, rain lashing a few feet away.

Srog smirked.

"Every day is a bad day here," he answered. "Yet it can also change on a dime. They say the Upper Islands experience all four seasons in a single day—and I have come to see that it is true."

Reece looked outside at a small, empty castle courtyard, populated with a handful of ancient stone buildings, gray, ancient, which looked like they blended into the rain. Few people were outside, and those that were lowered their heads against the wind and hurried from one place to the next. This island seemed to be a lonely and desolate place.

"Where are all the people?" Reece asked.

Srog sighed.

"The Upper Islanders stay indoors. They keep to themselves. They are spread out. This place is not like Silesia, or King's Court. Here, they live all over the island. They do not congregate in cities. They are an odd, reclusive people. Stubborn and hardened—like the weather."

Srog led Reece down a corridor and they turned a corner and entered the Great Hall.

In the room sat a dozen of Srog's men, soldiers with their boots and armor on, glumly sitting around a table near a fire. Dogs slept around the fire, and the men ate hunks of meat and threw the scraps to the dogs. They looked up at Reece and grunted.

Srog led Reece to the fire. Reece rubbed his hands before the flames, grateful for its warmth.

"I know you haven't much time before your ship departs," Srog said. "But I at least wanted to send you off with some warmth and dry clothes."

An attendant approached and handed Reece a set of dry clothes and mail, exactly his size. Reece looked at Srog with surprise and gratitude as he peeled off his wet clothes and replaced them with these.

Srog smiled. "We treat our own well here," he said. "I figured you'd need it, given this place."

"Thank you," Reece said, already feeling much warmer. "I've never needed it more." He had been dreading sailing back in wet clothes, and this was exactly what he'd needed.

Srog began talking politics, a long monologue, and Reece nodded politely, pretending to listen. But deep down, Reece was distracted. He was still overwhelmed with thoughts of Stara, and he could not shake her from his mind. He could not stop thinking of their encounter, and every time he thought of her, his heart fluttered with excitement.

He also could not stop thinking, with dread, of the task that lay ahead of him on the mainland, of telling Selese—and everyone else—that the wedding was off. He did not want to hurt her. But he did not see what choice he had.

"Reece?" Srog repeated.

Reece blinked and looked over at him.

"Did you hear me?" Srog asked.

"I'm sorry," Reece said. "What was that?"

"I said, I take it your sister has received my dispatches?" Srog asked.

Reece nodded, trying to focus.

"Indeed," Reece replied. "Which is why she sent me here. She asked me to check in with you, to hear firsthand what was happening."

Srog sighed, staring into the flames.

"I've been here six moons now," he said, "and I can tell you, the Upper Islanders are not like us. They are MacGils in name only. They lack the qualities of your father. They are not just stubborn—they are not to be trusted. They sabotage the Queen's ships daily; in fact, they sabotage everything we do here. They don't want us here. They don't want any part of the mainland—unless they are invading it, of course. To live in harmony, I have concluded, is just not their way."

Srog sighed.

"We waste our time here. Your sister should withdraw. Leave them to their own fate."

Reece nodded, listening, rubbing his hands before the fire, when suddenly, the sun broke free from the clouds, and the dark, wet weather morphed to a clear, shining summer day. A distant horn sounded.

"Your ship!" Srog cried out. "We must go. You must set sail before the weather returns. I will see you off."

Srog led Reece out a side door in the fort, and Reece was amazed as he squinted in the bright sunlight. It was as if the perfect summer day had returned again.

Reece and Srog walked quickly, side by side, followed by several of Srog's men, rocks crunching beneath their boots as they navigated the hills and made their way down winding trails toward the distant shore below. They passed gray boulders and rock-lined hills and cliffs peppered with goats that clung to the hillsides and chewed at weeds. As they neared the shore, all around them bells tolled from the water, warning ships of lifting fog.

"I can see firsthand the conditions you are dealing with," Reece finally said as they walked. "They are not easy. You have held things together here for far longer than others would have, I'm sure. You have done well here. I will be sure to tell the Queen."

Srog nodded back in appreciation.

"I appreciate your saying that," he said.

"What is the source of this people's discontent?" Reece asked. "They are free, after all. We mean them no harm—in fact, we bring them supplies and protection."

Srog shook his head.

"They will not rest until Tirus is free. They consider it a personal shame on them that their leader is imprisoned."

"Yet they are lucky he only sits in prison, and has not been executed for his betrayals."

Srog nodded.

"True. But these people do not understand that."

"And if we freed him?" Reece asked. "Would that set them at peace?"

Srog shook his head.

"I doubt it. I believe that would only embolden them for some other discontent."

"Then what is to be done?" Reece asked.

Srog sighed.

"Abandon this place," he said. "And as quickly as possible. I don't like what I see. I sense a revolt stirring."

"Yet we vastly outnumber them in men and ships."

Srog shook his head.

"That is all but an illusion," he said. "They are well organized. We are on their ground. They have a million subtle ways of sabotage we cannot anticipate. We are sitting here in a den of snakes."

"Not Matus, though," Reece said.

"True," Srog replied. "But he is the only one."

There is one other, Reece thought. Stara. But he kept his thoughts close to himself. Hearing all of this made him want to rescue Stara, to take her out of this place as quickly as possible. He vowed that he would. But first he needed to sail back and settle his affairs. Then he could return for her.

As they stepped onto the sand, Reece looked up and saw the ship before him, his men waiting.

He stopped before it, and Srog turned to him and clasped his shoulder warmly.

"I will share all of this with Gwendolyn," Reece said. "I will tell her your concerns. Yet I know she is determined with these isles. She views them as part of a greater strategy for the Ring.

For now, at least, you must keep harmony here. Whatever it takes. What do you need? More ships? More men?"

Srog shook his head.

"All the men and ships in the world will not change these Upper Islanders. The only thing that will is the edge of the sword."

Reece looked back, horrified.

"Gwendolyn would never slaughter innocents," Reece said.

"I know that," Srog replied. "Which is why, I suspect, many of our men will die."

CHAPTER NINE

Stara stood on the parapets of her mother's fort, a square stone fortress as ancient as the island, the place in which Stara had lived ever since her mother had died. Stara walked to the edge, grateful that the sun had finally broken free on this dramatic day, and looked out to the horizon, with unusually nice visibility, and watched Reece's ship set sail in the distance. She watched his ship parting from the fleet, watched for as long as she possibly could as his boat drifted for the horizon, each lapping wave taking him farther and farther from her.

She could watch Reece's ship all day, knowing he was on it. She couldn't stand to see it go. She felt as if a part of her heart, a part of herself, were leaving the island.

Finally, after all these years in this lonely, awful, barren island, Stara felt overwhelmed with joy. Her meeting with Reece had made her feel alive again. It had restored an emptiness within her that she hadn't even realized had been gnawing away at her all these years. Now that she knew that Reece would call off the wedding, that he would return for her, that the two of them would be wed, finally together forever, Stara felt that everything was going to be okay in the world. All the misery that she had put up with in her life would be worth it.

Of course, she had to admit, there was a small part of her that felt bad for Selese. Stara never wanted to hurt anyone else's feelings. Yet at the same time, Stara also felt that her life was at stake, her future, her husband—and she also felt that it was only fair. After all, she, Stara, had known Reece her entire life, since they were kids. It was she who had been Reece's first and only love. This new girl, Selese, barely knew Reece, and only for a short while. She certainly could not know him like Stara did.

Selese, Stara figured, would eventually get over it and find someone else. But Stara, if she lost him, would never get over it. Reece was her life. Her destiny. They were meant to be, they had been their whole lives. Reece was her man first, and if anything, the way she saw it, Selese was taking him away from her, and not the other way around. Stara was only taking back what was rightfully hers.

Regardless, Stara could not have made a different decision if she'd tried. Whatever her rational mind would have told her was right or wrong, she could not listen. Her whole life, everyone around her—and her own rational mind—had also told her it was wrong for cousins to be together. And even then, she could not listen. She absolutely loved and adored Reece. She always had. And nothing anyone would say or do could change that. She *had* to be with him. There was no other option in life.

As Stara stood there looking out, watching his ship become smaller on the horizon, she heard sudden footsteps, someone else on the fort's roof, and she turned to see her brother, Matus, walking quickly toward her. She was pleased to see him, as always. Stara and Matus had practically been best friends their entire life. They had been outcasts from the rest of their family, from the rest of the Upper Islanders, Stara and Matus both despising their siblings, and their father. Stara thought of Matus and herself as being more refined, more noble, than the others; she saw her other family members as being treacherous, untrustworthy. It was as if she and Matus had their own little family within the family.

Stara and Matus lived here on separate floors in their mother's fort, apart from the others, who lived in Tirus's castle. Now that their father was in prison, their family was divided. Her other two brothers, Karus and Falus, blamed them. She could always trust Matus to have her back, though, and she was always there for him, too.

The two of them talked long and often of leaving the Upper Isles for the mainland, joining the other MacGils. And now, finally, all of that talk was beginning to feel like it might become a reality, especially with all the sabotage the Upper Islanders had been inflicting on Gwendolyn's fleet. Stara could not stand the thought of living here any longer.

"My brother," Stara greeted him, in a happy mood.

But Matus's expression was unusually darkened, and she could see immediately that he was troubled by something.

"What is it?" she asked. "What's wrong?"

He shook his head disapprovingly at her.

"I think you know what's wrong, my sister," he said. "Our cousin. Reece. What has happened between you two?"

Stara reddened and turned her back on Matus, looking back out at the ocean. She strained to see Reece's ship in the distance, but it was already gone. A wave of anger rushed over her; she had missed the last glimpse of him.

"It is not your business," she snapped.

Matus had always been disapproving of her relationship with her cousin, and she'd had enough. It was the one point of contention between them, and it threatened to drive them apart. She did not care what Matus—or anyone else—thought. It was none of their business, as far as she was concerned.

"You know he is set to marry, don't you?" Matus asked her, accusing, coming up beside her.

Stara shook her head, as if to push the awful thought from her mind.

"He will not marry her," she answered.

Matus looked surprised.

"And how do you know that?" he pressed.

She turned to him, determined.

"He told me. And Reece does not lie."

Matus stared back, shocked. Then his expression darkened.

"Did you get him to change his mind then?"

She stared back, defiant, now angry herself.

"I did not need to convince him of anything," she said. "It was what he wanted. What he chose. He loves me. He always has. And I love him."

Matus frowned.

"And are you okay then to destroy this girl's heart? Whoever she is?"

She scowled, not wanting to hear this.

"Reece loved me far longer than he loved this new girl."

Matus would not relent.

"And what of all the carefully laid plans of the kingdom? You do realize that this is not just a wedding. It is political theater. A spectacle for the masses. Gwendolyn is Queen, and it is her wedding, too. The entire kingdom, and distant lands, will be there to watch. What will happen when Reece cancels? Do you think it will be taken lightly by the Queen? By all the MacGils? You will throw the entire Ring in disarray. You will set them all against us. Are your passions worth that much?"

Stara stared back at Matus, cold, hardening.

"Our love is stronger than any spectacle. Than any kingdom. You would not understand. You have never had love like ours."

Now Matus reddened. He shook his head, clearly furious.

"You are making the gravest mistake of your life," he said. "And of Reece's. You are going to bring down everyone with you. Yours is a foolish, childish, selfish decision. Your childish love should stay in the past."

Matus sighed, exasperated.

"You will pen a missive and send it on the next falcon to Reece. You will tell him you've changed your mind. You will instruct him to marry this girl. Whoever she is."

Stara felt herself swell with anger toward her brother, an anger stronger than she'd ever felt.

"You speak out of line," she said. "Do not pretend to give me counsel. You are not my father. You are my brother. Speak to me of this once more, and you shall never speak to me again."

Matus stared back, clearly stunned. Stara had never spoken to him that way before. And she meant it. Her feelings for Reece ran much deeper than her bond with her brother. Much deeper than anything in her life.

Matus, shocked and hurt, finally turned and stormed off the roof.

Stara turned and looked back out at the sea, hoping for any sign of Reece's ship. But she knew it was long gone.

Reece, she thought. *I love you. Stay the course. Whatever obstacles you face, stay the course. Be strong. Call off the wedding. Do it for me. For us.*

Stara closed her eyes and clenched her hands, and begged and prayed to every god she knew that Reece would have the strength to follow through. To come back for her. That the two of them would finally be together forever.

No matter what it took.

CHAPTER TEN

Karus and Falus, Tirus's two sons, walked quickly down the spiral stone staircase, descending deeper and deeper, heading toward the dungeon that held their father. They hated the indignity of having to descend to this place to see their father, a great warrior who had been rightful King of the Upper Isles. And they silently vowed revenge.

Yet this time, they brought news, news which could change everything. News which finally gave them cause for hope.

Karus and Falus marched right up to the soldiers standing guard at the entrance to the prison, men loyal, they knew, to the Queen. They stopped in their tracks, reddening, hating having to suffer the humiliation of needing to ask permission to see their father.

Gwendolyn's men surveyed them, as if debating, then nodded to each other and stepped forward.

"Hold your arms out," they commanded Karus and Falus.

Karus and Falus did so, bristling as the soldiers stripped them of their arms.

They then unlocked the iron gates, opened them slowly, and let them in, closing and slamming and locking the gates behind them.

Karus and Falus knew their time was short; they would only be allowed to visit their father for a few minutes, as they had, once a week, ever since he had been imprisoned. After that, Gwendolyn's men would command them to leave.

They walked to the end of the long dungeon corridor, all the cells empty, their father the only one down here in this ancient prison. Finally, they reached the last cell on the left, lit dimly by a flickering torch against the wall, and they turned to the bars and peered inside, searching for their father.

Slowly, Tirus emerged from the dark corners of the cell and came to the bars. He stared back, his face gaunt, his beard untended, grim. He stared back with the hopeless expression of a man who knew he would never see daylight again.

Karus's and Falus's hearts broke to witness it. It made them resolve even more to find a way to free him, and to get vengeance on Gwendolyn.

"Father," Falus said, hopefully.

"We bring urgent news," Karus said.

Tirus stared back at them, a flicker of hope at their tone.

"Out with it, then," he growled.

Falus cleared his throat.

"Our sister, it seems, has fallen in love again with our cousin, Reece. Our spies tell us the two plan to marry. Reece intends to call off his wedding on the mainland, and to marry Stara instead."

"We must find a way to stop it," Karus said, indignant.

Tirus stared back, expressionless, but they could see his eyes darting, taking it all in.

"Must we?" Tirus said slowly. "And why is that?"

They looked back at their father, confused.

"Why?" Karus asked. "We cannot have our family merge with Reece's. It would play right into the Queen's hand. Our families would merge, and she would gain complete control."

"It would remove any ounce of independence our people still have," Falus chimed in.

"The plans are already in motion," Karus added. "And we must find a way to stop them."

They waited for a response, but Tirus slowly shook his head.

"Stupid, stupid boys," he said slowly, his voice dark, shaking his head again and again. "Why did I raise such stupid boys? Have I taught you nothing all these years? You still look at what's in front of you, and not what's beyond."

"We do not understand, Father."

Tirus grimaced.

"And that is why I am in this position. That is why you are not ruling now. Stopping this union would be the stupidest thing you've ever done, and the worst thing that could happen to our island. If our Stara marries Reece, that would be the greatest thing that could ever happen for all of us."

They looked back, confused, not understanding.

"Greatest? How so?"

Tirus sighed, impatient.

"If our two families merge, Gwendolyn cannot keep me imprisoned here. She would have no choice but to set me free. It would change everything. It would not strip us of power—it would give us power. We would be legitimate MacGils, on the same footing as those on the mainland. Gwendolyn would be beholden to us. Don't you see?" he asked. "A child of Reece and Stara would be as much our child as theirs."

"But Father, it is not natural. They are cousins."

Tirus shook his head.

"Politics are not natural, my son. But this union will happen," he insisted, determination in his voice. "And you two will do everything in your power to make it happen."

Karus cleared his throat, nervous, uncertain now.

"But Reece has already sailed for the mainland," he said. "It is too late. Reece, we hear, has already made up his mind."

Tirus reached up and smacked the iron bars, as if wishing to smack Karus's face, and Karus jumped back, startled.

"You are even stupider than I thought," Tirus said. "You will make certain it happens. Men have changed their minds over lesser things than this. And you will make certain that Reece changes his mind."

"How?" Falus asked.

Tirus stood there thinking, stroking his beard for a long while. For the first time in many moons, his eyes were working, darting, thinking, formulating a plan. For the first time, there was hope and optimism in his eyes.

"This girl, Selese, the one he is about to marry," Tirus said finally. "She must be gotten to. You will find her. You will bring evidence…evidence of Reece and Stara's love. You will tell her firsthand, before he reaches her. You will be sure that she knows that Reece is in love with someone else. That way, in case Reece changes his mind before he reaches her, it will be too late. We will be assured of their breakup."

"But what evidence do we have of their love?" Karus asked.

Tirus rubbed his beard, thinking. Finally, he perked up.

"Do you remember those scrolls? The ones we intercepted when Stara was young? The love letters she penned to Reece? The letters he penned back to her?"

Karus and Falus nodded.

"Yes," Falus said. "We intercepted the falcons."

Tirus nodded.

"They remain in my castle. Bring them to her. Tell her they are recent, and make it convincing. She will never guess their age—and all will be finished."

Karus and Falus finally nodded, smiling, realizing the depth of their father's cunning and wisdom.

Tirus smiled back, for the first time in as long as they could remember.

"Our island will rise again."

CHAPTER ELEVEN

Thor sat atop his horse, leading it up and down the lines of Legion recruits, all of the eager boys lined up, standing at attention before him in the Legion's new arena.

Thor looked out at the dozens and dozens of new faces, examined each one carefully, and felt the weight of responsibility. New recruits had poured in from all over the Ring, all eager to join the newly rebuilt Legion. It was a daunting task to choose the next crop of warriors, the men upon whom the Ring would rely in the coming years.

A part of Thorgrin felt that he did not deserve to be here; after all, it was not so many moons ago that he himself was hoping to be picked by the Legion. As he thought back on it, it felt like a lifetime ago, before he'd met Gwen, before he'd had a child, before he'd become a warrior. Now here he was, tasked to rebuild it, to find replacements for all the brave souls that had been killed defending the Ring.

As Thor looked out past the boys, he saw the graveyard he'd had erected, all the markers rising from the earth shining in the late afternoon suns, reminding them always of the Legion they had known. It had been Thor's idea to bury them here, on the periphery of the new arena, so that they could always be with them, always be remembered, and watch over the new recruits. Thor could feel their spirits hovering over him, helping him, urging him on.

Knowing that his Legion brothers, Reece and Conven and Elden and O'Connor, were all spread throughout the Ring on various tasks, Thor felt comfortable, at least, that he was the one who remained here, close to home, to focus on this task. He'd also been Captain of the Legion, so it felt almost natural he should be the one tasked with rebuilding it.

Thor looked at the dozens of boys before him, and he had high hopes for some, but not for others. They did their best to stand at attention as he came close, and he could tell that some of them were just not warriors; others could be, yet they would need much training. There was an untested look in all their eyes, a look of anxiety, of fear of what was to come.

"Men!" Thor called out. "Because you are all *men* now, regardless of your age. The day you take up arms to defend your homeland, to risk your life with your brothers, you become a man. If you join the Legion, you will fight for honor, valor. That is what forms a man, not your age. Is that understood?"

"YES SIR!" they all screamed back.

"I have fought with men twice my age who have died beside me," Thor continued. "Being older did not make them any more of a man than I. Nor did it make them better warriors. You become a man by taking on manly duties; and you become a better warrior by bettering yourselves."

"YES SIR!"

Thor guided his horse slowly up and down the ranks, observing, weighing each recruit, looking them in the eye.

"A spot in the Legion is a sacred thing. There is no greater honor the Ring can bestow. It will be handed to no one. It is more than position. It is a code. A code of brotherhood. Once you join it, you no longer live to defend yourself. You live to defend your brothers."

"YES SIR!"

Thor dismounted. He walked slowly, turned and looked out to the field behind him, the newly rebuilt arena.

"There, in the distance, lie a dozen targets. Before you, spears lie on the ground. There is one spear for each of you. You have one chance to hit the target. Show me what you have," Thor said, walking off to the side, watching.

The boys rushed forward, each racing to grab one of the spears lodged in the ground. Excited, each one hurled his spear, each wanting to be first to hit the target of hay about thirty yards away.

Thor watched their technique with a professional eye. He was not surprised to see that nearly all of them missed.

Only a small handful of boys managed to hit their targets. And none of these hit the center.

Thor shook his head slowly. This would be a long and painful process, he knew. He wondered if he would ever find boys skilled enough to fill the shoes of the others. He had to remind himself what he and his brothers were like on their first day.

"Grab your spears, come back, and try again."

"YES SIR!"

They sprinted across the arena, heading for the spears, and as Thor watched, a voice startled him:

"Thorgrin."

Thor looked over and saw the face of a boy he dimly recognized, a boy who looked back at him with hope.

"Do you remember me?"

Thor squinted, trying to put a name to the face.

"I remember you," the boy said. "You saved my life. You may have forgotten, but it was something I will never forget."

Thor narrowed his eyes, beginning to remember.

"Where was it?" Thor asked.

"We met in the dungeon," the boy said. "You had been accused of killing King MacGil. I was there on charges of thievery. You saved my hand from dismemberment. It is a kindness I will never forget."

Thor suddenly remembered it all.

"Merek!" Thor said. "The thief!"

Merek nodded and smiled. He extended his hand, and Thor shook it.

"I have come to repay the favor," Merek said. "I heard you're recruiting for the Legion, and I want to volunteer."

Thor looked at him in surprise.

"I thought you are a thief?" Thor asked.

Merek smiled back.

"And what better skill could you want for the Legion? After all, to win battle is to steal men's weapons, to steal men's courage. A thief is quick and bold, willing to go where others will not, cunning, fearless. A thief takes what others want. He does not ask permission. And he does not hesitate. Aren't these the traits of victory?"

Thor examined him carefully, thinking it over.

"You have a way with words," Thor said. "I will give you that. And you have thought this through. But you are missing something. The most important thing, in fact, that a thief lacks. Honor. At the heart and soul of a warrior is honor. And it is honor that a thief lacks."

Thor sighed.

"You might be the best warrior here," Thor said. "But I cannot allow a stain upon our honor."

Thor turned away, but Merek placed a hand on his shoulder.

"Please," Merek said. "Give me one chance. I realize my ways have been dishonorable. Yet times were desperate for my family, and I had no choice if I was to support them. Surely I cannot be blamed for that. It is easy to speak of honor when one has the luxury of sitting in a tower and looking down on others who have nothing. No one handed me anything in life. I had to take what was mine."

Thor grimaced.

"No one handed me anything in life, either," he countered. "Yet I never stole from anyone."

Merek swallowed, desperate.

"Which is why I'm asking for forgiveness," Merek said. "And vowing to change my ways."

Thor looked at him.

"That's right," Merek said. "I vow to never steal from anyone again if you accept me into your Legion. I've come here not to steal. I've come here because I want a better life. I want to leave my old life behind. I want to become a better person."

Thor looked him over, debating. He remembered when he himself pleaded for a spot, for just one chance, whether he deserved it or not.

"You are very determined," Thor said. "And you seem sincere. And I suppose you are correct in that everyone makes mistakes, and everyone deserves a second chance." Thor nodded. "I will give you that chance. You may try out. Abuse it, and I assure you I will kick you out of our arena."

Merek smiled wide and clasped Thor on the shoulder.

"Thank you!" he said. "Thank you, thank you!"

Thor smiled back.

"Now go and grab a spear with the others, and let's see what you can do."

Merek, jubilant, ran off into the group of boys and grabbed a spear.

Merek was the last one to throw, and Thor watched with interest as Merek's spear sailed through the air and hit the target perfectly.

A bull's-eye.

All the other boys looked to him in shock, and Thor stared back at him in wonder. He was shocked, too. And impressed.

"Again!" Thor called out, wanting to see if it was a fluke, and if the other boys could get closer.

The boys ran off to retrieve their spears again, and as they did, Thor turned as a lone boy walked through the Legion training ground gates, and right up to him. Thor recognized this boy, too, standing there with his face and clothes covered in dirt, but from where, he could not remember.

The boy stared back.

"I've come to try out for your Legion, as you invited me."

Thor studied the boy, younger and smaller than the others, and tried to place him.

"I invited you?" Thor asked.

"You told me I could try out. Don't you remember? In the Empire. In my father's cottage. I saved your group from the monsters of the jungle. I've crossed the ocean to find you. I know I'm young. And small. But let me try, with the others."

Thor stared back, dumbfounded, it all coming back to him.

"Ario?" Thor asked.

Ario nodded.

Thor was in shock; he could hardly believe this boy had crossed the world to come here. That said more to Thor than just about anything. He remembered the boy in the Empire as being agile, fearless, attuned to every noise in the jungle. And he recalled him saving them from that Gathorbeast. If it weren't for him, they'd all be dead.

Yet, at the same time, Ario seemed so small, so young.

Thor kept one eye on the large group of boys, who had just finished hurling another round of spears. They all came closer this time, many more hitting targets, and Thor began to feel some hope.

"Bows and arrows!" Thor called out.

All the boys turned and ran to the long stretch of bows and arrows lined up along the side of the grounds, and all took aim for the distant targets.

One at a time, they fired, and Thor shook his head as too many of them missed.

Thor looked over at Ario, still standing there.

"I do remember," he said. "And we do owe you our lives. Yet you are so young. And small. I fear you would get hurt, boy. I asked you to come back when you are older—and you are hardly older. I am sorry you crossed the ocean. But I don't want to see you get hurt."

Ario frowned.

"I am more capable than any of these other boys!" he yelled, determined.

Thor smiled.

"Are you?"

Thor nodded to the bows.

"Is your aim more true than the others, then?"

Ario smiled back.

"Give me a chance."

Thor sighed.

"Okay," he said, giving in. "One chance."

Ario rushed forward, grabbed a bow, set an arrow, and fired, barely pausing to take aim.

Thor watched as the arrow sailed through the air, past the target, and realized the boy had chosen the farthest target on the field—and hit it perfectly.

Thor looked back at the boy, mouth agape. He had never seen such a fine shot.

"How did you do that?" Thor asked.

The boy shrugged.

"In the jungle, you learn to fire. It is a way of life. With these other boys, it's training. With me, it's survival."

Thor nodded back approvingly.

"You have proved me wrong," he said. "Join the others."

Ario smiled wide.

"Thank you, sire," he said, elated. "I shall not let you down!"

Ario ran off and joined the others.

"Retrieve your arrows and fire again!" Thor boomed out, and they all broke into action.

"Thorgrin!"

Thor turned, recognizing the voice, and was surprised to see Erec and Kendrick standing there in their armor, facing him earnestly.

"Can you leave the Legion affairs for a few moments?" they asked. "We have business. Join us. We have an important matter to discuss with you."

Thor wondered what the matter could be; they had never pulled him aside before.

Thor glanced back over his shoulder at the boys.

"Do not worry," Kendrick said. "You will return to them shortly."

Thor turned to the boys.

"Men, keep on firing!" he boomed out. "And don't stop until I return."

Thor turned and walked off with Kendrick and Erec, his heart pounding in suspense as he wondered where on earth these two men, whom he respected more than any men on earth, could be leading him.

CHAPTER TWELVE

Thor followed Erec and Kendrick as they led him through a meandering path in the forest, wondering where they were leading him. Thor knew that Kendrick and Erec were busy with their work with the Silver, and he wondered if something had gone wrong, if they needed his help somehow.

Kendrick, usually talkative, had hardly said a word to Thor, deepening the mystery as they all walked. He and Erec would not say where they were going, which was unlike them, too. In the time Thor had come to know them, Erec and Kendrick had taken Thor in as if he were a brother, treating him with respect. He did not understand what this was about. Was it a reprimand? Did he do something wrong while rebuilding the Legion? Had they decided to choose someone else?

Kendrick finally cleared his throat.

"Before you wed my sister," Kendrick finally said, walking beside Thor, "something very important must happen. My sister has found, in you, a man worthy of her status. And now you must have a rank worthy of your own."

Thor looked back, puzzled, still not understanding.

A forest clearing opened up before them, and Thor was surprised to see a dozen members of the Silver standing there, waiting to greet him in their shiny armor that reflected the afternoon suns. They were all expressionless, and Thor's sense of apprehension deepened. What could it be? Were they somehow upset with him that Andronicus had been his father?

Deepening Thor's confusion, standing amongst them was Aberthol, along with several members of the Queen's high council. Most surprising of all, standing amongst them was Argon, who stared at Thor with great intensity, his eyes shining, as he clutched his staff.

Thor could not help but wonder if he were on trial for something.

"Have I done something wrong?" Thor asked Erec and Kendrick as they came up beside him.

Kendrick shook his head.

"On the contrary," he replied. "You have been a true and noble warrior from the day you arrived at King's Court. You have defended our homeland selflessly. You have fought off the Empire, and brought us dragons. You have restored the Shield and returned the Destiny Sword. And all this in just so many moons."

Erec stepped forward and placed a hand on Thor's shoulder.

"Thorgrin, it is past time for you to have title and rank befitting who you are. You are no longer a mere boy. You are no longer a mere Legion member."

Erec studied him, and Thor's heart pounded as he wondered what was happening.

"Thorgrin," Kendrick said, "it is time for you to join our ranks. It is time for you to join our Ring's most elite fighting force. It is time for you to join the Silver."

Thor stood there, staring back, hardly able to think straight, the words ringing in his ears. The Silver. This was not what he'd expected—not what he had *ever* expected. It was honor reserved for the King's most elite, for sons of nobles, sons of kings, legendary, lifelong warriors. The greatest warriors who had ever served the Ring. It was an honor most people only dreamed of, an honor that Thor could hardly fathom, and one he had never expected to be given in his lifetime.

As he stood there, facing them, words stuck in his throat. He did not know what to say.

"The Silver?" Thor repeated. "Me?"

Erec and Kendrick smiled, nodded back.

If it were not for all these great men standing here in this forest clearing, before this lake, Thor would have thought this was all a joke.

But he could tell by the gravity of all their expressions that this was no joke.

Thor stared back at all the men, and he had never felt more accepted, more honored, in his life. There was no greater privilege he could dream of than to be one of these great men, to join their ranks, to don their armor, their insignia, their weapons, to be known as a member of the Silver.

"Do you accept this honor?" Kendrick asked.

Thor nodded, barely able to contain himself.

"I can think of no greater honor, my lord," he said, bowing his head.

Kendrick stepped aside with the others, all of them clearing a path, and as they did, Thor saw behind them the shining red lake. It was small, mystical, a light fog rising off of it, and Thor recognized it immediately: the Sacred Lake. It was a magical place, reserved for the elite, hidden deep in the woods, where one would come to pray to the gods, to transform oneself.

Argon stepped to the side of the lake.

"Come," he beckoned Thor.

Thor walked slowly to him, the men parting ways, until he reached the water's edge. Argon reached up and placed his palm on Thor's forehead, and closed his eyes.

Thor felt an intense energy, a burning heat, coursing through Argon's palm, radiating through his body, as he closed his eyes and focused.

Argon began to mutter in an ancient chant, his voice stark and rumbling, cutting through the silent summer afternoon.

"By the light of the seven dawns, by the grace of the westerly wind…"

Argon's chanting trailed off, stopping and starting, as Thor found himself getting lost in the ceremony. Argon switched to the ancient, lost language, and Thor no longer understood the words; but he recognized their intonation, recognized they were part of the formal, ritualized language of the Ring, the ancient language reserved for kings, for holy events.

Argon chanted again and again, and Thor felt as if he were melting into Argon's palm, as if he were surrendering his brain, transforming, becoming someone else.

Finally, Argon paused, then slowly removed his palm.

Thor slowly opened his eyes and the world was filled with an intense, bright light. He saw Argon standing there, looking down.

"Thorgrin of the Western Kingdom of the Ring," Argon proclaimed formally. "You are being endowed with the highest honor of the Ring. You are being inducted into a society in which every King has joined. You are being allowed into a sacred brotherhood, dubbed a warrior for all time. You will be the youngest member ever inducted into the Silver. This is an honor that can never be retracted, for your entire life, and for lifetimes to come. Now I ask you: is this an honor that you will accept?"

"It is," Thor said back.

"Do you vow to uphold the principles of the Silver, to protect the weak, to champion the poor, to lay down your life for your family, your people, for any woman in distress?"

"I do," Thor replied.

"Do you vow to protect your brothers in arms, to give up your life for them?"

"I do."

"Do you vow that any injury to your brothers is an injury to yourself?"

"I do."

Argon paused, taking in the silence, closing his eyes.

Finally, he nodded.

"Follow me," he said.

Argon turned, and Thor watched, amazed, as Argon walked out onto the water. Thor couldn't believe what he was seeing: Argon kept walking out onto the lake without sinking, his feet atop the water, as if he were walking on dry ground.

Thorgrin watched him go, then he followed, taking a step in. Thor walked in, unable to float as Argon did, and the water was unnaturally cold for this summer day. He continued to walk in, deeper and deeper, teeth chattering, until finally he was in up to his chest, standing beside Argon.

Argon reached down with his staff, placed the bottom atop Thor's head, and gently pushed down.

"Immerse yourself, Thorgrin," he commanded, "and rise a member of the Silver. Rise a Lord. Rise a Knight."

Thor felt Argon pushing his forehead down into the water, and Thor gave in.

Thor submerged, and soon his head was completely underwater, and his entire body felt the chill. He stayed there for several seconds, Argon's staff holding him down.

As he was underwater, Thor felt his entire life transforming, flashing before his eyes. He felt as if he were leaving one person behind, and becoming someone new.

Argon lifted his staff, and Thor rose, gasping for air, above the water. He stood there, water dripping into his eyes, breathing deep.

As he rose, the sun broke through the sky over the lake, and Thor no longer felt the cold. He turned and looked back, to all of his brothers in arms staring back at him from the shore, approval on their faces—and he felt reborn.

Finally, Thor felt as if he belonged.

They all raised their fists into the air.

"THORGRIN!" they cried out. "THORGRIN!"

*

Thorgrin, still elated from the ceremony, sat in the small stone workshop of Brendan, the royal armorer, warming up beside a roaring fire in the fireplace, wearing new, dry clothes given to him as he watched the armorer at work. In the room with him sat Erec and Kendrick, having led him here right after the ceremony, and watching over the handiwork, too.

Brendan, a short, stout man in his fifties, proud, with a big belly, a balding head, and a long dark beard, sat hunched over his forge, scrutinizing his work as if it were his only child. As he sat there, Brendan meticulously explained each piece of armor, what purpose it served, how it was made. He worked on a dozen small pieces at once, holding them up, reexamining them, fitting them onto Thor, then taking them off and adjusting them.

Brendan was putting the finishing touches on the shiniest, most beautiful, most ornate set of silver armor that Thor had ever seen. It shone beside the fireplace, and Thor could hardly believe that it was being made just for him. As Brendan pounded away at it with a hammer, flattening it against the stone at just the right angle, the sound rang throughout the room.

"Members of the Silver must wear the finest armor known to man," Erec explained, sitting near Thor, watching the armorer work beside the flames.

"No regular armor will suffice. It must be the strongest, reinforced a thousand times, stronger than any armor from anywhere."

"And also lighter," Kendrick added.

"Not to mention shinier," added Brendan, turning to them with a smile as he wiped sweat from his brow. "The armor must not only be the best, it must also look the best. Outward appearance is a point of pride for the Silver."

"Take pride in your appearance," Kendrick said, "and you will take pride in yourself."

Thor watched, transfixed, excited to wear it, as the armorer pounded away.

"This metal comes from a very special place," he continued, "before it is coated with silver. The refining process takes years."

The armorer finally finished with one piece to his satisfaction, and he reached up and placed it against Thor's shoulder, taking yet another measurement of Thor's shoulder and arm, making more fine adjustments.

"The pauldron," Brendan explained, gauging it with his eye. "It protects your shoulder, and it must also protect the joints. Good armor allows you to move and to breathe. It also guards your most vulnerable spots."

Brendan lowered the pauldron, set it back down, took up a smoothing tool, then polished it, working so fast, it all seemed like magic to Thor. The room was filled with the sounds of his work, and the smells of burning metal and the silver polish. Thor watched in awe as he worked.

Soon, Brendan turned and held up the breastplate against Thor's chest. He placed it, then hurried back around Thor, reached under his arm, and strapped it tight around him. He then placed the pauldron over his shoulder and arm, strapping it tight.

"And how does that feel now?" he asked.

Thor bent his elbow several times, reached his arm up and down, left and right, and was amazed. He had never worn armor so light, yet so strong. As he moved, his arm shined in the light, like a fish jumping through water. He felt different just having it on. He felt invincible.

"It is perfect," Thorgrin said.

"Of course," Brendan said, with a wink and a smile, "my work is always perfect."

Brendan gathered up the entire suit and placed it before Thor.

"We are ready, my lords," he said to Erec and Kendrick.

Kendrick stepped forward.

"It is a tradition, when a knight gets his first suit of armor, that his father put it on him," Kendrick said to Thor. "But since your father is not here, Erec and I are here to do it for you. If you allow us the honor."

Thor felt overcome with gratitude.

"There would be no greater honor," he replied.

Erec and Kendrick together began to put on all of Thor's pieces of armor, strapping them on one at a time. As they did, Thor felt as if he were being rebuilt. He felt supported not just by the armor, but by these two men, who were like fathers to him. It made up for the loss of not having a real father to accept him.

"Even if he were alive," Thor said, "with the father I have, I would not want him to be here for this. In some ways," he said, realizing, "I have no father."

Kendrick nodded.

"I understand," he said. "I have no mother—at least not one I've ever met. I have been known as the bastard of the royal court my entire life. There is something empty inside you when you are missing a parent—or even worse, when you have a parent you don't understand, or you don't like."

Kendrick sighed.

"But I'll tell you something I was told when I was young, something that stayed with me my entire life, something which has sustained me. Once I learned this, it changed my way of looking at the world."

Thor looked at him, curious, and he could see Kendrick thinking, brows furrowed, earnest.

"We have the ability to choose our parents," he said.

Thor looked back, puzzled.

"Choose?" Thor asked.

"We have biological parents. But inside, mentally," Kendrick said, pointing a finger at Thor's head, "in your mind, you can choose your parents. You can choose your father. You can choose one you admire, one you respect. And you need not only have one father. You can choose many fathers. In your mind, they can sit around a table, like a council. Like the King's council. Together, they can be your new father. Ones you admire and respect. Ones who admire and respect you back. Ones you wish to be like."

Thor thought about that.

"Whenever you think of the father you don't have, or don't like," Kendrick added, "think of these men instead. Picture them clearly in your mind. Place them in your head as if they are your father. Your real father. Over time, they will become your real father. As real to you—if not more so—than your biological father. And then you will see that your biological father is not that important after all. He is no authority for you. Eventually, you will come to see that these men are no authority for you, either. You choose your own authority."

Thor pondered all of this carefully, and he tried to do what Kendrick said. He imagined the council table, and around it, he put people he loved and admired and respected. He put Kendrick there. And Erec. He put Argon, and King MacGil, and Aberthol. He put some of the great warriors he had known and fought with….

Thor closed his eyes, and in his mind, all these men populated the table, and slowly he began to see them all as his father. Each of them comprising pieces of the father he never had. Slowly, he felt he had a father. A new father. Kendrick was right.

They finished securing the armor to Thor, and he could not believe how good it felt, how light, the silver custom-fitted to his body, conforming to every contour. He looked at a reflection of himself before a tall mirror, and he was shocked. It was one he did not recognize. He no longer saw a boy. He saw a man. A member of the Silver. A great warrior and knight. It took his breath away, and it made him feel differently about himself.

Thor put on his helmet, ornate, cut on sharp angles, its nose coming to a point, and it was the most beautiful Thor had ever seen. As he put it on, he saw he was a man to be feared.

Thor took off the helmet and held it in his hands, feeling the power radiating off of it.

"No suit of armor is complete without this," Kendrick said.

Thor looked down to see Erec place a dagger in his hand, a beautiful, ornate dagger, carved with the King's inscription.

"It bears the inscription of the MacGil family. You will soon wed my sister. You are a member of the royal family now. We are brothers. You deserve this."

Thor felt his eyes tearing up as he held the dagger, feeling its weight, honored to hold it, to have these great men in his life. There was nothing more he could want.

They opened the door and led him down the ancient hall of the armorer, Thor's new spurs clinking as they went, Thor feeling like a man among men. As Thor wondered where they were leading him, two attendants threw open a set of huge double doors, and Thor found himself ushered into a great hall.

He was shocked at what he saw: inside sat every member of the Silver, hundreds of men, all in armor, all waiting to greet him, all looking at his new armor with great respect. The greatest warriors of the kingdom, all eager to welcome him into the ranks.

"Thorgrinson!" they all chanted as one, raising their swords high in honor.

"Thorgrinson!"

"THORGRINSON!"

CHAPTER THIRTEEN

Romulus marched down the gravelly trail, through the barren wasteland on the outskirts of the Empire capital, flanked by his new councilmen and a dozen generals. He was preoccupied as he marched, his mind swarming with all the reports that had filtered in throughout the day of the rebellion popping up throughout the Empire. News of Andronicus's and Romulus's ascension had continued to spread, and provinces everywhere saw this as their chance for freedom. Some of his own commanders, his own battalions, had been staging rebellions, too. Romulus had been dispatching his soldiers to every corner of the Empire to crush them. It seemed to be working. Yet every day, fresh reports of revolt arrived. Romulus knew he needed some decisive action to put an end to the instability for good, to reassert the dominance of the Empire. Without that, he feared, the Empire might begin to fragment.

The revolts did not worry Romulus too much. His army was vast, and thus far loyal, and over time he felt certain he would crush them all ruthlessly and cement his power. What worried him more—much more—were the reports of the dragons. Word had it that they were bent on vengeance since the theft of the sword, and were spreading havoc throughout the Empire, setting fire to towns and cities, taking their revenge. A great wrath had been unleashed, one not seen since the time of his father, and it spread with each passing day. With it spread the clamor of the people to quell it. Romulus knew that if he did not do something soon, the dragons would reach the capital—and even those loyal to him would revolt.

Over these last moons, Romulus had sent his men on a quest to every corner of the Empire to find a magical spell to combat the dragons. He had followed countless false leads, through murky swamps, and bogs, and forests, listening patiently to sorcerers who gave him various spells and potions and weapons. All of them had turned out to be dead ends. In his rage, Romulus had murdered each and every sorcerer—and the leads had stopped coming in.

Yet now, another lead had come in, and Romulus grimaced as he hiked, following yet another lead, this one through the desolate wastelands. His hopes were low; most likely, it was just another charlatan. He marched quickly, impatient, meandering down the twisty trail, through a field of thorns, already in a bad mood. If this sorcerer was false, Romulus resolved to murder him by hand.

Finally, Romulus crested a ridge and saw before him a tall limestone cave, an eerie greenish glow coming from inside.

He paused before it, something about it putting him on edge. This place felt different than the others—a creepiness crawled up his arms. His advisor came up beside him.

"This is the place, Supreme Commander," he reported. "The sorcerer dwells inside."

Romulus glowered down at him.

"If this one, too, wastes my time, I will kill not only him, but you with him."

His advisor gulped.

"Many have sworn by him, Commander. He is rumored to be the greatest sorcerer of the Empire."

Romulus marched forward, leading the pack of men directly into the cave. The luminescent green walls let off a glow, just bright enough to see by, and Romulus led the way deeper and deeper into the cave. Odd noises echoed off its walls, sounding like moans, screeching, like trapped spirits, and it made Romulus, a man afraid of nothing, think twice. The air was thick, humid, and a stench wafted on the air from somewhere in the distance.

Romulus felt an increasing sense of foreboding, and he was beginning to lose patience as he marched deeper into the blackness.

"If you are wasting my time," Romulus said, turning to his advisor, reddening, preparing to turn around, starting to wonder if this were another dead end.

His advisor gulped.

"I swear no time is being wasted, Commander. I was told that—"

Suddenly, Romulus stopped short, all his men beside him, as he sensed a presence a few feet away. The stench was overwhelming.

"Come closer still," came a dark, gravelly voice from the other side of the cave. It sounded like the voice of a demon.

Romulus peered into the darkness, and suddenly the cave lit up as a ring of fire rose up on the floor before them. It illuminated a small man, standing on the far side, with no legs, his thumbs resting on the ground, wearing a red cloak with no hood, his bald head covered in warts. His shrunken hands were also covered in warts, his face was round and puffy, and he had slits for eyes. He opened them as he stared back at Romulus, his black eyes aglow in the blaze.

"I have what you seek," the man added.

Romulus took several steps forward, to the edge of the ring of fire, and looked across the flames to the sorcerer.

As he stared at this creature, Romulus felt something different inside him. He felt a tingling of excitement. He felt as if, for the first time, perhaps this sorcerer was the real thing.

"You have a way to stop the dragons?" Romulus asked.

The sorcerer shook his head.

"No," he replied, "I have something more powerful."

"And what could be more powerful than that?" Romulus asked.

The sorcerer peered back at him, his eyes demonic, frightening, flashing against the flames.

Romulus, inside, shuddered.

"A way to control them."

Romulus stared back, unsure, trying to understand. There was something about him, something authentic. Authentically evil.

"Control them?" he asked.

"For one moon cycle," the sorcerer replied, "the dragons will be yours. You shall control them as you will. Direct them anywhere you wish. Your own personal army. A chance to change the Empire forever. To do anything you wish. You will be the most powerful man alive."

Romulus narrowed his eyes, wondering, his heart pounding. Could such a thing be true? he wondered.

"And if this is all true," Romulus said, "what do you want from me in return?"

The sorcerer laughed, an awful grating noise, sounding like a thousand chipmunks.

"Why, only your soul," he said. "Nothing else."

"My soul?" Romulus asked.

The sorcerer nodded.

"Upon your death, your soul be mine. Mine to do with as I wish. You see, I collect souls. It is my hobby."

Romulus narrowed his eyes, the hairs on his arms tingling.

"And what do you do with these souls?" he asked.

The sorcerer frowned, displeased.

"That is none of your concern," his voice boomed, suddenly amplified, echoing off the walls, so loud it nearly split Romulus's ears.

Romulus stared back at the creature, and wondered what he was. He felt an intense creepiness hanging over this cave, and a part of him wanted to turn and run.

"Master, don't do it," Romulus's advisor said. "Let us leave this place at once."

But Romulus shook his head and stared at the sorcerer. He could sense that he was real. That he had what he needed. And he could not let that go so easily.

To control the dragons. Romulus imagined all that he could do with that sort of power. He could crush all the revolts. Consolidate his power for all time. Control the Empire. And even take control of the Ring. He would be the most powerful man who had ever walked the earth. More powerful than even he had ever imagined. Even if it were only for one moon cycle, it would be worth it, worth giving his soul. After all, he was going to hell anyway. Once he was dead, who cared what happened to his soul?

"What do I need to do?" Romulus asked.

The sorcerer smiled back.

"Look down. Into my ring of flames. Into the reflecting water. That is all you must do."

"That is all?" Romulus asked, disbelieving. It couldn't be that easy.

Romulus looked down, slowly, and saw his reflection looking back up in the firelight. As he looked, his face contorted, changing shapes and sizes. He was terrified to watch.

"Good," the sorcerer purred. "Now hold your arms out to your sides."

Romulus did so, slowly, warily.

"Now fall. Fall face first into the pool of reflecting water."

"Fall?" Romulus asked.

For the first time in his life, he was afraid.

"When you strike the water, you will be transformed. You will rise Master of the Dragons."

Romulus felt his entire body vibrating, and he felt it to be true. He stood there, arms out at his sides, and slowly, he fell face first, bracing himself for impact against the shallow pool, only a few inches deep. He expected his face to hit the ground hard.

As Romulus fell past the flames, he was shocked to feel himself submerging as he hit the water. It was impossible, he knew; the water was but an inch deep. Yet still, he submerged, deeper and deeper, his whole body immersed. He felt his entire body being penetrated by some force, as if it were being pierced by a thousand small needles. He screamed underwater, but no sound came out.

Suddenly, Romulus rose up, sprang out of the water, bursting back up into the cave, water showering down all around him.

He landed on his feet, shocked, and he felt twice the size, twice the strength he was before. He felt like a giant. He felt himself overflowing with strength. He felt like nothing in the world could stop him.

Romulus leaned back and roared, feeling the new power coursing through his veins, an earth-shattering roar which bounced off the cave walls.

And as he did, he could hear, in the far distance, the roar of a host of dragons, answering him, ready, he knew, to do whatever he bid.

CHAPTER FOURTEEN

Thor held Guwayne in his arms as he walked beside Gwen, the two of them leading the procession of thousands to the mountaintop. Krohn was at their feet, and behind them followed an endless line of Gwen's devoted subjects, well-wishers, all excited to witness the initiation ceremony of the baby, the sacred ritual that would mark the baby's transition into life. As Guwayne was born into the warrior class, and as he was a member of the royal family, Argon himself would be the one to preside over the ancient and mystical ceremony, which would be held at the very peak of King's Hill.

Usually, a baby's initiation was witnessed by a devoted few; but Gwen and Thor were so loved by the people—who were so excited for their child—that the flock behind them was growing and growing. The Ring was ecstatic. After all the gloom, finally, the people had cause, true cause, to celebrate. An heir to the throne had been born, and even better, it was Gwendolyn's boy, the child of a Queen they loved more than any who had come before her. All the outpouring of love they had for Gwendolyn, they could now direct to her boy as well.

Thor, too, was equally loved amongst the people—most of whom viewed him as their savior, as the greatest warrior they had ever had, already the stuff of legend—and for a child to arrive who was the product of Thorgrin and Gwendolyn's union, it might as well have been the child of the people itself. They all followed Thor and Gwen excitedly, like overeager grandparents, and as Thor glanced back over his shoulder he saw thousands and thousands of people, snaking around the mountain, all the way back to the gates of King's Court.

The initiation was more than a mere ceremony; it was also a sacred time, a time of great omens, and the entire kingdom would watch carefully to see if any signs or omens would mark the initiation of this child. Already, legend had spread far and wide of Guwayne's auspicious birth, of the signs and omens that had appeared with the arrival of the child; already, the kingdom saw this child as more than a mere person. There already existed rampant speculation about the destiny of this boy, and these people no doubt were eager to see for themselves if any omens were present at the child's initiation.

Thor's heart pounded himself with excitement and anticipation. As he held his son in his arms, wrapped in his blanket, close to his chest, he felt a heat and power rush over him. Thor felt a tremendous bond with his child, more than he could ever express. As Thor looked down into his son's face, Guwayne opened his eyes and stared back into Thor's, and Thor felt a connection with him from another time, another realm. He had a child. A *son*. He still could not believe it. He felt an overwhelming rush of love for him, and felt more protective of him than he could say.

Thor also felt protective of Gwendolyn, who walked slowly by his side, still recovering from her delivery. They walked as slowly as they could, at her pace, pausing every so often so she could catch her breath. Thor was elated to see she was okay, back on her feet. It had been an emotional few days for her, not only with the birth of the baby, but with the ongoing death watch for her mother. She still lived, but the entire kingdom was anticipating the royal bells that could ring out at any moment, any day, any hour, to announce her death. It was an ominous time. Yet it was also a propitious time, and it was all keeping Gwendolyn in an emotional storm.

Thor thought back to how intense it had been, at Gwen's mother's bedside, watching the two of them interact. It had made Thor think of his own mother. Seeing Gwen's mother dying like that had made Thor realize how precious life was, had made him feel a renewed sense of urgency to see his own mother. What if, he thought with dread, his mother died before he ever even had a chance to greet her?

He would never be able to live with himself; it would leave him with an emptiness, and a sense of guilt, that he could not fathom. It would also make him feel as if his own destiny were incomplete. Thor resolved, once again, to go and seek her out as soon as he could. Now that his child was born, he felt it was time. First, of course, he must stay for his marriage to Gwen; he could not depart before that. But as soon as it was over, he decided, he would depart. He had no choice. He loved Gwen and Guwayne desperately, and he would come back for them and stay by their side his entire life. But first, he had to complete his destiny. He felt, he did not know why, that the very future of the Ring was at stake.

"I am proud of you," Gwen whispered to him, turning to him and smiling and laying a gentle hand on his wrist.

"For what, my love?" Thor asked, puzzled.

"The Silver," she said. "I heard. *Sir* Thorgrinson," she added, her smile broadening.

Thor smiled back; he had been so preoccupied with Guwayne, he had not even thought of it. But now that she mentioned it, it all came rushing back, and he replayed in his mind the ceremony, the armor. He felt like a new man inside. Stronger. More substantial.

As they walked, circling higher and higher up the mountain, Thor was taken aback at the sweeping vistas, the views from up here in the Valley of Fire. This was a strange and haunting place, just west of King's Court, a valley of ancient and dried up volcanoes, dozens and dozens of them, rising up from the earth, dormant, as they had been for thousands of years. They towered over King's Court, an ancient reminder of what had once been. It also, of course, made for a natural defense for the city, which was why, Thor figured, King's Court had been built here to begin with.

As Thor ascended higher and higher, he could see the peaks of the dried up volcanoes, none of which he had ever seen in his lifetime. They were beautiful, gaping. There was a slight smell in the air, as if of a sulfur that had once been, that had seeped into the ground. Thor's boots slid in the dry dirt and gravel beneath his feet as they neared the mountain top, a strong breeze getting stronger as they crested its peak, carrying a cool wind despite the summer day.

Thor looked down and saw summer's bounty spreading out all over King's Court, fields of grain swaying in the wind, entire valleys of orchards, abundance beyond belief. Except for here, this dead Valley of Fire, like a stark reminder that all this bounty could one day disappear.

"He's here," Gwen said, beside him.

Thor looked up and saw Argon standing at the top, dressed in his white cloak and hood, holding his staff, looking down on them all, expressionless, like a shepherd awaiting his flock. Thor flooded with relief. Without Argon, the ceremony could not take place—and one never knew if Argon would appear.

They crested the very top of the ancient volcano, and as Thor and Gwen took their place at its peak, beside Argon, the three of them turned and looked down into the center of the volcano. The terrain sloped down gently, for about twenty feet, loose sand and rock, then leveled out in a plateau at the top, shaped in a perfect circle, perhaps a hundred yards in diameter, on which sat an ice-blue lake. It reflected the sky, the clouds, and the two suns, and the sight took Thor's breath away. They made their way to the water's edge, and behind them, Thor heard the gentle footsteps of thousands of people cresting the ridge, coming up behind them to the shores of the lake.

As they stood there, Argon turned to Thor, held out both hands, and looked to the child.

Thor found himself clutching his boy, reluctant to let him go; he felt a gentle hand on his forearm, and looked over at Gwen, and she nodded back.

"It's okay," she said. "Let him go."

Thor reluctantly reached out and placed Guwayne in Argon's arms.

The second he did, the silent sky filled with the sound of Guwayne's screams and cries. Thor felt his heart break at the sound. Thor felt an emptiness, a hollow feeling, as Guwayne's warmth left his arms.

Argon held Guwayne close, and slowly, his crying stopped. Argon unswaddled him, one layer at a time, until Guwayne was completely naked. Argon then held the boy up high to the sky, over his head, and he turned and faced the people.

"In the name of the seven forefathers, in the name of the ancient pillars, in the name of the fields of light and the fields of gray, of all four winds and the great divide, I call upon all the gods that ever were and all the gods there will ever be to bless this child. Endow him with the strength of his father, the spirit of his mother. Infuse him to carry on the royal bloodline of the MacGils. Give us all a great warrior, and a great leader of men."

The congregation cheered in approval, and Argon turned, knelt beside the water, lay the baby on his back, and immersed him in the water.

Gwen gasped and rushed forward instinctively to save him—but Thor clutched her wrist. It was now his time to reassure her.

Argon raised him from the water, and Guwayne screamed. Argon immersed him again. Then, a third time.

As Argon finally raised him up high overhead, the crowd all took a knee and lowered their heads. Guwayne screamed, and as he did, Thor was shocked as the earth beneath him suddenly began to shake. Everyone looked to each other in fear and wonder, as a great earthquake shook the ground, all of them stumbling, Gwen clutching Thor's wrist.

"What is happening?" she asked. "Is it the boy?"

Suddenly, all around them, there came tremendous explosions.

Thor looked up, and he was amazed to see all the volcanoes around them exploding, bursting up into the air, great plumes of smoke filling the summer sky, and sparks and molten fire following. The volcanoes were far enough away that Thor could not feel their heat from here. But he was in awe at the sight, at their beauty, dozens of volcanoes shooting molten fire into the air, volcanoes that had been dormant for centuries. It had happened at an auspicious moment, and Thor knew it had tremendous meaning. All the people looked to each other in terror and wonder. Even Argon looked down at the boy in wonder, clearly awestruck.

Who was this boy?

Thor did not know. But he did know, he could sense it in every ounce of his being, that his child was more powerful than anything he had ever known.

CHAPTER FIFTEEN

Alistair stood on the roof of the small fort, running her hand along the ancient stone parapets as she looked out over the countryside of the Ring on this brilliant, beautiful summer day. From up here, surrounded by nothing but rolling hills, she looked out and saw fields of tall lime-green and violet grass, swaying in the wind, shining in the sun, rustling, as if happy to be alive. The weather was perfect, the two suns shining, and Alistair leaned back and breathed deep, and took it all in.

For once, Alistair felt relaxed, content, at home in the world. Finally, she had love in her life, had met a man who loved her, and had also met her brother. Soon, she would marry. And Argon was helping her understand who she truly was. For the first time in her life, Alistair was beginning to feel that she was not some sort of freak, not an outcast. She was starting to understand that what was different about her was what made her special. That her powers were a normal, natural part of her. A part of her she did not have to be ashamed to claim. She felt empowered, especially after her trip to the Netherworld, after their battle against the Empire, and seeing just how powerful she was.

Ever since Thor had killed her father, Alistair had felt an immense sense of peace in the world. She felt relieved that everyone, especially Erec, knew her secret, knew that her father was a monster. She'd been so afraid that if he discovered it, he would leave her. And she would not blame him. But Erec had remained loyally at her side. Never once had he blamed her, or looked at her differently; on the contrary, his compassion for her had only deepened, and she could feel that he didn't see her any differently. After all, he had insisted, we are not our parents. For the first time in her life, she was beginning to realize that.

Alistair had taken a break from all the wedding preparations to ride down here and visit Erec, a half-day's ride from King's Court, as he was immersed in the work of the Silver, rebuilding and re-arming fortifications, as he had been for moons. Alistair looked out over the parapets and saw below dozens of members of the Silver, their armor shining in the morning suns, and Erec in the middle of them, as he always was, directing the men as they were hard at work on rebuilding fortifcations. Other knights charged on their horses in their impromptu training grounds, engaged in exercises, sparring, keeping their skills sharp.

Alistair looked out and saw four major roads passing through this small town, saw how strategically situated it was, here the middle of the country, and knew that Erec had an important job to do here, to keep all these villagers secure. Erec had been carefully stationing his men at different points all throughout the countryside, helping to mend roads, to raise gates, to deepen moats, and to quarry the stone they needed to repair the damage that Andronicus had done. It was amazing that anything was left of this fort at all. In many of the other towns throughout the Ring, forts which had stood for centuries were completely wiped out, unsalvageable.

Alistair heard a distant rumble. She looked up at the horizon and saw a lone rider charging for the tower, kicking up dirt on the dusty road. She watched as he rode right up to Erec, knelt before him, and handed him a scroll. She wondered what it could be that would make him ride with such haste?

Erec stood very still for a long time, reading. Finally, he turned and walked toward the fort. He looked lost in thought, his brow furrowed, and whatever it was, Alistair sensed from his body language that it was not good.

Alistair heard a muted shuffling of feet coming up the spiral stone staircase, then Erec appeared on the roof of the fort, holding the scroll, looking grim.

"What is it, my lord?" Alistair asked, rushing over to him.

Erec looked down and shook his head. She could see his eyes well with tears.

"My father," he said, grimly. "He's gravely ill."

Alistair felt overwhelmed with compassion for Erec, and she leaned in and hugged him, and he hugged her back. He had never spoken to her of his father, or of his people, and she did not know much about them. All she knew was that Erec hailed from the Southern Isles.

"What will you do?" she asked.

Erec stared out at the horizon, thinking.

"I must go to him," he said. "I must see him before he dies."

Alistair's eyes widened.

"To the Southern Isles?" she asked.

He nodded, earnest.

"It is a long voyage, my lady," he said. "Harsh and unforgiving. I will have to cross the Southern Sea, which takes more lives than it lets pass. It will be safer for you to stay here. I shall return to you."

Alistair felt a rush of determination, and she shook her head.

"I will never be apart from you again," she said. "I vowed to myself. And I intend to keep it. Whatever the price. I will join you."

Erec looked back, seeing her determination, touched.

"But Gwendolyn's wedding," he answered. "You are her maid of honor."

Alistair sighed.

"If you must go now," she replied, "then I must go with you. Gwendolyn will understand."

Erec embraced her, and she embraced him back. She held him tight, and wondered. What would their voyage be like? What were the Southern Isles like? What was his family like? Would they like her? Accept her? Would he make it to see his father before he died?

And most of all, how would this affect their wedding? Would it delay it?

Would Gwen really understand? Would Thor? Would she ever see her brother again? Would they really return to the Ring?

For some reason, she had a sinking feeling that they would not.

*

Alistair rode through King's Court, having just said goodbye to Gwendolyn, and her heart was still breaking. It had been painful to break the news, even though Gwen had received it well. She felt terrible telling Gwen, especially at this time, right before her wedding. But the way she saw it, she had no choice. Erec would be her husband, and she could not stand to be separated from him again. Gwen had been understanding, stoic, and had made it easy on Alistair. But Alistair sensed, deep down, that Gwen was hurt, that she would have wanted her there at her wedding. Alistair wished things could be different; but this was the hand life had dealt her.

As Alistair rode out of court, she was determined, before riding back to Erec, to see her brother one last time, to break the news to him, too, that she was leaving. She braced herself. When all this was over, Alistair vowed silently to return, to find a way to come back to the Ring, to be with Gwendolyn and

Thor, and all of her people, again. After all, she and Gwendolyn had been through so much in the Netherworld together, and Gwen felt like a true sister to her, like the sister she'd never had. Alistair also felt protective of Gwen. She felt attached to her, especially since hearing the news of her new child.

Alistair could hardly believe that she had a nephew. When she'd held him, she had felt his energy course through her, and had felt a greater connection to the child than any she had ever known. Her brother's son. It was hard to imagine. As she held him, she knew without a doubt that the two of them would have a close relationship their entire lives.

Alistair rode through the newly rebuilt stone gates leading to the Legion training ground, past all the new recruits lining up on the field, all hoping to catch her brother's attention for a spot in the coveted Legion. She spotted her brother, and rode across the courtyard and dismounted before him.

Thor must have sensed her coming, because before she even got close to him, he turned and met her gaze, his light gray eyes alight in the morning sun, standing there so noble and proud, all the hopeful warriors of the Legion looking to him. Her brother was clearly a leader, and all these boys, some older than he, looked up to him as if he were a god. She could understand why. Not only was he a skilled warrior, but he also exuded an energy, something mystical, almost like a light shining around him. It was hard to put her finger on exactly what it was about him. It was almost as if she were looking at the stuff of legend, while he was still alive. There was also a fleeting air to him, as if somehow, he, burning so bright, might not live very long, like a shooting star racing across the sky. She flinched at the thought, and tried to suppress it.

But as Alistair walked up to him, she suddenly choked up. She had a flash, saw something she could not suppress. It was a vision: she saw her brother dead. At a young age. She saw death—and glory—all around him.

Alistair stopped before Thor, about to hug him, and her smile morphed to a frown, as she barely stopped herself from crying. They had become close these past moons, and Thor was the only real family she had, and the idea of losing him now, after she had just met him, was too much for her to bear.

"What is it, my sister?" Thor asked, looking at her, puzzled.

Alistair merely shook her head, biting her tongue. Instead, she leaned in and hugged him, and he hugged her back. Over his shoulder, she quickly wiped away tears and forced herself to smile.

She pulled back.

"Nothing, my brother," she said.

He watched her, skeptical, concerned.

"Yet you seem disturbed," he said.

"I have come to say goodbye," she replied.

Thor looked at her, surprise and disappointment in his face.

"Erec departs for the Southern Isles," she said, "and I must join him. I am sorry. I will not be here to see you wed."

Thor nodded, understanding.

"At Erec's side is where you should be," he said. "He is the greatest warrior of our Ring—and yet, he needs you. You are even greater. Protect him."

"As are you," she said back.

Thor flushed with embarrassment.

"I am but a boy from a small farming village," Thor replied humbly.

Alistair shook her head.

"You are far, far more than that."

Thor sighed and looked off into the distance, watching his recruits train.

"I will be departing myself, soon," he said.

101

Alistair suddenly gained an insight into his mind, as she often did when she was around him.

"You will go to seek out our mother," she said, more of a statement than a question.

Thor looked at her, surprised.

"How did you know?" he asked.

She shrugged.

"You are an open book around me," she said. "I don't know why. It is as if I can see what you see."

"What else do you see?" Thor asked, excited, narrowing his eyes. "Will I find our mother?"

Alistair had a sudden flash of Thor's future. She saw that he would indeed find her. But then the vision was obscured by darkness, as if it were being deliberately masked by the fates. She saw Thor in a great battle, one beyond even his powers. She saw darkness all around them, and she quickly closed her eyes and shook her head, wanting to quash the vision. It was too dark, too terrifying.

She didn't want to scare Thor, and she forced herself to remain composed. She shuddered inside, but did not let him show it.

"You will find her," she replied.

Thor looked at her, unconvinced.

"And yet...you hesitate," he said.

Alistair shook her head and looked away.

"Last time we spoke of Mother," she said, "I was beginning to tell you that I have something of hers. It is fitting that you have it. I do not know if I shall ever see her."

Alistair reached into her pocket and extracted an object.

"Hold out your wrist," she said.

Thor did so, and he looked down as Alistair held out a golden wrist bracelet, six inches wide, and clasped it around his wrist. It covered Thor's wrist, halfway up his forearm, shining, shifting colors in the light.

Thor examined it in wonder. She could tell he was awestruck.

"The Land of the Druids is a fearful place," she said. "A place of great power. But also of great danger. You will need this more than I."

"What is it?" he asked, running a finger along its smooth golden surface.

She shrugged.

"It is the only thing that Mother left me. I do not know what it is, or what it does. But I know that you will need it where you're going."

Thor leaned in and, clearly grateful, embraced Alistair tight; she embraced him back.

"Be safe," Thor said.

"Send Mother my love," she said. "Tell her I love her. And one day, I hope to meet her, too."

CHAPTER SIXTEEN

The attendants opened the double doors, and Reece braced himself as he entered his mother's sick chamber alone. He felt a pit in his stomach as the darkened room embraced him, lit only by a flickering torch. Nurses hovered over his mother's bedside, patting her forehead with salves. Hafold stood closest to her. Reece had been worried his entire trip here that he would not reach her before she died—and he was so grateful that he had. He had come here first, the second the ship touched shore, before even going to break the wedding news to Selese.

The thought of his mother dying tore Reece apart. Of all of the children, Reece, the youngest, had always been closest to his mother. They confided to each other, and she had been kinder and gentler to him than all the others. She had sheltered him from his father's occasional wrath, and had always made sure he had the best of everything. The thought of her dying made him feel as if a part of him were dying, too. He'd wanted more than anything for her to be alive for his wedding.

Thinking of the looming wedding confused Reece. The entire ship ride home, his mind had been filled with thoughts of Stara, of their encounter, of his love for her. Throughout the trip, he remained determined to make her his wife, to steel himself to tell Selese the news.

But now that he had reached home again, had entered King's Court, seen all the furious wedding preparations, it gave him pause. It was a spectacle. King's Court looked more beautiful than it ever had, and thousands upon thousands of people were finally arriving from all corners of the Ring, and the world, getting ready to watch. And Reece would be at the center of it. He would be letting down not only Selese, but also his sister, and Thorgrin, ruining everyone's special day, for which they had worked so hard to prepare. He would also be letting down the thousands of people who were anticipating this great event.

How could he do that? How could he betray his people? And most of all, how could he betray Selese? The thought of hurting Selese pained him to no end. She, most of all, who had been so kind and loyal to him. Was he right to follow his passions, his heart? Or was he being selfish, wrong to betray everyone around him?

Reece now felt completely at a loss as to what to do. He felt like a traitor, like the worst betrayer in the world.

Except, of course, to Stara.

Reece thought of her, and a rush of love washed over him, so strong, like a wave washing over his entire world. It was a love that prodded him on, a love strong enough to defy everyone and everything he knew and loved.

As Reece approached his mother's bedside, he forced himself to snap out of it and focus on her. She opened her eyes as he laid a hand on her wrist, and gestured to Hafold, who quickly rounded up all the servants and hurried from the room.

Reece and his mother were alone, and Reece, as he had his whole life, wanted to confide in her, to ask for her thoughts, her opinion. But he did not know if he could. He did not know if she was in a state to hear it all, or to respond, and as pressing as this was, and as torn as he was, he didn't want to upset her right now, in her final moments. Also, she had given him her royal ring to use to propose to Selese, along with her blessing. How could he tell her that he wanted to marry someone else?

Reece took his mother's limp hand in both of his, a tear rolling down his cheek as he lowered his forehead to the back of her palm. He was overwhelmed with a whirlwind of emotions.

His mother sat up a little in bed, looked down at him, then coughed and coughed, the sound reverberating in her chest. It was a cough he'd never heard; the cough of an old woman. It terrified him, and he squeezed her hand.

"Mother, I'm so sorry," he said. "I'm sorry I could not be here sooner."

"You were away on important business," she said. "The Queen's business. After all, the Upper Isles are important, too."

His mother looked at him with a knowing look he knew well.

"And I hear you had more business than that," she added.

Reece looked back, stunned. How had she known? Even here, now, across the ocean? He'd underestimated her. Nothing escaped her. He should have known; his whole life, his mother had always known everything. She had spies in every corner of the kingdom, and she always knew something before he did, before even his father. He could get away with nothing. There was a saying in King's Court: when the halls whispered, the Queen MacGil heard it before the echo.

"How did you know?" Reece asked, knowing it was a stupid question.

She merely shook her head.

"How could you do this?" she asked, displeased.

Reece reddened, ashamed.

"I gave you my ring," his mother added. "The ring your father gave me. A ring of honor. A ring that signifies your word that you would not betray someone else. For any reason. It was a ring for all eternity, the ring I blessed for you to give to Selese, and you have made a mockery of it."

She looked at him with scorn, and Reece looked away, humiliated, unable to look back. His confusion heightened, and he felt increasingly unsure.

"I'm sorry, Mother," he said. "I did not mean to disappoint. I did not mean to fall in love with Stara. I did not even seek to see her."

"Yet when you saw her, you did not turn away. That was your choice. Those were your actions. You might make one lonely woman happy. But think of how many others you will hurt."

His mother shook her head.

"It is no longer about you," she added. "You will come to see, as you grow, that lust is oft mistaken with love, and lust is a childish thing. As you get older, you'll find that love, true love, is about commitment, responsibility. Especially for you—a member of the royal family. We are not regular people; we are all actors here. The entire kingdom looks to us. We are a spectacle for the masses, and little more. Don't fool yourself. Pacified masses means the royal family can rule. Your life is not private. People look to you. You cannot cast a pall of dishonor on the royal family. You have given your word, and you must honor it, above all else. Without that, what would we be? What worth would the royal bloodline have?"

Reece's forehead was covered in a cold sweat, and he reached up and wiped it with the back of his hand. His mouth was going dry as he contemplated his mother's words, so piercing, as always.

"I'm sorry, Mother," he said again. "I have lived my entire life for honor. I do not mean to dishonor anyone."

"Indeed you do," she retorted.

"I did not set out to dishonor Selese," he insisted. "Yet I love Stara. Is it not wrong to ignore one's feelings?"

"Feelings are temporary," she scoffed. "Actions are permanent. You could follow your passions if you were a commoner. But you are not. You are a King's son. You don't have the luxury to follow your feelings. You do what is right, what is expected of you. You do not betray the one to whom you have given your word, who has put her faith in you."

She sighed.

"Stara will be hurt, true. But that is one person. The rest of the kingdom will be happy. You may regret it your whole life. You may hate it; you may hate me. But that is the price you pay to be in the royal family. There are many forms of honor. The honor sung of in battle is the easiest kind. Honor in daily life— that is hard. You must display honor in love as you would on the battlefield. One is not more important than the other. Show me an honorable warrior who has betrayed his wife, and I'll show you a man who is worth less than nothing."

His mother's tone was harsher than Reece had ever heard, and he realized they were the sounds of a woman on her deathbed, a woman with no time left, with nothing left to lose, and with urgency in her message. It was a tone Reece barely recognized.

Worst of all, he knew she was right. He hung his head low, wishing he were anywhere but here in this stifling chamber. He wished this dilemma had never fallen into his lap. How had his life become so complicated so quickly?

"You are not a boy," she said. "You are a man now. Which is why you are taught honor from other men. Not from women. But that means you are only being taught half of what true honor means. It is past time you learned it from a woman's side. For only then will you become a true man."

Reece felt his entire face flush hot red. He felt more ashamed than he ever had in his life.

"You are right," he said finally, his voice broken, the words difficult to speak. "My actions have disgraced our royal name. I gave my word, and I must keep it. Whatever the cost. Whatever the price."

Reece hung his head, his world spinning, and he wished he could just die. Most of all, it hurt him that he had hurt his mother like this, especially on her deathbed. He wished he could take it all back. He wished now that he had never visited the Upper Isles.

Reece felt his mother squeeze his hand with surprising strength, and he looked up at her, tears in his eyes. He was surprised to see her smiling down at him—the old affectionate mother he'd always known.

"I'm proud of you, my son," she said. "Your father would be too. You have listened, and you will do the right thing. Now go, and make Selese your wife. Use my ring in honor. And wipe the name Stara from your mind. The Upper Isles only breed trouble—they always have."

Reece smiled, feeling a rush of love for his mother; at the same time, he also felt devastated that he would be losing her soon, his best advisor, the one person he trusted above all.

He leaned over and hugged her tight, crying over her shoulder at the thought of losing her, and she reached up and hugged him back, her frail arms gripping him.

"I love you the most, Reece," she said. "Of all my children. I always have."

Reece cried, overcome by emotion, as he knew what he had to do. He had to hurry to Selese, and before another moment passed, tell her how much he loved her. Tell her that he wanted her, and only her, to be his wife.

CHAPTER SEVENTEEN

Selese exited the house of the sick and removed her frock, a broad smile across her face, done with her healing duties for the day. It was a beautiful summer afternoon, both suns shining, the wind blowing back her hair, and she breathed in deeply. She set off through a field of flowers, feeling a buoyancy she had not felt in years, dreaming with every minute of her wedding.

She felt butterflies in her stomach. Her wedding to Reece, the love of her life, was but a few days away, and she could hardly think of anything else. All morning, even as she was tending the sick, the hours had flown by as she'd imagined the wedding to come, saw her and Reece walking down the aisle together, saw the thousands of spectators that would be there to witness the joyous ceremony, the double wedding with Gwendolyn and Thorgrin. Most of all, she imagined Reece kissing her, holding him, taking their vows to be together for the rest of their lives. She imagined the joy she would feel in knowing that she was finally his wife, after all these moons of waiting, that nothing could ever tear them apart.

It was all that Selese wanted. Reece had taken her heart the moment she had laid eyes and him, and being officially wed to him would be the greatest day of her life—and the beginning of her new life. In some ways, she felt her life had begun the day she met him.

Selese broke into a jog, skipping through the fields, anxious to get back to King's Court and finish all of her wedding preparations for the day. There were last-minute dress fittings, choices of flowers and bouquets, and sundry other matters awaiting her, and she did not want to be late for any of them.

"Selese!" rang out a voice she did not recognize.

Selese turned, caught off guard by the stranger's voice, and was surprised to see, riding toward her through the fields, a man she did not know. He wore an armor of another place, and it took her a moment to recognize it was the dress of the MacGils of the Upper Isles. She wondered what he could be doing here on such urgent business, and how he knew her name.

"You are Selese, yes?" he asked, as he approached and dismounted, short of breath.

Her heart fluttered upon seeing the serious expression on his face. She knew Reece had recently traveled to the Upper Isles—she anxiously awaited his return—and she suddenly wondered if this man came bearing bad news, perhaps that Reece was ill or wounded, or that something bad had happened to him.

"Is everything okay?" she asked quickly, alarmed.

"My name is Falus. I'm the eldest surviving son of Tirus, of the house of MacGils of the Upper Isles. I come bearing bad news, I'm afraid."

Selese's heart pounded at his grave tone. She felt her hands begin to tremble.

"Bad news?" she echoed.

She immediately stopped, frozen, bracing herself for news that something bad had happened to Reece.

She rushed forward and grabbed the man's wrist.

"You must tell me—is he okay?" she pleaded.

Falus nodded, and she sighed with relief.

"Reece is fine. That is not the news I bring."

She looked at him, confused. What other news could he possibly have for her?

Falus held out a scroll, then placed it in her hand. Selese looked down at it, confused.

"I'm sorry to have to bear this news but we, the MacGil family of the Upper Isles, take our honor very seriously, and we thought it pertinent that you should know this right away. The man you love, Reece, is preparing to betray you. He is in love with someone else."

Selese felt her entire body go cold at his words, as she stared back at him, baffled, trying to process what he was saying. She lost all sense of time and place; it was like a terrible nightmare unfolding before her.

She found herself unable to speak.

"My sister, Stara," he continued, "Reece's cousin, she is in love with him. And he is in love with her. Their love affair has blossomed ever since they were children. Years before the two of you met. On his recent trip to the Upper Isles, Reece sought out Selese and pledged his love, and vowed to marry her. In secret."

He sighed.

"The scroll you hold bears proof of their love. You will see her letter to him, and his to her, each professing their love. You will, no doubt, recognize Reece's penmanship."

Selese's heart pounded in her ears so loudly she could barely think. With shaking hands, she unrolled the scrolls, hoping this was all some awful lie, some terrible mistake.

But as she began to read, she recognized Reece's handwriting at once. She felt like throwing up as she read his profession of love to Stara. The scroll seemed old, brittle, yet somehow she did not recognize that. She only focused on Reece's words.

She felt her entire world splitting in two.

How could this be? How could someone like Reece, so proud and honorable, so noble and devoted, do such a thing? How could he betray her like this? How could he have lied to her? How could he love someone else?

Her head swarmed, trying to understand. None of it made any sense. Just a minute ago she was prepared to marry him.

This was a man she loved him with every fiber of her being, a man who had made her whole life, and she had been sure that he loved her, too. Had she been so wrong? She had not taken Reece for a dishonest person. Was she such a fool?

"I'm sorry to bear this news," Falus said. "But we thought you should hear it from us first. Reece has humiliated you before both kingdoms."

Selese burst into tears. It was more than she could take. She wanted to respond, to tell Falus to leave her alone, to drop dead.

But her voice was stuck in her throat, and he had already turned, like a messenger of death, and taken off on his black steed, kicking it and charging farther and farther away, disappearing into the horizon. He rode through the fields of flowers, but now she could no longer see their color. Now they appeared as fields of thorns.

Selese looked at the scrolls in her hand, sobbing, her tears making them wet, running the ink. She reached down and tore them into pieces, again and again and again.

"NO!" she screamed.

With every tear, she felt her entire life being torn into pieces. Everything she had imagined, everything she had ever thought she knew, was now being torn to nothing.

CHAPTER EIGHTEEN

Kendrick stood before the bridge spanning the Western Crossing of the Ring, overseeing his men, supervising scores of Silver as they were hard at work on securing it, rebuilding it as it once used to be. Joined by several of his illustrious friends, including Atme and Brandt, Kendrick helped the men as they rolled a boulder, guided a new stone into place, repaired the railing. This bridge had undergone extensive damage since the Shield had been down, and too many creatures from the Wilds had used the opportunity to cross into the Ring during the Empire's invasion.

Kendrick stood for a moment and looked out, and on his side of the canyon, he saw the countless corpses of those beasts scattered about the grass. As he watched, several of his men picked them up and hoisted them over the canyon's edge. Over these last moons, scattered reports had filtered in of a random beast that had terrorized a village. Now, after all these moons of Kendrick and the Silver hunting them down, killing any beasts that had slipped in while the Shield was down, the reports were stopping. Kendrick was determined to make the Ring as secure as it had ever been. One day at a time, they were repairing all the damage that Andronicus had done.

Kendrick was thrilled to be back with his men, back with the Silver, strengthening the Ring—it was what, he felt, he had been born to do. He was thrilled that Gwendolyn had tasked him with leading the Silver, together with Erec, and making the Ring stronger, more secure. Erec had headed southeast to rebuild the forts at strategic points throughout the Ring, and had taken half of the Silver with him, while Kendrick had taken the rest of the men to fortify the canyon.

Kendrick turned and looked out over the canyon, and saw, on the other side, several beasts lurking in the Wilds, watching their work. With the Shield up, these creatures wouldn't dare try to cross. Yet they still stood there, the Wilds teeming with them, waiting for their chance, whenever it should come, to cross again. Kendrick was determined not to ever let that happen.

"Raise that stone higher!" Kendrick called out to several knights, and they raised a particularly large boulder and secured it in place.

Kendrick surveyed the landscape, and still saw tremendous work that lay ahead for them. There remained countless villages here that needed securing, walls that needed to be repaired, bridges that needed to be rebuilt, crossings that needed guards. He would need to distribute the knights of the Silver strategically at certain posts, make their presence known to prevent lawlessness, and to remind the people of the power of King's Court. The people needed to know they were being protected, watched over. And Kendrick had to prepare, in case for some reason there was ever another invasion of the Ring.

"My lord," came a voice.

Kendrick turned to see his new squire running toward him, out of breath as he knelt. Kendrick was surprised to see him; he hadn't seen him in moons, and he thought back to the last time he'd dispatched him. Kendrick had sent him, far and wide, to crisscross the Ring to see if he could discover any news about Kendrick's birth mother, whom he had never met. It had been gnawing at Kendrick, and he had felt an ever-burning desire to know her, to know whom he hailed from. He hated the idea that he was a bastard in the world. And knowing that King MacGil was his father was not enough for him.

Seeing this squire return got Kendrick's heart racing with anticipation. Had he discovered some news?

Kendrick had always hoped and dreamed that his mother was a princess in her own right, maybe in some other land, far away. Maybe that would explain why she had never come back for him. Perhaps she was separated by a vast ocean. Mostly, he just hoped that she was alive. He hoped that he could lay eyes on her, just once, if for no other reason than to ask her why she had abandoned him. Why she had never claimed him. Did she even know he existed?

Kendrick's heart pounded as his squire stood, still catching his breath. From the look on his face, Kendrick sensed he bore news.

"My lord," his squire said, gasping, "I think I have found her."

Kendrick's throat went dry as his squire reached out and placed half of a medallion in his palm. He looked down at the bronze medallion, held it up to the light, and slowly removed the necklace he had worn for as long as he could remember— half a medallion, bronze. His father had always told him that the other half belonged to his mother.

He held them up and was shocked to see it was a perfect match. There was a hole in the center, and the holes aligned, room enough for a thread to pass through, and for it to become one necklace.

It was authentic. His hands trembled to hold it; he had dreamed of this day his entire life.

"Where did you find this?" Kendrick asked, barely able to speak.

"In a small village in the northern part of the Ring, my lord. In a shop. I bought it from them. They told me a woman sold it to them."

"A woman?" Kendrick asked. "Sold it?"

Was it his mother? he wondered. How could she sell it, the one and only connection she had to him? Had it happened many years ago?

His squire nodded.

"Just a few moons ago," he said. "They told me where she came from. And her name: Alisa."

Kendrick stared back, dumfounded.

"Your mother lives, my lord."

Kendrick felt his hand go limp, the medallion burning inside it, as he gazed out at the horizon.

His mother. Alive.

After all this time, he wanted to put it out of his mind; for a moment, he even regretted sending his squire on this mission.

Yet the more he considered it, the more he knew he could do nothing else. A burning curiosity rose up within him. His mother. Alive. What did she look like? Did she resemble him? Would she be happy to see him?

Kendrick looked out at the horizon, and knew he had no choice.

He had to find her.

CHAPTER NINETEEN

Luanda, finally on the right side of the Highlands, in the Western Kingdom of the Ring, breathed with joy as she rode with Bronson down the long road leading back to King's Court. It felt so good to be home again. Waves of relief washed over her as she spotted her home, the place she had grown up, saw all the people—her people—milling about, the throngs heading into the city for her mother's funeral. Finally, she was home.

Luanda was shocked to see King's Court so resplendent, rebuilt, and more magnificent than she had ever seen it. It made her realize how long she had been away. For so many moons she had been banished, like a common exile. She could hardly believe what her sister had done to her.

And yet now she felt vindicated, being summoned back here by her sister for their mother's funeral. Obviously, Gwendolyn had had a change of heart, had realized she had been wrong, and was changing her mind and allowing her to come back home.

Luanda breathed deeply as she rode behind Bronson, clutching his waist, the two of them riding down the slope towards King's Court, feeling rejuvenated despite the somber event. Soon, Luanda would re-enter the gates of King's Court, finally back to a civilized city. Perhaps, too, there were other reasons Gwendolyn had invited her back—perhaps word had spread of the fantastic job Luanda had done in helping put down the revolt, in killing all those McClouds and setting that hall on fire. Among the MacGils close to the Highlands, Luanda was now considered a hero. Maybe Gwen realized that, and was giving in to popular demand to have her return.

Since that night, since her ruthless quashing of the rebellion, no McCloud had acted up. The MacGils now had a tighter grip on the McCloud city than ever.

More and more MacGils, she knew, now looked to her, Luanda, as their true leader. Bronson had wavered, had shown weakness, and Luanda had been the one to exhibit the necessary strength and resolve. The dynamic had shifted, and they were viewed as a husband and wife ruling a city, with Luanda the decisive player. Bronson seemed to be fine with that; he was overwhelmed with the situation, and not a man inclined toward force. Luanda, though, had no hesitation.

Bronson had never thanked or applauded her for her ruthless actions that night; yet he had not chided her, either. Perhaps he was still in shock; or perhaps, deep down, he also held admiration for what she had done.

As Luanda thought back to that night, she realized she owed Bronson much, too. After all, if it wasn't for Bronson stepping forward and saving her, she would be dead right now. She clutched his waist tighter as they passed through the gates. The more they had grown together, the more she realized that Bronson was the only one she truly loved in the world—the only one she could count on, the only one, despite any weakness he might have, that she cared about and respected. She owed him her life. And that was not something she took lightly. She was determined to stay by his side. And if ruthlessness and brutality were things he was lacking to rule, then she would gladly supply them for him.

They entered through the soaring gates of King's Court, joining in with a throng dressed in black. They dismounted, and as they did, Luanda anticipated being welcomed as a returning hero. What a difference a few moons made, when not so long ago, she had entered here in disgrace. Now she was being invited back by the Queen, after her heroic actions on behalf of the MacGils, and now she would participate in her mother's funeral. She would take her spot once again as an honored member of the royal family.

Luanda smiled wide, as she was beginning to realize that her time of exile was over. She anticipated greeting all of her siblings there, all of them applauding her, apologizing to her, allowing her a place back in court, with Bronson. Luanda couldn't wait to find out what rank and position Gwen gave her, and to settle down here. She vowed to never leave King's Court again—and most of all, to never cross the Highlands again.

Luanda and Bronson weaved their way through King's Court with the masses, passed through yet another arch, exited the other side of the city, and followed the funeral procession up a hill. Bells tolled with every step they took.

Finally, they all came to a stop. The crowd was so thick, Luanda could barely see over their heads, could barely catch a glimpse of the tomb of her ancestors.

Determined, Luanda pushed her way through the masses, clutching Bronson's hand. As the people turned and looked at who she was, they parted way for her, and she was allowed to come all the way to the front, the guards stepping aside.

Luanda stopped at the clearing, taking in the sight. Before her was the ancient marble tomb of her ancestors, built into the hillside, its roof covered in grass—the final resting place of her father, and his father before him, and all those before them. There sat a small clearing before it, in which lay her mother's sarcophagus, carved of marble and, thankfully, closed.

Beside it stood Argon, facing the masses, and around him, in a semicircle, stood her siblings: Kendrick, Godfrey, Reece—and, of course, Gwendolyn. Luanda did a double take as she saw Gwendolyn holding an infant. She was shocked. The last time Luanda had seen her, she had barely been pregnant.

The sight of the baby inflamed Luanda with jealousy. She had been kept so out of the loop, she hadn't even been informed of the baby's, her nephew's, birth. Worst of all, there stood Gwendolyn, her younger sister, holding a baby—while she, Luanda, the eldest, stood there, barren. It was unfair. It brought up a fresh wave of resentment in Luanda, who resolved quietly to double her efforts to have a child with Bronson—if for no other reason than to trump her sister.

Beside Gwendolyn stood Thorgrin; beside Godfrey, Illepra; and beside Kendrick, Sandara. Down at Gwendolyn's feet, there stood Krohn, that animal that Luanda had never liked. Krohn turned and snarled at Luanda as she stepped into the clearing to take her spot beside the others in this place reserved just for the family, Bronson at her side.

Bronson stood there, as if afraid to enter the clearing reserved for the family, but Luanda grabbed his hand and yanked him, and the two of them walked right up to the sarcophagus, taking their place beside the others.

The crowd grew silent, thousands of them, all standing, watching, as Gwendolyn and her siblings turned and faced Luanda, seeing her for the first time in moons. There was a look of cautious surprise on their faces; this was certainly not the big warm welcome she had anticipated. Then again, she reasoned, this was a somber event.

Luanda looked at Gwendolyn, and was surprised to see how different she looked since her pregnancy. Gwen looked much older now, aged beyond her years. She saw the lines in her forehead, under her eyes—and she could tell that being Queen had taken its toll. Yet it was a toll that Luanda had wanted taken on herself.

Luanda searched Gwen's face, looking for any signs of apology or remorse; she was baffled to see none. Gwen stared back, cold and hard, the same look she wore on the day she'd banished her. All the warmth and compassion of the younger sister she'd once known was gone. Luanda could not understand why. After all, had she not summoned her back here? Her younger sister, she felt, was becoming harder and harder to understand the older they grew.

There was no time to talk to her now. Argon stepped forward before the sarcophagus and raised both arms high, and everyone lowered their heads and closed their eyes.

"We come here today to celebrate the death of a beloved member of the royal MacGil family," he boomed, his voice carrying on the wind in the silence. "The matriarch of the family, our beloved King MacGil's devoted wife. A beloved Queen herself for so many years. A woman we all knew and loved. A woman who will finally have a chance to lie with her husband, who was taken from her too soon."

Argon's words made Luanda think of her mother, and of their relationship. It had been a relationship Luanda had always felt confident in, had always thought she understood. Yet as Luanda grew up, she had begun to wonder if maybe she had read it all wrong. When she was young, Luanda had always assumed that she, being firstborn, was her mother's favorite, her pride and joy, the one she had groomed to become a great ruler and Queen. They had never fought.

Gwendolyn, on the other hand, had always been the one that her mother had the most difficulty with, was the one who she had always been arguing and screaming with. But Luanda and her mother had always gotten along. When Luanda had been married off to the McCloud kingdom, Luanda naturally assumed that that was because her mother had expected her to be a woman of great power, and had condoned this marrying off, which would give Luanda the position of strength she deserved. At the same time, she had assumed that her mother had not thought of Gwendolyn for any great position, and that she kept her here, to remain in King's Court, where no woman could obtain power, for an empty life.

Yet now, so much older, Luanda was wondering if she was all wrong. Now, looking back, she saw things differently. Now she saw that the relationship may have been quite the opposite. Perhaps Gwendolyn was the one that her mother had had faith in all along, the same way her father had. Perhaps all of her fighting and screaming with Gwen had been a sign that she was, paradoxically, closer to her. Perhaps Luanda's lack of fighting with her was not a sign of their bond but rather a sign of her mother's disappointment and indifference; and perhaps her mother had married her off to get her out of the MacGil side of the kingdom.

Luanda wondered. She had always assumed her mother had admired her ambition; yet now, looking back on it, seeing the great spot reserved for Gwendolyn, Luanda wondered if her mother actually detested her ambition. Luanda was beginning to look at all of her siblings with a fresh eye; she now saw that she was not the leader, the one most respected—but rather the outcast, and the one least loved. It pained her to realize it. And to realize how delusional she had been. How could she not have seen it? How could she have been so wrong for so long?

Luanda felt old feelings rise to the surface, and she felt a fresh wave of anger and indignation. She looked at her mother's stone sarcophagus, and she had no tears to shed, like her siblings. She felt a cold wave of neutrality.

Perhaps, Luanda reasoned, she had been born into the wrong family. She should have been born into a family that appreciated her. She deserved that. After all, what was so wrong with her? What was so wrong with ambition? She had been born into a royal family with tremendous ambition. Wasn't that what she was supposed to model? Why wasn't her ambition appreciated? She had tried to model everyone around her—and yet, somehow, she had failed.

Argon slowly lowered his hands, finishing his chanting and recitation, and the siblings stepped forward. They each reached out and placed a small rock on the lid of the sarcophagus, as was the ancient custom.

Luanda stepped forward and slowly placed on the lid a beautiful, small white rock she had found on the banks of a river, a beautiful rock which she had carried across the kingdom. She felt pleased with herself. But then Gwendolyn stepped in and placed a rock right after hers, and Luanda saw it was a large, yellow rock, shining and sparkling in the sun, the most beautiful rock she had ever seen, and Luanda felt a fresh wave of resentment and jealousy. Even in death, Gwendolyn outdid her every step of the way. Was there nothing left for Luanda? No place left where she could excel? Not even in this?

Several attendants stepped forward and carried the sarcophagus into the tomb, and soon, it slipped into the blackness—and her mother's body was gone.

Luanda released her breath, realizing how anxious she was. She turned to face Gwendolyn, expecting, now that the ceremony was over, for all of her siblings to welcome her.

Yet Luanda was shocked to see Gwendolyn turn her back on her and begin to walk away.

"Gwendolyn!" Luanda called out, her voice strident, cutting through the air.

Gwendolyn turned and faced her, as did all the other siblings, and a thick, tense silence settled around them.

"Have you no words for me?" Luanda asked, stunned. "Will you not welcome me home?"

"Welcome you home?" Gwen repeated, sounding baffled. "You are not home. And you are not welcome here."

Luanda stood there, stunned.

"Of what do you speak? You invited me back home," Luanda pleaded, slowly feeling her world collapse around her. Was this some sort of sick joke?

Gwendolyn shook her head, firm.

"You were summoned back for our mother's funeral," Gwen corrected. "At our mother's request. Not mine. Your sentence has not been lifted. You will return to your home, on your side of the Highlands, now."

Luanda felt her entire body flush with rage, a prickling of her skin. She felt as if a dagger had been plunged into her heart. She could not even process Gwendolyn's words, her entire world spinning all around her. Could it be true?

"I am *home!*" Luanda insisted, barely thinking clearly, "and I will never go back to the far side of the Highlands! Ever!"

Now Gwendolyn reddened, facing her, equally determined.

"The choice is not yours to make," she said. "Your choice was made for you on the day you betrayed us all. Your punishment deserved death. I was merciful, and gave you exile."

Luanda felt like crying.

"And for how long?" Luanda asked. "Will you never let me back?"

"You are alive," Gwendolyn said. "Be grateful for that."

Luanda wanted to kill her sister.

"You have become a cruel, cold-hearted Queen," Luanda said. "An awful sister who has forgotten mercy."

Gwendolyn sneered.

"And did you show mercy the day you offered for Andronicus to kill us all?"

Luanda frowned.

"Those were different times," she countered.

Gwendolyn shook her head.

"You have not changed, Luanda. And you never will."

Luanda stared at her sister, wanting to hurt her somehow. She did not know how, but she had to say something before she left, something that would really strike at her. Luanda, reeling, looked down and fixed her eyes on Gwendolyn's baby.

"I curse your child!" Luanda screamed out loud.

A horrified gasp spread through the crowd.

"I curse him that he should suffer the same punishment that I am made to suffer! That you never enjoy his presence as long as you live! That he be taken away from you, that you be divided, never to enjoy him!" Luanda screamed, pointing at Guwayne and shaking.

Gwendolyn turned bright red, looking as if she might lunge at her sister.

"Get this creature out of my sight," Gwendolyn said to her men.

The guards rushed forward, grabbed Luanda, and dragged her away.

"NO!" Luanda kicked and screamed as the masses of onlookers stared at her, dragged backwards through the crowd, Bronson trying to get the guards off of her, but unable. "You can't send me back there! Anywhere but there!"

Luanda felt her heart sinking as she was dragged, knowing she would be escorted all the way back to the other side of the Highlands, to her vision of hell, never allowed to set foot in her home again.

CHAPTER TWENTY

The second sun hung low on the horizon, a huge red ball in the sky, and Selese looked up and watched it, her face covered in tears. In her hand, she clutched the scraps of parchment that she had torn up, the letters curled up in her palm, the ones proving that Reece loved someone else. After tearing them to pieces, she had saved the shredded parchment. After all, it was all that she had left of Reece in the world. It was his handwriting, and despite everything, despite how he had hurt her, she still loved him—more than she could say. And she needed to hold onto something of Reece's as she came here, to the Lake of Sorrows.

Selese looked up at the blood red sun and did not look away, staring at it long enough to sting her eyes. She no longer cared. This, she decided, would be the last sun she ever witnessed.

Selese looked out at the Lake of Sorrows, glowing a bright red, reflecting the sun. It looked alive, as if it were a lake on fire. It sat perfectly still, only a lonely wind passing through, the trees rustling, a high-pitched noise, as if crying, as if knowing what Selese was about to do.

Selese cried and cried as she took her first step into the water, clutching the fragments of Reece's letter. She thought of all the time she had spent with him, of how alive he had made her feel, of how much she had been looking forward to their wedding, to their life together. Her love for him was so strong, she could barely comprehend it; she would cross the Ring for him, do anything for him. But if he did not love her back as much, she had no desire to live.

Their love had given her life a new purpose, and all these moons preparing for their wedding had swept her up, had been the greatest time in her life. Yet now, she was about to be publicly humiliated, scorned by Reece, his wedding proposal retracted. Embarrassed in front of the entire kingdom when he left her alone at the altar.

It was too much for Selese to comprehend. Not the humiliation, or the scorn—she could handle that—but most of all, Reece's lack of love for her. It pained her so much to think that he did not love her back. Even worse—that he loved someone else more.

Selese took another step into the water, then another.

Soon, she was up to her knees, clutching the shreds of parchment. The water was cold, unforgiving, despite the summer season, and she began to shiver.

Selese heard the screech of a bird, high up, and she craned her neck to see a falcon circling, screeching. She dimly recognized it as Thorgrin's falcon. Estopheles. He screeched and screeched, as if trying to convince her not to step any further.

Selese tried to shut out its cries. She looked down at the water before her and took another step, now up to her thighs.

Selese reached out, both fists clutching the torn parchment, and gently placed the pieces in the still waters of the lake. As she opened her hands and let them go, she watched as the little shreds of parchment floated away, farther and farther, until the parchment filled with water, and the pieces began to sink, one at a time. Selese spread open her empty palms and let the cold water touch them.

She took another step.

Then another.

She was up to her chest now. She heard herself crying and crying, her body wracked with sobs. She never thought her life would end in this way. In this place. At this time. Alone. Without Reece.

Life had been so kind to her. And yet it had also been so cruel.

Selese heard another screech, high up in the sky. She turned and floated on her back, drifting, weightless, toward the middle of the lake. She lay perfectly still, floating atop the water, and looked up at the sky.

It was filled with a million streaks of red, the two suns almost touching, the most beautiful sky she had ever seen. She floated on her back for she did not know how long, until finally, slowly, her limbs grew cold, heavy, numb, and she felt herself begin to sink.

She did not fight it. She let the water bring her down until her face was submerged. She closed her eyes and in the icy cold blackness felt her body sinking slowly, deeper and deeper, down to the depths of the Lake of Sorrows.

One final thought came to her, before her world turned black:

Reece. I love you.

CHAPTER TWENTY-ONE

Reece sprinted along the trail in the woods, scratched by branches and not caring, his heart pounding as he made for the Lake of Sorrows. After his visit with his mother, Reece had realized the wrong of his ways, and had raced through King's Court searching for Selese, determined to tell her that he loved her, and that he could not wait to marry her.

Reece had decided that his love for Stara had been momentary craziness. Whether his feelings had been real or not, he realized he needed to strike Stara from his mind. He had to be with Selese, regardless of how he might also feel for Stara. It was the right thing, the honorable thing, to do. And he also loved Selese, very, very much. He realized he might not have quite the same level of passion for her, but he also loved Selese in a different way, and while in some ways, his love for her might not be as strong, in other ways, it might just be stronger.

When Reece had arrived at the House of the Sick looking for Selese, he had instead encountered Illepra, who had told him the terrible news: one of Tirus's sons had paid her a visit, had shown her a scroll, and ever since that moment, Selese had not been the same person. She had been devastated. She had withdrawn into herself, and would not tell Illepra what it was about. All that Illepra knew was that she had fled toward the Lake of Sorrows. Illepra was baffled.

Illepra handed Reece one of the torn-up fragments of the scrolls, and his blood curdled and his skin grew cold as he recognized his own handwriting. He realized, with shock, that it was an old scroll, from his childhood, professing his love to Stara.

But Selese wouldn't have known that, he realized. She would assume it was fresh.

Reece realized—it all came washing over him in one horrible moment—that Tirus had set in motion an elaborate treachery; he had sent one of his sons to convince Selese that Reece loved Stara. To tear Reece and Selese apart, to assure Reece ended up with Stara. No doubt, to serve his own purposes. Tirus wanted power—and Reece's union with Stara would assure that for him.

Reece had flushed with rage and humiliation when he'd realized it all, realized that Selese now thought that he loved Stara and was going to call off their wedding. The thought of how it must have pained her, especially to hear it from a stranger, tore him apart.

When Illepra mentioned the Lake of Sorrows, Reece immediately thought the worst. He had turned and sprinted for it, and had not stopped sprinting since.

Please, God, he thought as he ran. *Let her be alive. Just give me one chance, one chance to tell her that I love her, that I will marry her, that Tirus's scroll was treachery, that it was all a mistake.*

Reece ran until his lungs burst, and finally, as the second sun began to dip below the horizon, he burst from the woods, to the shores of the Lake of Sorrows. Reece had hoped and prayed to see Selese standing there.

But as Reece arrived, his heart dropped to see the shore was empty. He looked down at the sand, and his heart fell to see torn-up fragments of the scroll. He realized that Selese had been here. That she'd held the scroll. Had torn it up. None of this could be good.

Reece looked out at the water, panicking, hoping for any sign of her. Yet still, he saw none. He scanned the treeline, desperate for any indication of her, any sign for where she might have gone. Yet still, there was none.

As the sun dipped lower and twilight spread across the sky, Reece squinted into the darkness, and he spotted an outline of something at the shore of the lake, a figure lying on the sand.

Reece sprinted, his heart pounding, praying it was Selese, and that she was okay.

"Selese!" he called out.

But she did not move.

Reece reached the body and dropped to his knees in the sand beside it, gasping for breath. He turned the body over, praying she was okay.

Please, God. Let this be Selese. Let her be okay. I will give you anything. Anything.

As Reece turned her over, he felt his entire world go numb.

There was Selese. Eyes wide open. Her skin too pale. Her skin, ice to the touch.

Reece leaned back and shrieked to the heavens.

"SELESE!"

Reece broke into sobs as he reached down and hugged her, lifting up her body, holding her tight in his arms as he rocked her back and forth. He wanted with all he had for his warmth to seep into her, to bring her cold, lifeless body back to life. He would give anything. He had been stupid. So stupid. And now this poor girl, who had loved him so much, had paid the price.

"Selese," he moaned, again and again. "I'm so sorry."

Reece held her, tighter and tighter, wondering how fate could be so cruel. Why? Why had it all had to happen like this? Why couldn't he have arrived here just a few minutes sooner? Why couldn't he have a chance to explain?

It was too late for all of that now. As he held her dead body, he collapsed on the sand with her, his entire body wracked with sobs, knowing that he would never, ever, be the same.

CHAPTER TWENTY-TWO

Gwendolyn stood beside Thor, surrounded by attendants, in the sprawling grounds of King's Court, watching the final preparations for her wedding unfold in the night. The plaza was lit by a thousand torches, nearly as light as day, and an army of servants rushed to and fro, lugging thousands of flowers, shaping hedges, even bringing in exquisite rows of flowering trees. Other workers set up chairs, decorations, while others put the final touches on the altars for the ceremony. There was not just one altar, but two, one each for Gwendolyn and Thorgrin and Reece and Selese. The entire Ring prepared for their joint wedding. It would be the biggest and grandest wedding that King's Court had ever seen, and Gwendolyn was determined for that to be the case.

Gwendolyn knew that this was what her people needed. She loved all of this splendor for herself, too, of course, but it was her desire to please her people that drove her to make this spectacle what it was, to make it over the top. Sometimes, she knew, her people needed shelter and protection; other times, though, what they needed was joy, distraction. Entertainment, after all, was as vital a human need as any other. What would life be merely with food and shelter? Life needed a soul, a supreme distraction. Her father had always told her that good rulers considered the people's needs; great rulers considered their hearts.

Gwen walked slowly through the ceremony space, large enough to hold a city, overseeing the workers and making small adjustments to the army of servants creating decorations, putting her stamp on the wedding to make it as beautiful as it could be. She wished her mother could be with her now to see all this, to celebrate with her. It was hard to go from a funeral to a wedding, and a part of her wondered whether they should; yet another part of her knew that that was exactly what they needed to do, what the people needed, and what her mother herself would have wanted.

Gwen was also driven by her love for Thor, and for her love for their new baby. She wanted this to be the most beautiful celebration to ever take place. Thor deserved it. Their love deserved it. She and Thor had been through too much together for it to be anything less.

Reece wanted it to be magnificent for Reece and Selese, too. After all, Reece was her brother, a member of the royal family, and he, too, was deserving of the greatest, grandest wedding the kingdom had to offer. Her father and mother, if they were alive, she was sure would want no less. And since they were not here to oversee it, as they had been for Luanda's wedding, it all fell on Gwendolyn's shoulders. She felt she needed to act not just as Queen, not just as a bride-to-be, but also as the missing parent for Reece. It was easy, though, being as close as she was to Reece, and as close as she was to Selese, who already felt like a sister to her.

Attendants followed Gwen, busy behind her, fitting her with a spectacular wedding dress. They had been working on the dress for moons, and now they were putting the final touches on it. Gwen tried to hold still as they made adjustments, twisting the fine silks around her arms and legs and wrists, measuring, adjusting.

Gwendolyn looked it all over and was content—yet deep inside, she was restless. She found herself thinking, brooding, like her father used to do. She looked out, beyond the plaza, to King's Court, her kingdom and beyond, and she pondered affairs of state. She worried. She worried the way a good Queen should worry. Everything here was perfect, shining, resplendent, more beautiful than it had ever been. Yet still, somehow, she could not help feel as if some terrible storm were brewing.

"My lady?" an attendant prodded. "We should not wait longer."

Gwen looked at him and realized he was right. She felt overcome with a wave of anxiety as she wondered, for the millionth time, where Reece and Selese could be. Selese should have been here hours ago, and Reece, she knew, had recently arrived from the Upper Isles and had seen their mother before she'd passed. Reece, too, should be here. Where was he? Could the two of them have forgotten somehow?

She did not think it likely.

It was getting late, and Gwen knew the rehearsal needed to continue, and she nodded her consent.

A horn sounded, and Gwen and Thor walked down the endlessly long wedding aisle, holding each other's hands, and each holding a single lit torch out on either side of them. They were followed by a trail of attendants as they walked down the aisle for their rehearsal, heading slowly toward the altars. On either side of them, thousands of chairs sat empty, waiting. Soon, Gwen knew, they would be packed with people. She felt butterflies. It was all becoming real.

It was the final rehearsal before the big day, and Gwen's heart was fluttering with excitement—yet she was also nervous. It would be the biggest day of her life, and she wanted everything to go smoothly. The entire kingdom would be watching, and knowing her people, they would be searching for any signs of omens.

They reached the altars, and they placed their torches in the holders, and Thor helped Gwen as they stepped up onto the platform.

Gwen looked about the altars and wondered. Where was Argon? He was supposed to be here, to preside over the rituals and ceremony. Had he not appeared because it was just a rehearsal? Would he show up on the wedding day?

Gwen stood there, feeling an increasing sense of foreboding. She saw the two other torches on the altar, placed where they'd been all night—Reece's and Selese's—and Gwen turned and looked out at the darkness.

She felt something was wrong. It was unlike her brother not to show up, and unlike Selese, who had been here with her for all these moons, through every step of the preparations. They were all getting married together, after all, and she knew how much it meant to Selese.

Had the two of them gone somewhere?

Gwen peered onto the darkness and began to feel her stomach turning. *Not on this day*, Gwen thought. More than anything, she wanted nothing to be wrong on this day.

As Gwen looked out into the blackness, past the rows and rows of torches, she began to see something. Her royal messenger was racing her way. He ran faster than she had ever seen him, and he was flanked by two attendants. She saw by the look on his face that whatever news he carried, it was not good.

Gwendolyn took Thor's hand and stepped down the steps, back to the aisle. All of her attendants parted as they looked, puzzled, at the messenger. He came running forward and Gwendolyn watched, a sinking feeling in her chest, as he knelt before her.

He bowed his head low, then looked up at her with bloodshot eyes.

"My lady, I bear news," he said, then hesitated. "News which no man should have to bear."

Gwen's heart pounded, as her mind raced with a million scenarios.

"Out with it then," Gwendolyn said harshly.

"It is…" The messenger trailed off, stopping himself, wiping away tears. He took a deep breath. "My lady, it is Selese. She has been found dead."

Gwen gasped, as did Thor beside her—as did all of her attendants. She reached down and clutched her chest, feeling as if she had just been stabbed.

"Selese?" she said. "What? How? It is not possible."

Gwen looked around at all the wedding preparations, half of them for Selese. None of it made sense. She was alive. She had to be.

"Was she attacked?" Thor demanded, his brow furrowed in anger as he clutched the hilt of his sword.

But the messenger shook his head sadly, to her surprise.

"No, my lady. I am sorry to say…her life was taken by her own hand."

Gwen gasped again, horrified by the news. She clutched Thor's hand, and he squeezed hers back. She could not fathom it.

"I don't understand," she said. "Why would Selese…take her life? Our wedding…it is but one day away. She looked forward to this day, more than anything on earth…"

"I do not know, my lady," the messenger continued. "All I know is that your brother is by her side. At the Lake of Sorrows."

Her close friend dead, the night before her wedding? The night before the biggest day of her life? How could it be?

Gen felt herself reeling, felt all her carefully laid plans falling apart around her.

She turned and looked at Thor, who looked back at her, equally grave, equally puzzled. This night of the highest joy had so suddenly been turned into a night of deepest mourning.

138

"Bring me to him," Gwen demanded, already walking, her people filing in behind her, determined to understand what had happened.

*

Gwendolyn held Thor's hand as they walked, squeezing his hand, it giving her the reassurance she desperately needed. She closed her eyes and hoped this was all a nightmare, some terrible mistake, as they all made their way through the forest path, toward the Lake of Sorrows. But a part of her could not help but feel that it was all real.

Gwen was crying silently, and she quickly wiped a tear, knowing she needed to show the strength of a Queen. But inside, her heart was breaking as the news was settling in. Selese, dead. One of her closest friends. Her future sister-in-law. The love of Reece's life. Her wedding partner. And her life taken by her own hand.

How could it all be?

It made no sense. Gwen knew how much Selese had been looking forward to the day. Why would she do such a thing? Selese had always been brimming with joy, the first to help someone else in need, to volunteer her time in the house of the sick.

Gwen sighed. Just when she had envisioned all the darkness behind them, just when she had envisioned them breaking free from sorrow and into times of joy, now, the times of darkness seemed to have returned. It was as if a curse lingered over the royal family, one they could never quite escape.

They finally broke through the clearing of the woods, and Gwen gasped as she saw the Lake of Sorrows before her, and her brother, kneeling on the shore, huddle over Selese's body.

Her blood ran cold as she heard Reece's cries. She knew, with dread, that all of this was real.

Gwen approached, Thor beside her, her entourage trailing her, and as she neared, she saw the pale white face of Selese, her long hair spilled out on the sand, lit under the moonlight. Gwen clutched Thor's hand tightly.

Gwen stopped but a foot or two away and looked down at her brother. She had never seen him so devastated, wracked with sobs, looking as if his whole life had been destroyed.

Gwendolyn, crying herself, knelt down and laid a reassuring hand on Reece's shoulder. She hardly knew what to say. She wanted answers, of course. But now was not the time.

Reece turned and looked at her, his eyes bright red, tears sliding down.

"My brother," she said.

She leaned in, but instead of giving her a hug, Reece turned and looked back at Selese, staring at her, running his hand along her face, as if still trying to bring her back.

"She died by my hand," Reece said, his voice that of a broken man.

Gwen looked back in shock.

"By your hand?" she repeated.

He nodded.

She was perplexed.

"I was told she took her own life," Gwen said.

Reece shook his head.

"She did the deed," he said. "But the fault is mine. I might as well have wielded the dagger."

Gwen furrowed her brow.

"I don't understand. How is the fault yours?"

Reece sighed.

"Selese received word, through subterfuge, that I was in love with another woman. That our wedding was off."

Gwen gasped, shocked.

"And is it true?" she asked.

Reece shrugged.

"It was a partial truth, a truth obscured by lies. It is true, I fell in love again with my cousin, Stara. But since then, I had changed my mind. I had come to find Selese, to tell her I loved only her. That I wanted to marry her. But Tirus deceived her. He sent his son, who convinced her I did not love her. I have been betrayed. But the fault is mine."

Reece sobbed.

"If only I could take it back, I would give anything. But now it's too late."

Reece sobbed, and Thor laid a reassuring hand on his shoulder.

"Whatever the situation is," Thor said. "You did not kill her. As you say, she was deceived. And whoever was behind this treachery shall be brought to justice."

But Reece ignored him, wracked with sobs.

Gwendolyn felt her heart breaking as she tried to process this terrible tragedy. She felt a need to take action, to do *something*. She saw that Selese's corpse was stiff with cold, and that Reece had been here too many hours, and she knew something needed to be done.

"She will be given a proper burial," Gwendolyn said. "With all the honors and glories of our kingdom."

Reece shook his head.

"No she won't. The royal cemetery will not accept her. Suicides are not allowed, remember?"

Gwendolyn thought, and she did remember. It was the one rule that her father had been strict about: no one who took their own life could be buried with their royal ancestors.

It came to Gwen that the time had come to make a strong decision.

"I am Queen," she said, confidently, "and I write the law. Selese will be buried with all glories and honors in the Royal Cemetery."

Reece looked up at her, and for the first time, he seemed to have some sense of peace.

"My lady, that would set a terrible precedent," Aberthol said, stepping forward.

"I am Queen, and she will be buried as I say," she said, giving Aberthol a withering look until finally he backed away.

Gwen laid a hand on her brother's shoulder, and he turned and looked at her, slightly mollified.

"She will be buried, my brother, as befits her. Our wedding shall be called off, and tomorrow, instead, we shall have her funeral. Will you bring her to the cemetery, so that her body can be prepared?"

Gwen needed to find a way to include Reece, so that he could feel as if he were a part of it, and so that they could begin to move on.

Reece looked at her, as if debating, and finally, he nodded, seeming satisfied.

"If she will be buried as you say, with all honors, then yes, I will take her."

Gwen's attendants came forward to take the corpse, but Reece shoved them away. He was mad with grief, and he would let no one else close to her.

Instead, Reece reached down and scooped her up himself. He stood there, holding her in his arms, then slowly walked off with her, into the forest trail, the men closing in with torches behind them.

Gwendolyn and Thor lingered behind. They stood there and looked at each other, their faces filled with grief and shock beneath the moonlight.

"Our wedding will have to be postponed," Gwen said, her voice filled with sorrow and disappointment. "The grief that will run through our kingdom will be deep. I fear our wedding may not take place for many more moons."

Thor nodded, agreeing.

"Our wedding bells will be replaced by funeral bells," he said. "Such is the way of life."

Thor embraced her and she embraced him back, hugged him tight.

Over his shoulder, Gwen cried silently, overwhelmed with grief, with loss. She could not help but think that this was the beginning of the end, of a new, even greater stretch of darkness, and that nothing would ever be the same in King's Court again.

CHAPTER TWENTY-THREE

Romulus marched down the wide country road, gravel crunching beneath his feet, leading thousands of soldiers, an entire division of his army following him into war. Romulus marched with confidence, taking long strides, fearless, with his shirt open and his large, glowing green amulet prominently visible on his chest.

Romulus felt like a new man since that ceremony in the cave. After he had risen from the waters, his initiation into the puddle of fire, that sorcerer had given him this amulet, along with the prophecy that he would wield it to become lord of the dragons. He assured him that, for the next moon cycle, nothing on this planet would stop him, not even the dragons, and not even the Ring. It would all—anything he could imagine—be his.

Romulus felt it to be true. Since leaving that cave he had put it to the test, consolidating his power over the Empire, ruthlessly assassinating all of his enemies, instilling fear in all of his men, and taking over, force by force, all of the legions that had once belonged to Andronicus. He had abolished the Empire Council, and he now ruled alone with an iron fist, leaving a wake of blood in his trail. He had been successful, no one able to stop him, managing to get the entire Empire to cower at the sight of him. The ceremony had worked.

And yet today, Romulus knew, would be the ultimate test of his power. Romulus's people now believed in him, because of the prophecy, because of the rumors they had heard. They all already saw him as lord of the dragons.

But Romulus had not proven it yet, and his people knew that. He knew this final test would be the most important one: to become a ruler of legend, once and for all, to assure himself a place that no man could topple, he would need a dazzling display of power. He would need to demonstrate to his people that he could indeed stop the dragons.

Romulus marched with all of his men through the southern fields of the Empire, heading toward the city of Ganos, a once-great Empire city that now lay in ruins, ransacked by a host of dragons. Over these past moons reports had filtered in of the trail of devastation left by the dragons, who had been provoked when Romulus had entered their territory and tried to steal back the Destiny Sword. Now, the dragons were taking revenge. They were sweeping across the Empire, raining fire, wiping out one great Empire city after the next. There had been no way to stop them; Romulus had sent many divisions to try, only to see them obliterated. The Empire was losing ground, and the people were losing faith in him. If he didn't do something fast, there would be a revolt.

Now, it was time for Romulus to offer a stunning display of his newfound power. To prove to his people that he indeed was lord of the dragons. If he could stop and control the dragons, that meant that the other prophecy was true, too: that he would shatter the Shield and enter the Ring. He smiled at the thought. He would control every inch of every corner of the world, and be the greatest ruler of all time.

Romulus's heart pounded as he marched to Ganos, preparing to risk his life to face the dragons. If he died, at least he would go down in a blaze of glory—and if he survived, well, his life would never be the same.

"My liege, are you certain you want to attempt this?"

Romulus turned to see his lead generals behind him, panicked as they began to crest the final hill before their arrival in Ganos. He could see the fear in their eyes, these men who were never afraid. He understood; as soon as they crested this ridge, they would be spotted and would have no choice but to

145

confront the dragons. And if they fared the same as every other army in the Empire, they, too, would soon be dead.

"My liege, please turn back," another general said. "All of our men have died by the dragons' breath. What if the prophecy is false? After all, you are but a single man."

Romulus ignored them, marching faster and faster, cresting the top of the ridge, smiling to himself. He felt he would win. But if not, he didn't care. He'd be glad to be burned alive with all his men. In fact, he would find that quite fun. He had no fear of death like these men. He knew it was coming for him soon enough. And if he was not meant to be ruler of the world, he would rather just embrace his death now.

Romulus crested the ridge and stopped in his tracks, his breath taken away at the sight. The entire vista below opened up, and Romulus saw dozens of dragons flapping their great wings in the air, screeching, arching their backs, intertwining in the air, soaring, diving down, rising up, pillaging the city below. Some of them breathed fire down on already smoldering buildings. Others swooped down with their great talons and tore up ancient buildings on the ground, as if playthings, carrying them into the sky, then dropping them. They were enjoying their destruction.

Romulus's men came up beside him and stopped, and he heard their audible gasps. He could sense their fear, as the air was filled with the smell of sulfur, as the heat reached them from here, and as all around them the dragons screeched.

But Romulus stood unafraid. He could feel his new amulet throbbing on his chest, could see it throbbing green, and he felt himself infused with a strength he did not understand. It was a primal strength. The strength of other realms. He did not fear an encounter with the dragons; he craved one.

The host of dragons, as if sensing his presence, suddenly turned in his direction. They stopped what they were doing, arched their backs, and roared, infuriated. They then all came flying toward him at the speed of lightning, diving right for him.

Romulus stood his ground, unafraid, while many of his men turned and fled, screaming. Romulus waited and waited, as these huge, ancient creatures blackened the sky, swooping down, right for him. They opened their great mouths and breathed fire.

Romulus felt the heat as a wave of fire came his way. He knew this was his moment.

But he still was unafraid. Instead, he raised a single palm, held it out toward the fire, and watched as the dragons stopped in midair, several feet before they reached him. He threw his palm forward, and as he did, the rain of fire descending for him suddenly reversed, shooting up in a storm, engulfing the dragons.

The dragons screeched, then they all lifted up, away from Romulus, in a rage.

They circled around, determined, swooping down for him again with their great talons extended, their huge jaws open—and this time, Romulus extended both palms.

A blue light shot forth, up into the sky, encasing all the dragons. He felt the amulet throbbing, the newfound strength coursing through his body, and within moments, he felt himself controlling the dragons. He raised his arms higher, and as he did, the dragons all froze in the air. Romulus lifted them higher and higher, until he stopped them exactly where he wanted them to be.

They looked down at him, confused, flapping their wings, unable to move, unable to breathe fire at him.

They stared down at him with a new expression. It was the look of a beast staring back at its master.

CHAPTER TWENTY-FOUR

Reece knelt in the black of night, atop the cliffs, cradling Selese's body in his arms, as he had been for hours, numb to the cold and to the wind and to the world around him. Thousands of people held torches in the night, a massive funeral procession, all crowding around the open grave, all waiting quietly, patiently, for Reece to let go of Selese's body.

But Reece could not let go. He had been holding her for hours, weeping so much that he had no tears left to shed, and feeling completely empty to the world.

He still felt it had all been his fault. How stupid and reckless and irresponsible he had been to give in to his passions in the Upper Isles, to even look twice at Stara. How stupid he had been for his lapse of reason.

Because of his stupid feelings, because of his lust for Stara, this beautiful girl, who had been so devoted to him, who had risked it all for him, now lay dead.

All Reece had wanted was a chance to make up for his mistake. If it hadn't been for Tirus's son, Reece surely would have had that chance. After all, no one else even knew of his encounter with Stara, of his affections for her. Selese never would have known, and she'd be alive today. If it hadn't been for Tirus's son, Reece would be marrying Selese now, instead of burying her.

Reece hated himself. But even more so, he hated Tirus and his sons.

As Reece knelt there, he felt that Selese's soul cried for vengeance. And he would not rest until he exacted it.

"Reece," came a soft voice.

Reece felt a soft hand on his shoulder, and he looked over to see Gwendolyn kneeling beside him.

"It is time to let her go. I know you don't want to. But holding her here will not bring her back to us. She is gone now. The fates must take what they demand."

Reece was overcome with anguish at the idea of letting her body go. He just wanted her to wake up again. He just wanted this nightmare to be over. He just wanted one more chance to make things right. Why couldn't he have just one more chance? Why did his one mistake in life have to be a fatal one?

As Reece clutched her tightly, he knew on some level that Gwendolyn was right. He could not bring her back. Time for that had passed.

Reece leaned over and slowly, gently, lowered Selese's body into the open grave, into the earth below.

He wept as her body slid down into the fresh dirt. Selese's body spun around and landed face first, looking up to the sky, her eyes open. One of her arms propped up, her finger pointed toward Reece. Reece's blood ran cold. He felt it was pointed at him accusingly. He wept and wept.

Reece looked on as others all around him began to shovel fresh dirt on Selese's corpse.

"NO!" Reece shrieked.

Several strong men held him back, and soon, Selese's body disappeared beneath the soil. It was all like a horrific dream. Dimly, Reece was aware of people he knew and loved, Gwendolyn and Thorgrin, his Legion brothers, faces that were now all just a blur of grief. They all tried to console him. But he was past consoling.

The love of his life—the true love of his life—was now dead and buried. He could not bring her back. But he could exact vengeance.

Reece slowly began to harden inside, as a resolve began to set hold. He looked out into the black of night, into the howling winds, and vowed that, no matter what it took, vengeance would be his.

CHAPTER TWENTY-FIVE

Steffen sat on the top of the mountain ridge, on a small plateau, looking out at the countryside spread out below, and, still reeling from his encounter with his family, wiped away a tear. After instructing the royal caravan to wait down below, he had hiked up here, alone, to this spot he remembered as a child, the spot he would always come to be alone. The ridge, made of rocks and gravel, climbed steeply into the air, the crater at the top now a small, shallow reflecting pond, with a radius of perhaps twenty feet. It was a quiet, empty place, a place to reflect with nothing but sky, rocks, water, and wind.

A gust of wind pushed back his hair, and Steffen looked down at the rippling waters, reflecting the two suns in the sky. Being up here brought back his childhood. Too many times he'd come up here to get away from all of them, to stare into these waters and hope to see a different person staring back. A person who was not disfigured. A person with a perfect body and perfect shape, like all of the others. A person who was tall and strong and broad; a person his father could be proud of.

Usually, after a certain point, he'd stop looking. He'd look away instead, disappointed in himself, as usual, and understanding why others were disappointed in him, too.

This time, as he sat there, Steffen forced himself to keep looking, to stare into the waters. He saw his crooked shape, his short height, and he examined himself carefully. He did not have the good looks of all the others; and yet, this time, he also saw something else. He saw that his eyes, a light cream, were not terribly unattractive; neither was his auburn hair, thick and wavy, falling past his ears. If it were not for his shape, his body, he was not the ugliest man in the world.

When he looked into his face, he saw a face too big for his body—but he also saw a long, strong jaw and chin, saw a man who was proud and determined. A man who would not let others keep him down. A man who would not treat others the way he had been treated. Steffen took pride in that. He had a bigger heart than all of them, than all of those cruel people down in that village. It made him wonder: who, indeed, was the misshapen one? Why did he empower those people?

He would never have his family's approval, but he could live with that. His own approval, he was starting to realize, could be enough.

"Steffen?" came a voice.

Steffen wheeled, surprised anyone else was up here—and even more surprised to see a beautiful woman standing there, perhaps twenty, wearing the simple garb of the villagers.

She looked down at him sweetly, not with the hate of the others, the same sweetness he'd detected in her voice. Very few people spoke to him in that sort of tone, kind and compassionate. He stared up, blinking, and wondered for a moment who she was.

"Do you not remember me?" she asked.

Steffen examined her closely. Her face was beautiful, her eyes almond-shaped, her jaw and cheekbones chiseled, with big wide lips, light brown eyes, and light brown hair to match. She was tall and thin, and as he examined her, he noticed her right hand was missing two fingers.

His eyes lit with recognition as it all flooded back to him.

"Arliss?" he asked.

Arliss nodded sweetly, and smiled.

"May I sit with you?" she asked.

Steffen looked up at her in wonder. He could barely catch his tongue. He could hardly comprehend how long it had been since he'd seen her, how beautiful she had become—and the fact that she had come all the way up here and actually wanted to sit with him. He looked up at her, wide-eyed with shock.

"When was the last time I saw you?" he asked, reeling.

She smiled sweetly.

"When we were six," she said.

He looked at her, flabbergasted.

"You have grown," he said.

She laughed.

"As have you."

He blushed, not knowing what else to say.

Steffen had never forgotten her. Growing up, Arliss had been the only one in his village who had been kind to him. Perhaps it was because she had been missing two fingers—imperfect, like him, it made her understand; the others had been cruel to her, too. But Steffen had always seen her as beautiful—the most beautiful girl in the village—and had always been so grateful for her kindness. Indeed, it had been the one thing that had sustained him up to the time he'd left, had taken away his darkest moments. He had never forgotten her, and had always wondered if he would ever see her again.

"May I sit with you?" she repeated.

Steffen remembered himself; he immediately slid over, making room for her to sit beside him.

"What are you doing up here?" he asked.

"Word spread you'd come to town, and I figured this is where you would be," she replied.

Steffen sighed and shook his head.

"Some things never change," he said.

"Did you see your family, then?" she asked.

He nodded, looking down.

"I should have known better," he said.

"I'm sorry," she said, understanding in her voice, knowing everything immediately, as she'd always had. She understood all too well.

"I do not live near here anymore," he said. "I live in King's Court now. I serve the Queen."

"I know," she said, smiling back at him. "Word spreads quickly here."

Steffen smiled.

"I forgot. The houses in this town have no walls."

She laughed, a light carefree sound that restored Steffen, made him forget his woes.

"You coming through here with that royal entourage is probably the most exciting—and humiliating—thing that has ever happened to this excuse of a village. I think they're all sitting down there in shame right now—at least, I hope they are."

Steffen frowned.

"It is not my intention to shame anyone," he said, humbly. "I came here because the Queen sent me. Otherwise, I never would have again."

Arliss laid a hand on his wrist.

"I know," she said, reassuring. "I know who you are. We grew up together. I've never forgotten you."

Steffen turned and looked at her, and he saw her staring back at him with eyes filled with love and compassion. No one had ever looked at him that way before, and his heart began to pound. Was it possible? His entire life, Steffen never received the gaze of a woman's affection; he'd had no idea what it felt like. But now, unless his eyes were deceiving him, he thought he was seeing exactly that.

"I never forgot you either, Arliss," he said. "I assumed you'd grown up and gone away. That you'd likely married some local lord."

Arliss laughed.

"Me? Marry a lord? Are you crazy?"

"And why not? You were the most beautiful woman in this village."

Arliss blushed.

"In your eyes, perhaps. Not the eyes of the others. In their eyes," she said, holding up her hand missing the fingers, "I'm a freak."

Now Steffen laughed.

"And I am not?" he countered.

Arliss laughed back, and they laughed together. It felt so good to Steffen to laugh, something he rarely did, and all the tension of the day began to dissipate. Just sitting next to Arliss made him feel good. Someone who actually cared for him; someone who shared something with him, who was equally oppressed by this place; someone who understood.

"So?" Steffen asked. "Did you ever marry?"

Arliss shook her head, looking down.

"It is a small village. Not many men to choose from. Not that any man here ever looked at me with anything but scorn."

Steffen felt himself surge with hope upon hearing she was unwed.

"Would you like to leave this place?" he asked.

It was the boldest thing he'd ever said, and the words just poured out of his mouth, without his even taking a moment to think of what he was saying. They just felt right. Arliss was clearly trapped here, and Steffen wanted to free her from this bondage, from this awful place of small-minded people. Yet if he had given it some thought, he probably would not have worked up the confidence to ask her. But it was more than just that; he also, as he'd always had, loved her.

Arliss looked at him, her eyes wide in surprise and wonder.

"And how might I do that?" she asked.

"You can come with me," he found himself saying, his world a blur as he was speaking, the words stumbling out, changing his life, and hers, forever. "Come with me to King's Court. You can stay in King's Castle. There are many rooms."

"I'm sure the Queen would love that," she said, sarcastic.

Steffen shook his head.

"You don't understand. I am one of the Queen's right hands. If I ask for something—and I never ask for anything—she would grant it. More than that, she sees through people. She would see your good nature. She would love you. I'm certain of that. In fact, she would be happy to have you there."

Arliss' eyes flooded with tears, and she laughed as the tears slid down her face. She wiped them away quickly and looked away, then right back at Steffen.

"No one has ever spoken to me the way you have," she said. "I do not know whether to believe it. I'm so used to being made fun of."

"As am I," he said.

Steffen realized he needed to let her know how serious he was.

He rose and held out a hand, looking down earnestly. Slowly, hesitantly, Arliss took it.

"Those days are behind you now," he said. "Never, in my presence, shall you be made fun of again."

Arliss rose, holding Steffen's hand, and looked into his eyes, long and hard. They each held the stare, and Steffen felt himself getting lost in her eyes, lost in another world, lost in something greater than himself—something he had never experienced before.

Arliss did not look away, and Steffen, suddenly, found himself overcome with emotion, and leaning in to kiss her.

Arliss did not back away. Instead, she waited, and at the last second, she leaned in, too, her lips trembling on his.

They kissed, the first time Steffen had ever kissed a woman, and to him it felt like it lasted forever. When it was over, he felt like a changed man. He felt he understood what love meant.

"Forgive me, my lady," he said, unsure. "I did not mean to be too forward."

Arliss looked down, squeezed his hand, and held it tight. Then she looked back up and smiled.

"Nothing," she said, "has ever made me happier."

CHAPTER TWENTY-SIX

Alistair walked beside Erec, each holding their horse by its reins, a dozen Silver behind them. She was thrilled to finally be dismounted and have some time to walk quietly with Erec. This journey, heading south so that they could embark for the Southern Isles, had been taxing, most of all because Alistair hadn't had much quiet time with Erec. Now, finally, she and Erec walked out in front, the two of them alone, walking close to each other. They had all ridden most of the way, but as they reached this narrow mountain pass, they had all dismounted to walk with the horses, the trail too rocky, the fall-off too steep in either direction.

Alistair welcomed the break, welcomed the opportunity to be able to walk beside Erec, to finally have a chance to speak with him without the sound of galloping horses in their ears. There was so much she had wanted to say to him. Most of all, she just wanted to be close to him. She was a bit nervous about leaving the Ring, crossing the ocean, about the huge adventure that lay ahead of them. They'd be leaving her homeland, entering a foreign kingdom. Would his people like her?

Alistair felt as if she never had a chance to spend time alone with Erec, to get really close to him—there were always some events coming in between them. And now that they were finally alone, there were so many things she wanted to ask him. So many, in fact, that her mind froze up, and she could think of none.

That was okay, though; just being with him in the silence was enough.

As they walked side by side, Alistair was awestruck by the vista that spread out before them. She looked out at sweeping valleys and ridges, lit beneath the beautiful summer suns, fields of tall, orange grasses swaying in the wind. How incredibly beautiful the Ring was, she thought, especially now, in summer, entire valleys filled with trees of every color. It was a place of incredible bounty, of such prosperity and peace. A part of her never wanted to leave.

Alistair felt overwhelmed with conflicting emotions as she thought back to all she was leaving behind. Her brother, Thorgrin, just as she was beginning to know him. A part of her wanted desperately to seek out her mother, too.

There was also her new sister-in-law and friend, Gwendolyn. Alistair had been looking forward to her wedding so much, and a huge part of her wanted to stay behind and be there for it, as she had promised Gwendolyn. She felt as if she were letting both her and her brother down.

What bothered Alistair most of all was her premonition, no matter how hard she tried to shake it, that terrible things were coming for the Ring. She tried to ignore it, to discard it as nonsense. After all, the Ring had never been more secure. What bad could possibly come here?

Alistair reached over to take Erec's hand, and as she did, she could feel the warmth coming off of it, and she knew, above all, she had to be here, by her husband's side. She *wanted* to be here. Despite everything, there was nowhere else she wanted to be. Her people needed her, but her husband needed her more—and she would not be happy if she were not by his side.

Erec squeezed her hand.

"Thank you for coming with me," he said. "It is a journey I would not wish to take without you. I can't wait for you to meet my people."

Erec smiled at her, and she smiled back as she held his hand. It was the right decision. After all, his father was dying, and it was past time for him to return to his homeland. And once they reached the Southern Isles, they would marry. Nothing meant more to Alistair than that.

"I would journey with you to the ends of the earth, my lord," she replied.

They walked until the trail forked, and they all came to a stop. To the left, atop the ridge they had been walking, the path continued—but it also forked to the right, sharply down, curving off in a different direction.

Erec and his men all began to take the path downward, but Alistair stopped in her tracks, her entire body suddenly feeling cold. Her eyes opened wide as she sensed something—a powerful feeling. She stood there, frozen.

Finally, Erec and the men realized, and they all stopped, too, and turned and looked at her.

Erec looked at her with concern.

"What is it, my lady?" he asked.

Alistair looked down in terror at the trail they were about to embark on.

"We cannot go down there," she said. "The trail is not safe."

"What do you mean, my lady?" one of the Silver said. "This trail has been traveled for centuries. And against warriors such as us, no thieves stand a chance."

Alistair stared at the trail, and she did not back down. She felt something off.

"I do not know what it is," she replied, "but I know it is not safe. If you take that path, you will die."

They all turned and looked down at the trail, wondering, skeptical.

Erec walked over to her and took her hand. He faced the men.

"If my lady says the trail is unsafe, then it is unsafe. We shall follow her."

"But my lord," one of them protested, "that trail offers the most direct way to the ship. To go another way would lose us days. We could miss the ship. And for what? A premonition?"

Erec's jaw tightened in Alistair's defense.

"I said we shall not take that trail," Erec repeated firmly.

Erec turned and, taking Alistair's hand, forked to the upper trail. Reluctantly, all his men fell in behind him.

As they walked, Erec squeezed her hand, leaned over, and whispered in Alistair's ear: "I trust you, my lady."

Alistair was about to reply, but before she could, suddenly, there came a great rumbling. They all turned and looked below, and they watched as there suddenly came a tremendous rockslide, huge boulders separating from the steep mountain ridge, rolling down. In moments, they completely filled the trail below them—the trail they all would have been on had they chosen the opposite fork just moments before.

They all stopped and turned to Alistair in awe.

She could feel all the eyes on her. They all knew that if they had gone the other way, right now, they would all be dead.

Alistair didn't know where her power came from. A part of her did not want to know.

Was it even greater than she could ever imagine?

CHAPTER TWENTY-SEVEN

Kendrick dismounted as he reached this small, lonely village in the northern part of the Ring, this desolate part of the country where the villages lay far and few between. He had ridden a long and dusty road, winding ever north, and had spent the entire ride wondering if the news could possibly be true. Kendrick had followed so many false leads over the years, each bringing him to a woman who was clearly not his mother.

Yet this time felt different. Kendrick's heart pounded as he clutched both halves of the medallion in his palm.

Kendrick had followed directions meticulously, weaving his way through the Ring, galloping to this lonely town in the northern country, until it had led him here. This town was slightly bigger than the others, with too many taverns; Kendrick passed too many crude types roaming the streets, stumbling, drunk even in the day. His heart pounded as he scanned the faces of all the people, wondering if any of them could be his mother.

Another part of him told him it was not possible. Why would his mother live in a place like this? Wasn't she a princess? He had always imagined her living in a castle—but as he looked around, he saw nothing but humble dwellings. It made no sense to him. Had his squire made a mistake?

Kendrick wondered, for the millionth time, if his mother had known about him. Surely, she must have. After all, Kendrick was famous as the King's bastard son. Why, he wondered, had she never claimed him? Had the King's people scared her away?

Kendrick secretly hoped so. He secretly hoped he would find a woman who was alone, sad without him, jubilant to see him, restored once again from some deep sadness she had suffered with all of these years. She would have the perfect explanation for why she had been away. He hoped she would tell him that she had searched for him his whole life, had wanted to come see him, but had been forbidden, kept away for some reason.

Kendrick walked through the streets with high hopes, feeling as if one of the defining moments of his life was about to happen.

He scanned the faces, unsure who to look for. He looked for a middle-aged woman who might resemble him. He looked for the face he'd pictured in his dreams his whole life.

Yet he found no one.

Kendrick hurried up to an old woman who sat before a tavern and watched everyone who passed by, and wondered if perhaps she would know.

"Excuse me," he said, "but do you know a woman named Alisa?"

The woman peered at him suspiciously.

"Alisa?" she repeated slowly. "Everyone knows her. What do you want of her?"

Kendrick's heart quickened.

"Please, tell me where she is. I am her son."

The woman's eyes opened wide.

"Her *son*?!"

The old woman broke into hysterical laughter, a cackle that set Kendrick's hair on edge.

"Her son!" she repeated, laughing, as if she found that the funniest thing in the world.

Kendrick blushed, annoyed, baffled at her response and beginning to lose patience. He did not understand why she found it funny.

"You insult me in some way I do not understand," Kendrick said. "I am a member of the Silver. Show your respect and hold your tongue."

The woman's cackle slowly subsided, her face morphing into fear.

"Your mother can be found at the Red Horse Inn," she said. "The last building at the end of the street."

Kendrick turned and walked away, and her laughter rose up again. He did not understand what it all meant, and he brushed it off as the musings of a crazy old lady. After all, this was a small town, far removed from any big city, and the people here seemed rude to him. Again, he wondered what his mother could be doing here. Was he in the wrong place?

Kendrick finally reached the Red Horse Inn and tied his horse to a post outside. His heart pounding, his palms sweating, he turned to the door—when suddenly, three men burst out of it, wrestling each other down to the ground. Kendrick stepped aside just in time as they drove each other down, stirring up dust. They were drunk, cursing and kicking each other.

Kendrick turned and looked inside the open door, and heard shouts and laughs coming from inside, and wondered how this could be the right place. This appeared to be a tavern of ill repute, one not even befitting a member of the Silver to enter—much less the *leader* of the Silver.

Kendrick steeled himself, strutted inside, and slammed open the door with the back of his Silver gauntlet, banging it hard to make every head turn.

The room quieted as every man stopped and examined Kendrick. There was a look of respect and fear in their eyes, as Kendrick strode into the room, his spurs jingling on the hardwood floors. He walked right up to the bartender.

"I seek a woman named Alisa," Kendrick said.

The bartender gestured with his head.

"The back room," he said. "The red hair. But I think it's too early for her," he added.

Kendrick did not understand with the bartender meant, but before he could ask he had already moved on to another customer.

Kendrick turned and hurried to the back room of the tavern, an increasing sense of foreboding rising within him. This all felt wrong. None of this was making any sense. He was certain now that his squire must have been mistaken. What would his mother, the one-time partner of a King, be doing here?

Kendrick pushed back a black, velvet drape partitioning the back room, and he stopped short, shocked at what he saw.

Before him were dozens of women, scantily clad, paired up with men behind thinly veiled partitions. Dozens more women roamed the place, and Kendrick flushed as he realized immediately what this place was: a brothel.

Before he could turn to walk out, Kendrick's blood ran cold as he saw a woman walking toward him, a smile on her face, middle-aged, the only one in the room with red hair. He felt his world slowly crumbling as he examined her face, and realized she looked exactly like him. An older, female version of him.

She smiled as she approached.

No, he thought. *This cannot be. Not her. Not my mother.*

"How can we serve you?" she asked Kendrick, smiling, laying a hand on his shoulder. "A real member of the Silver in our place. To what do we owe the honor?"

Kendrick's face collapsed in dismay as he stared back at the woman, feeling all his hopes, ever since he was a child, crushed.

"I have come to see my mother," he replied, his voice soft, humble, broken, his eyes filled with sadness.

Suddenly, the face of the woman crumbled; her smile dropped as she looked at him with confusion, then dawning recognition. She flinched and pulled back her hand, as if she had touched a snake, and her face fell with shame as she quickly covered herself up, wrapped the shawl around her shoulders modestly.

She raised a trembling hand to her mouth as she stared back at him, wide-eyed.

"Kendrick?" she asked.

Kendrick stood there, frozen, numb, not knowing what to say. He was overcome with dread and horror. Shame. Repulsion.

Most of all, disappointment. Crushing disappointment. His entire life had been spent as a bastard, and secretly, he'd always hoped to prove the world wrong, to prove that he had come from a royal mother, to prove that he had nothing to be ashamed about.

But now he saw the others were right all along. He was nothing but a bastard. He had never felt so low.

"How did you find me?" she asked.

But Kendrick had nothing more to say to her. He could not reconcile the image he saw before him with the vision he had always held in his mind. This woman could not be his mother. It was not fair.

"I've searched for you all my life," he said slowly, his voice broken. "Unlike you—who never bothered to search for me. Now I understand why."

His mother's face flushed with embarrassment.

"You shouldn't see me here," she said.

"You're my mother," he said, accusingly. "How could you do this? How could you live your life like this? Have you no noble blood running through your body?"

She scowled, turning red. It was a look he recognized; he wore the same look when he was angry.

"You don't know the life I've lived!" she replied, indignant. "You are no one to judge me!"

"Oh yes I am," he said. "I am your son. If not me, then who?"

She stared back at him, and her eyes flooded with tears.

"You should go now," she said. "You shouldn't be in this place."

He stared back at her, his own eyes welling with tears.

"And you should?" he asked.

She suddenly broke into a sob. She held her face in her hands.

Kendrick could not stand it any longer; he turned, drew back the velvet drape, and hurried through the tavern.

"Hey!" a beefy man said, reaching out and grabbing Kendrick's wrist roughly. "You went behind the drape and you didn't pay. Everyone pays, whether you sample the merchandise or not."

In a rage, Kendrick swung the man's arm around, twisting it behind his back, and brought the man's face down on his knee, smashing it into the silver armor and breaking it.

The man collapsed to the ground, and the rest of the men in the tavern froze, thinking twice about coming anywhere near him. The entire bar stood still, as the men stared, silent.

Kendrick turned and strutted out the door, into the daylight, determined to wipe this place from his memory, and to never, ever think of it again.

CHAPTER TWENTY-EIGHT

Conven, finally home, marched into his village, ragged, weary, his legs numb from trekking all these miles. Conven had come all this way alone, on foot, walking ever since he had departed from the Legion, deciding he had nowhere left to go but here. Home. Still besieged by grief over his brother's death, he needed the time to clear his head. To be alone from everyone and everything.

A part of Conven felt he should be back in King's Court, celebrating with his other Legion brothers; but another part of him, the bigger part, was still numb to the world. Thoughts of his dead twin brother consumed him, making it hard to focus on anything else. He was unable to shake his grief—and he didn't want to. His twin brother was like a part of himself, and when he had died back in the Empire, the best part of Conven had died with him.

Conven had been numb to the world the entire time he had marched here, trekking aimlessly, barely thinking of where he was going, not wanting to take part in any celebrations.

Yet now that he had arrived, now that he stepped foot through the gates of his old village, for the first time in a long time, something within him stirred. He looked up, recognized the old streets, the old buildings, the place where he and his brother were raised, had spent so many years, and he began to remember why he had come back here. Something within him began to wake, and for a moment, he began to feel a sense of purpose again. For the first time, thoughts of something else, aside from his dead brother, entered his mind.

Alexa. His wife.

Throughout his journeys in the Empire, back when his brother had been alive, thoughts of Alexa had sustained

Conven; he had thought of little but her, sad to have had to leave her. He had promised to return to her, to come back to this village when he returned from the Empire.

Conven and his brother had gotten married in a double wedding, and ever since, each had talked endlessly about returning for their brides, starting life over in their village. Conven felt guilty to be coming back here without his brother; yet at the same time, as he looked through the streets, thoughts of Alexa rose within him, and he recalled why he came here. Thinking of her made him feel a spark of optimism for the first time.

Alexa was the one thing Conven felt he had left in the world, the one thing left that he could cling onto, that made him feel he might have a chance to start life again. After all, Alexa always understood; she always had a way to make him feel better about everything. She knew his brother, she would understand, better than anyone. She would be able to relate to Conven's grief. Maybe, just maybe, she could bring him back. She had the ability to. She always had.

Conven walked through the village, ignoring the people bustling all around him, heading single-mindedly right for his old cottage, where he knew he would find Alexa. He turned the corner and saw it, the small, bright white cottage with the yellow door, which sat ajar. From inside he could hear a woman's voice, singing joyously—and his heart lifted at the sound. Alexa. It was his wife's voice.

She was singing, and it brought it all back, Conven remembering her singing, as she always did, the sound giving him more joy than anything on earth.

Conven's heart beat faster, and he rushed forward, eager to see her face, to hold her tight, to tell her everything. He felt that once he got it all off his chest, he would feel better, so much lighter. Then maybe, just maybe, he would be able to start life over again.

Conven rushed forward and pushed the door open further. He stepped inside, his heart pounding, so anxious to surprise her, already anticipating the joy he would find on her face. He stepped in without knocking and stood there, expecting to see her standing with her back to him, cleaning her bowls at the window, singing to herself, as she always had.

But Conven stopped short in his tracks at the sight before him, unable to process what he saw. There was Alexa. Singing, smiling. Happy as ever.

But she was not cleaning her bowls. Rather, she was looking into someone else's eyes. A man's eyes.

Alexa was leaning forward, smiling, and kissing a man, who kissed her back.

Conven stood there, frozen, numb, wanting to curl up and die inside.

How could it be? Alexa? His wife? With another man?

Suddenly, Alexa turned, looked at Conven with a horrified expression, and screamed. The man next to her jumped back too, both of them startled.

Conven just stood there, staring back, expressionless. He hardly knew what to say. He felt the ground sinking beneath him.

"Who are you?" the man yelled out to Conven.

"Who are you?" Conven yelled back, trying to control his rage.

"I am Alexa's husband. How dare you trespass into our home!"

Conven felt his heart grow cold at the man's words.

"Husband?" he said, baffled. "Of what do you speak? *I* am her husband!"

The man turned and looked back and forth between Alexa and Conven, puzzled.

Alexa burst into tears, quickly covering herself with a shawl, and looked at Conven with a horrified expression.

"Conven," she said, "what are you doing here? I thought you were dead."

Conven felt himself unable to speak, too shocked for words.

"They told me you had died!" she added, pleading.

Conven shook his head.

"No, my brother died. Though, seeing this, I wish it was I."

Alexa cried and cried.

"I waited for you!" she yelled out, between tears. "I waited for you for so many moons! You never came home. They told me you were dead, Conven!"

Weeping, she crossed the room toward him.

"You must understand. They told me you were dead! I married someone else."

Conven felt his eyes welling with tears.

"You must understand!" she pleaded, crying, rushing forward and grabbing his hands. "I had no idea! I'm sorry. I'm so sorry!"

Conven snatched back his hands, as if they were bitten by a snake.

"So is that it, then?" Conven asked, his voice broken. "Our marriage means nothing anymore? I do not return in time, so you run off and marry someone else?"

Alexa burst into fresh tears, her face reddening.

"I had no idea!" she cried. "You must believe me!"

"Well, here I am," Conven said. "Alive. Back home. I have returned for you. I am your husband, after all. This was my home."

Alexa closed her eyes and shook her head again and again, as if willing for it all to go away.

"I'm so sorry," she said. "I had to move on. It was all too painful. I have a new life now. I'm sorry. But I can't go back now. I have a new life. It's all too late."

Conven lowered his head in despair, and Alexa approached and put her arm around him. He marveled at the injustice of the world, at how despair bred more despair. Hadn't he suffered enough?

Most of all, he felt like a fool, felt so ashamed. He had assumed her love for him was still alive, was as strong as ever. He had assumed that his journeys would not change that.

Now, finally, he had no one left. Not his brother. Not his wife. No one.

Without another word, Conven turned and walked out of the cottage.

"Conven!" Alexa cried out behind him.

But he had already slammed the door behind him, on her voice, on her world, and everything with it.

*

Conven walked in a daze through his town, not seeing or feeling the world around him. People bumped into him, and he bumped off of them like the walking dead, not realizing. How could it be? How could it be that everything he'd loved in the world had been taken away from him?

Somehow, perhaps by instinct, Conven found himself entering a tavern, sitting at the bar. He didn't even remember ordering mugs of ale, but they appeared before him, and he drank them, one after the next. He sat there, closing his eyes, shaking his head, trying to shut it all out.

It couldn't be. Just moons ago, Coven had had it all. He had been happily married, in a double wedding, with his brother. He had been offered a coveted spot in the Legion, along with his brother. They had a plan to return successfully from their quest of glory into the Empire, returning heroes, Thorgrin retrieving the Destiny Sword. They had a plan to become knights, to return home, and to live a charmed life.

How had it all gone so wrong? Conven could not process it at all.

As Conven drank another ale, he entertained thoughts of ending it all. After all, the way he viewed it, life held nothing for him anymore.

Suddenly, Conven almost felt off his chair, as he was bumped by a big, tall fat man, who sat down next to him, his back to him. Conven regained his balance as the man turned to him.

"Watch where you sit, skinny boy," he said.

Conven stared back at him, his mind seething with rage in his drunken state.

"Don't look at me like that," the man smirked. "Unless you want me to knock that look off your face."

Conven stood there, seething, debating what to do, when the man suddenly jumped up from his chair, swung around, and before Conven could see what was happening, slapped him hard across the face with his beefy, sweaty, palm.

The smack rang throughout the room, and the bar suddenly grew quiet, all heads turning.

Several men slowly gathered near the big man, clearly friends of his, as if hoping for a fight.

That was when it happened. Something inside Conven snapped. He became a man pushed too far, too close to the brink of despair, and he could not restrain himself any further.

Conven lashed out like an animal backed into a corner, and he leapt for the man, grabbing his wooden chair, raising it high, and bringing it down across the man's face.

The man cried out, reaching up and grabbing his bloody face as he stumbled—but Conven did not wait. He jumped forward and kicked the big man in the gut so hard that he keeled over, then Conven reached up and kneed him in the face.

The man's nose broke with a cracking noise, then he fell down to the floor, like a dead tree, shaking it.

The man's friends, as big as he, each rushed for Conven, clearly itching for a fight.

Conven, eager to wreak more havoc, did not wait; on the contrary, he leapt for them first.

The first man came at Conven with a club, and Conven snatched it from his hands, backhanded him, then used his club to crack him across the head.

Conven then spun around and clubbed the other three men, knocking crude knives from their hands and forcing each down to the ground.

A dozen more men, clearly all friends of these people, charged Conven, surrounding him.

Conven fought like a man possessed, kicking and punching and elbowing and clubbing his way through the room, taking down one man after another after another. He picked up one man and threw him high over his head, across the room, breaking a bar table in half. He head-butted another, elbowed another across the jaw, and threw another over his shoulder.

Conven was a one-man wrecking machine, not caring, prepared to throw himself recklessly into death. He had nothing left to worry about, and nothing left to live for. He would gladly die in this place, and take as many men as he could with him.

Conven drew on his skills as a Legion member; even when drunk, he was a better fighter than the best man in here, and before he was through, Conven had managed to knock out nearly every patron in the place—when he, out of breath, heard a metallic sound behind him, of shackles.

Conven glanced back over his shoulder, but too late—he saw a dozen lawmen leap on him from behind, raising clubs, bring them down on the back of his head. He fought with these men, too, despite the odds, kicking and struggling.

But he was already spent, and there were just too many of them. One after the next, the blows rained down him, and in moments Conven felt himself shackled from behind, first by his wrists, then his ankles.

Unable to move, more and more blows rained down. Soon, his eyes were closing, heavy with bruises, and as his world went black, he heard the sound of soft thumping. His final thought, before his eyes swelled shut, was that he wished his brother was here to fight beside him.

CHAPTER TWENTY-NINE

Matus, annoyed, marched into his father's former castle, clenching his jaw as he prepared to confront his two brothers. He marched through the corridors of this place, a place that used to be filled with his father's presence, used to be the gathering place of the Upper Isles, but was now used by Matus's two brothers, Karus and Falus, as a gathering hall, a place to foment revolution and rebellion since their father's imprisonment.

Matus just did not see the world the way his brothers did. He never had. He was cut from a different cloth than Karus and Falus, who were nearly clones of his father in every way—even physically, tall and lean, with the same intense, shining black eyes and straight hair. Matus, by contrast, was shorter, with the brown eyes and curly hair he inherited from his deceased mother. Being the youngest, he'd always been somewhat apart from them, and ever since his father was in prison, he'd never been more estranged from them than he was now.

Matus had never agreed with his father's actions, with his duplicitous betrayal of Gwendolyn. If his father had disagreements, Matus felt, he should have aired them openly—and if he could not come to terms, then he should have taken his cause openly to the field of battle—not in a sneaky way, not in an act of betrayal. It was wrong for his father to violate the code of honor, for any reason. In his family's eyes, the end justified the means. In Matus's eyes, it never did. Honor was more sacred.

In Matus's eyes, his father deserved to be imprisoned, which was a generous act on Gwendolyn's part.

His brothers, though, could not feel more differently—and as Matus marched into the room, he was met by the hostile glare of Karus, who sat around their long, wooden table, scowling, debating with several other soldiers sitting with them. Scheming, as usual. Matus wondered where Falus was. Surely, he assumed, up to no good.

"Why did you attempt to poison Srog?" Matus demanded.

"Why are you loyal to that fool?" Karus shot back.

Matus grimaced.

"He is the Queen's regent."

"Not our Queen," Karus countered. "Your judgment has become clouded. You do not know where your loyalties lie. Your task is to defend your brothers. Your father."

"Our father rules no more," Matus said. "It is past time you faced the times. Change is here. Srog is our ruler now, and he answers to Gwendolyn. Our father sits in prison, and he will never rise again."

"Oh, he will," Karus said, determined, standing, pacing, as he walked over and tossed another log on the fire. He threw it with such anger that he just missed a dog, who jumped up and ran out of the way as sparks flew all over the stone floor.

"If you think he's going to sit there, rotting in jail for the rest of his life, you're entirely wrong."

Matus looked back in shock. His brothers never stopped.

"What are you scheming, exactly?" Matus asked.

Karus turned and looked knowingly at the other soldiers in the room, crude men, mercenaries who were loyal to his father. Karus hesitated, as if withholding some secret and debating whether or not to let Matus in on it, too.

"I have plans," he answered, cryptically.

"What sort of plans?" Matus pressed. "You'd be foolish to risk any sort of rebellion. Gwendolyn's army, the Silver, the

MacGils, are far more powerful than we. Have you not learned your lesson?"

"Are you with us or against us?" Karus demanded, slamming his fist on the table, stepping forward. "I need to know."

"If you advocate defying the crown, I am against you," Matus replied proudly.

Karus stepped forward and smacked Matus hard across the face.

Matus, stunned, stared back at him.

"You are a traitor to our father," Karus said. "You choose the Queen over your family, strangers over us. You'd let your father rot in jail for the rest of his life for trying to advance our cause, for trying to instill *us* as rulers of the Ring, for trying to give us a better future. If you love the mainland MacGils so much, go live with them. You are no longer part of this family."

Matus was stunned from the words as much as from the blow.

"You are not loyal to our father, either," Matus replied, his voice dark, steel. "Don't pretend you are. You are loyal only to yourself. To treachery. To betrayal. You disgust me. I am for honor, whatever the cost. If that makes me against my father, against you, then I am."

Karus sneered.

"You are young and naïve. You always have been. You and your chivalry and your honor. Where has it gotten you? You're no better than any of us."

Karus pointed a threatening finger.

"Interfere in our affairs again, and Srog won't be the only one who will have to watch his drink."

Several of the nobles stood darkly, supporting Karus.

Matus, disgusted by all of them, feeling betrayed, like an alien in his own family, amongst his own people, turned and began to march out of the chamber.

But more soldiers suddenly moved before the door, blocking his way.

"I am not through with you yet, brother," Karus called out.

Matus, indignant, bunched his fists and slowly turned.

"Open this door," he snarled.

Karus smiled.

"I will. When I'm ready. But before you go, there is something I wish for you to know."

Karus paced, his smile broadening, and Matus felt a sinking sense of foreboding in that look. He sensed that, whatever it was, the news would be very, very bad.

*

Stara ascended the spiral stone staircase, heading to the castle roof, eager to watch for any falcons, to see if any new scrolls arrived from the mainland. She was desperate to know what had happened with Reece, if he had already broken the news to Selese—and when he would return for her.

Stara took the steps three at a time, then suddenly stopped, halfway up, as she heard a muffled shouting coming from one of the castle's chambers.

She turned from the stairwell and hurried to see what it was about.

Stara passed several soldiers until she reached her brother's chamber. Two guards stood before the door, barring her way.

"My lady, your brothers are in a heated exchange. I would not advise entering."

Stara could hear the shouting behind the door, and she wondered what on earth was happening.

179

She shot the soldier a dark look.

"Open the door for me at once," she commanded.

The soldier stepped aside and opened the door, and Stara entered a room filled with shouting.

She was surprised to see Matus and Karus arguing, heated, face to face, neither giving an inch. They were so engrossed, neither even turned to acknowledge her.

"It is the stupidest thing you could have done!" Matus yelled, red-faced.

Karus, on the other hand, looked smug, self-satisfied.

"You don't know what you're talking about. They are Father's orders. Everything is about to change. The way is cleared for their marriage."

Matus shook his head.

"It will be considered an act of treachery," he said. "Our country will now have to brace itself for war."

Karus scoffed.

"What is going on here?" Stara finally interjected, confused, and having a sinking feeling, upon hearing the word "marriage," that this all had something to do with her.

They both turned and looked at her, startled at her presence, and both fell silent. They stood there, breathing hard, each flush with anger.

"We have accomplished your goal for you, my dear sister." Karus smiled, holding out a scroll. "From today's falcon."

Stara felt a vague sense of catastrophe as she grabbed the scroll, quickly opened it, and scanned it. She read the words, but the lines blurred, and she felt as if she were spinning.

"Selese is dead?" she asked aloud, reading from it, hardly believing the words. "Taken by her own hand...a royal funeral."

"Exactly what you hoped for, isn't it?" Karus asked with a satisfied smile. "Your rival is cleared from your path. Reece is yours now to wed."

Stara's hands began to shake, and her entire body went cold as she dropped the scroll with disbelief. She looked up at Karus.

"That's right," he said. "Falus paid her a visit on the mainland and delivered the news of your and Reece's courtship. He did his job quite effectively, apparently. She took her life before Reece could even reach her."

Stara felt her whole world shaking. She could not believe what she was hearing. She loved Reece. But she would never want her rival dead. Especially due to her.

Worse, as she thought of the implications of it all, she realized that this would only harm her relationship with Reece. A royal funeral...Reece would be overwhelmed with guilt...the entire kingdom would blame him. Blame her.... It would drive them apart.

Stara felt like crying inside. This would all force Reece *never* to marry her. He would have no choice now.

"You FOOL!" she shrieked, hurling the scroll back into Karus's face. "You have ruined everything!"

Karus stared back, uncomprehending.

"What do you mean?" he asked.

"Do you really think Reece will want to marry me after his beloved's life has been taken by her own hand? Due to our family's treachery? You have just made me, have made our love, the enemy of the Ring. You have destroyed our chance at marriage!"

"What are you talking about?" Karus said. "You should be happy. This was what you wanted. This was what Father wanted. He said it would assure your marriage."

"Father is a fool!" she yelled. "A shortsighted fool! He knows nothing of affairs of the heart. He has ruined everything. He's an idiot. And that is why he is where he is today."

"Do not speak against our father," Karus warned.

"She is right," Matus said. "You have created an enemy not only in Reece, but in the entire mainland of the Ring. All hopes we had for any union will now be crushed."

Stara felt her entire world collapsing around her as she thought of the implications. She burst into tears, realizing that whatever she'd had with Reece was over. It could never survive this. They—her brothers, her father—with all of their ridiculous scheming—had destroyed her only real love in life.

Even worse, Stara felt the guilt of this poor woman's blood on her hands.

Stara's eyes darkened as she set her sights on Karus.

"I HATE you!" she yelled.

She sprinted forward and raised her hands and clawed at his face, scratching him. Caught off guard, he raised his hands to his face, but too late, as she sent him flying backwards across the table and collapsing onto a chair with a crash.

Stara then turned and sprinted from the room, opening the door and slamming it behind her, running through the castle corridors, never stopping, weeping, knowing that all she cared for in the world had been taken away from her for good.

CHAPTER THIRTY

Thor stood in the center of the Legion training grounds, watching recruit after recruit race past him, galloping on their horses, holding out their lances as they tried to pierce the center of a small hoop. As Thor stood there in his new, shining Silver armor, his new dagger at his belt, he replayed in his mind again and again his initiation into the Silver. Being recognized amongst all those men. It was surreal. It was the greatest honor he could have ever hoped for, one he would not even dare to dream of his entire life. Now, wearing this armor, he felt like a different man. He looked down, saw himself gleaming in the afternoon suns, and he felt invincible.

Thor heard galloping horses and looked up to see several Legion recruits galloping past him, charging earnestly for the hoop, but missing. One after the next missed, and Thor shook his head, worried at the sorry state of some of these boys.

As he watched, a few managed to pierce the larger hoop with their lance, collecting the metal rings on the tip; but as they kept charging on to the next hoop, even smaller, they missed. Only one recruit, Ario, the small boy from the Empire, managed to pierce one hoop after the next with his lance. Thor watched in surprise as he finished the entire course in a broad circle, triumphantly holding up his lance, filled with small metal rings.

They all dismounted, and the other boys, breathing hard, looked over at him, envious.

Thor walked up and down the lines, examining them. After many days of trials, he was starting to see some of the recruits excelling at certain exercises, and failing at others. It was a mixed crop. Thor saw promise in many of them; but for some others, it was already clear they would not make the cut.

Thor felt bad sending anyone away, but he knew there was no point prolonging the inevitable.

"You, you, and you," Thor said, signaling out three recruits. "I'm sorry. But it's best if you leave now."

A tense silence filled the air as the three recruits came forward and walked, dejected, for the gates. One of them stopped and turned to Thor.

"But Thorgrin, sir, I do not understand," he said. "I hooped the rings. Many of the other boys did not. Why would you choose to send me home?"

Thor shook his head.

"You do not understand," Thor replied. "This exercise was not about hooping the rings. That was incidental."

The boy looked at him, puzzled.

"Then what was it about?" he asked.

"Your lance," Thor said. "Is it yours?"

The boy looked over at the lance he'd left behind, and seemed flustered.

"It is. I retrieved it as we all rushed for the weapons."

Thor stared back at him, evenly, calmly, waiting for the proper response. A different response.

Finally, the boy seemed to realize what Thor knew, and he looked to the ground, ashamed.

"I grabbed it from a boy's hands," he admitted.

Thor nodded, satisfied.

"Being a member of the Legion is not just about being a skilled warrior," Thor explained. "It is about looking after your brothers. When you're in battle, what makes you strong is each other. The finest warrior is he who thinks of his brothers first. Only by thinking of others will you save yourself. That is valor. That is what we strive for here. I don't want only the best warriors; I want the best band of brothers."

The boy finally walked away, head down, realizing.

Thor turned to the others. They all looked back at Thor with fear and respect.

Thor surveyed the training ground, looking over all the weapons, wanting to test the boys with something they had not yet tried. His exercises and trials were winnowing the boys out, one at a time.

"Heavy swords!" Thor commanded.

As one, they all ran to a rack lined up with long swords, twice as long and thick as the others, so heavy, they needed to be wielded with two hands. Thor watched as each struggled to hold one.

"They are heavy," Thor called out, watching them hold these swords with effort, wobbling. "They are designed to be. They are training swords, heavier than anything you'll wield in battle. Now, I want each of you to hoist a second sword, and hold these two swords together."

They all turned and looked at Thor as if he were crazy.

"Two swords, my liege?" one boy asked. "It will be too heavy."

Thor stared back, unwavering, until they all did as he commanded, each grabbing two heavy swords and struggling to lift them.

"These two swords you hold are heavier than any sword you will wield. These are the swords that will make you strong. Each of you will turn to the man beside him, and with those ropes you see lying there, you will bind his two swords together, and make them one."

The boys broke into action, binding each other's swords. When they were done, each boy held up two swords, bound together, struggling with both hands to raise it into the air, twice as thick as any sword.

Thor nodded with satisfaction.

185

"Each of you raise your swords high, and hold them still before you."

As Thor watched, each boy raised the double swords, arms trembling, struggling to keep them steady. They wavered in the wind, some boys dropping them down with a grunt. Only a handful of boys were able to hold them. Thor took note.

"But it is too heavy, sire!" one boy, sweating, shaking, called out. "No one will ever be able to wield a sword like this!" His sword crashed to the ground. "What is the point?"

Thor turned and marched over to him, staring him down.

"That is exactly the point," Thor said. "In battle, you must be able to wield weapons twice as heavy as your opponent. You must become faster than them, stronger than them. You must be able to wield a sword heavier than one you'll ever wield. Only then will you be able to outfight your opponent. It is speed, even a second, that will save you from life and death."

Thor turned and surveyed the line, and he saw that only a dozen boys remained still holding their swords, groaning and struggling. The boys that remained were all the biggest, tallest, broadest-shouldered boys, clearly stronger than the others.

All except for one: Merek. The thief. He was not as big as these others, and yet he proved himself to be even stronger than most. He managed to hold the sword steadier, and higher, than boys twice his size. Thor was impressed.

"Good!" Thor called out.

The remaining boys dropped their swords with relief, all breathing hard, exhausted.

"We lasted longer than the others," one boy said. "Does that mean that we get into the Legion?" he asked hopefully.

Thor shook his head and smiled.

"That means only that you get to fight each other. Everyone, form a circle around them!"

186

The dozen boys turned to Thor in wonder as the others gathered around them.

"You are now going to spar with each other," Thor said, "using your double swords! Pair off, and let's see what you can do!"

The boys rushed to formation, pairing off with each other. Their swords were so heavy they could barely lift them, and when they did manage to lift them high overhead, some fell backwards, while others slashed in such a slow and clumsy way that they did not come anywhere near their opponent.

Their opponent, though, was equally slow, barely able to lift his own sword to block or parry.

Thor walked between the sparring boys, shaking his head in disgust.

"You are so slow," he called out, "I can walk between you!"

As one boy raised his sword high, Thor leaned back and used his foot to shove him in the chest, sending him backwards. Thor bumped another boy with his shoulder as he raised his sword, knocking him down.

One at a time, Thor knocked each of them down onto their butts, each dropping with their heavy swords. Soon, they were all collapsed on the ground, gasping, exhausted.

"And could you do any better?" one of the recruits, sitting there red-faced, barked out to Thor.

All boys turned, aghast at the show of disrespect to Thor. It was a large, pockmarked kid from a northwestern province, a kid Thor did not like. He had kept him on because of his size, but he was not surprised by his disrespect.

"Let's find out," Thor said. "Take a single sword, and hand me a double."

The boy lit up at the idea; he rushed and grabbed a single light sword and faced off with Thor with an arrogant smile, certain of victory.

187

Thor raised the double sword easily; then he switched hands, throwing it back and forth between them, holding it with just one hand, to the shocked stares of all the boys.

"A third sword!" Thor called out.

The boys looked on in wonder as one rushed forward, took a third sword, and bound it with ropes to Thor's two.

The boys watched, mouths agape, as Thor wielded three swords with both hands, red-faced from the effort of it.

The boy opposite Thor looked back, now looking very unsure—and very afraid.

Thor did not wait; he charged the boy, raising his triple sword high and swinging it down with such speed that, as the boy raised his single sword, Thor chopped it in half, the sound cutting through the air.

Thor then plunged his sword down into the earth and used it as a pole, grabbing the hilt and pushing himself up and over it, and kicking the boy in the chest, sending him flying back down to the ground, onto his butt.

Thor stood over him as the boy looked up at him, shocked.

"You can go home now, too," Thorgrin said. "You may return if you learn to speak to your superiors with respect."

The boy turned and crawled off, running at a jog to get away from the Legion training grounds. All the other recruits turned and looked at Thor with awe.

"Only three swords then?" called out a gleeful voice.

Thor turned, elated at the sound of the familiar voice, and was thrilled to see his closest friends, his Legion brothers Elden and O'Connor, approaching.

Elden walked right to the double swords, picked one up, and held it high overhead with a single hand.

"It seems the standard for Legion training is slipping then, from what I remember," he said with a smile.

Elden rushed forward, holding the swords high, and with a battle cry sliced a log hanging in the training ground. With a great splitting noise, the thick log slice in half.

All of the boys stared at Elden in wonder.

Elden dropped the swords, came over to Thor, and embraced him, as did O'Connor. Thor was thrilled to see his old Legion members again. All this training, every day, had kept them close to his thoughts.

"It seems you have a sorry group of recruits here," Elden said out loud, so all the boys could hear. "I wonder if any shall make the cut?"

"Perhaps a few," Thor replied loudly, so the boys could hear.

"What is next on the day's training?" O'Connor asked with a smile.

"Well, funny you should ask—it's time for bows."

Thor had an idea, and he turned and faced the group.

"Is there anyone here who thinks they could fire an arrow better than my friend O'Connor? If anyone can, they will be granted an immediate spot in the Legion."

They all looked O'Connor up and down, and apparently decided, given his frail frame and his boyish smile, red hair, and freckles, that he was not a worthy opponent.

They all raced forward, grabbed one of the bows lined up along the edge of the field, and took aim at the large stacks of hay about thirty yards out. Only a handful of them hit the target, only a few came close to the inner circle, and only one of them hit a bull's-eye. He was a tall, thin boy, twice as tall as the others, with long straggly brown hair that he wore in a ponytail. He stood there, satisfied with himself, clearly the best shot of the bunch. Thor took note.

O'Connor, smiling wide, raised his bow off his back, took a step forward, licked his finger, and held it up to the wind. He looked up, as if examining the sky, then lowered his head, raised his bow, and fired three quick arrows.

The three arrows sailed through the air in a high arc, and went flying past the target. They continued to sail, and they all landed in the farthest target, fifty yards away. All dead center.

The boys watched, mouths agape—yet O'Connor was not done. He placed one more arrow, took aim, and fired. The arrow sailed, and it hit the arrow of the boy who had landed a bull's eye, the shot so precise that it split the boy's arrow down the middle.

The boys all stood there in awe at O'Connor's skills, and Thor smiled wide.

"O'Connor is the product of years of Legion training," Thor called out. "If you have what it takes, and train hard enough, you will be fighting with us. And this is what we will demand of you. Think about this as you sleep tonight, and decide if you want to come back in the morning. Now off with you!"

The boys slowly turned and began to walk off the training grounds, each slumped over, exhausted from the grueling day.

Thor turned and looked at Elden and O'Connor. Seeing them brought back memories, and he missed them dearly.

They looked Thor's new armor up and down, eyes aglow.

"Look at you!" Elden exclaimed. "A member of the Silver!"

"That armor of yours is so shiny, I shall have to block my eyes!" O'Connor added, pretending to shield his eyes.

"Imagine that," Elden said, "one of our own—a Silver!"

"We knew you'd make it one day," O'Connor said.

They clasped him on the shoulder, elated, as if they had been the ones inducted, and Thor basked in their approval.

"Thank you, my brothers," he said, proud, "and thank you for returning here on such short notice."

"For you, anything," Elden said.

190

"My hometown visit can wait," O'Connor said.

"I'm sorry for that," Thor said. "But I need you here. I want you two to be the first to know: I'm leaving the Ring."

They both stared back, clearly stunned.

"I must seek out my mother," Thor said. "I'll be embarking to the Land of the Druids."

"Alone?" Elden asked.

"We shall join you!" O'Connor implored.

Thor shook his head, clasping each on the shoulder.

"There are no others I would rather join me," he said, "but it is a journey I must take alone. I will be riding Mycoples. I must find my mother, and then I shall return. I will come back stronger. And I will help make the Ring stronger."

Thor watched the recruits leave.

"In the meantime," he added, "the training for the Legion must go on. Who else could I trust but my Legion brothers? I need you to take over for me while I'm gone. Can you turn these boys into men?"

Elden's and O'Connor's faces hardened into expressions of honor and appreciation.

"We are Legion brothers to the end," Elden said. "What you ask is a sacred task. We are honored you should ask it."

"When you return, these boys will be men," O'Connor added. "Then you can choose who you want to stay."

Thor was greatly relieved; he was about to respond, when suddenly, Merek approached, standing just a foot away, as if anxious to speak to him.

"I'm sorry, my liege, for interrupting," Merek said. "But I bear news that cannot wait."

"What is it, then?" Thor asked, suspicious.

Merek turned and looked at Elden and O'Connor, as if unsure whether to speak in front of them.

191

"Any news fit for me, my brothers can hear, too," Thor assured.

Merek nodded and began: "One of my associates, who wallows still in the dungeons from our days of thieving, knows everyone who comes and goes down below. He has just told me that one of your Legion brothers has been imprisoned in the royal dungeon. Conven."

Thor, Elden, and O'Connor all looked at each other, shocked.

"Conven?" Thor asked. "Are you certain?"

Merek nodded.

"Thank you," Thor said. "You have done your duty well. I shall not forget this."

Merek nodded and hurried off.

"I must go to him at once, and find out what has happened. He must be freed."

"We shall come with you," Elden and O'Connor said. "He is our Legion brother, too."

Thor nodded back, and the three of them turned and hurried off, mounting their horses and charging for the royal dungeon, Thor determined to free his brother from whatever bondage he was in.

*

Thor marched up to the main gates of the royal dungeon, flanked by Elden and O'Connor, and several guards stood to attention, shocked at his presence. They saluted and threw open the gates, and they all marched through.

As the three of them hurried down the stone staircase and into a low, arched ceiling hall, their boots and armor echoing, Thor wondered what on earth Conven could have done to end up in this place. Whatever it was, he knew it was not good, and

192

he feared, as he often had, for his brother's future. The veil of grief, Thor was coming to realize, did not lift off of some as easily as others.

They strode down the dim, drafty corridor of the dungeon, prisoners making noises on all sides of them, banging the bars with their tin cups. They walked past them, all the way to the end of the corridor, passing cell after cell, until finally, the guards led them to a large cell at the end of the passage.

The guard hoisted his skeleton key and unlocked it, the metal reverberating in the cell corridor.

As the door swung open, Thor looked into the lonely cell and saw, slumped in the corner, barely visible beneath the flickering torchlight, his Legion brother. Conven sat hunched over, completely dejected, unshaven, his hair long and tousled, and Thor felt a pit in his stomach at the sight. How had he sunk to this? Conven, once so happy, so jovial, a proud and fearless member of the Legion. Now, here he sat, thrown into his cell as if he were just another common prisoner.

Thor could not stand the sight. No Legion member should be treated this way.

Thor still felt tremendous sadness for the death of Conval. It had never left him. But Thor had been able to move on.

Conven clearly had not. He had been on a downward spiral ever since, and it had led him to this place. Thor feared that if something didn't change, his friend wouldn't live much longer.

Thor walked into the cell, Elden and O'Connor following, and walked right up to Conven, standing over him. Conven barely even looked up at their presence.

Thor squatted down before Conven, looking him in the eyes. He looked like all the life and spirit had gone out of him. Whatever love and joy had once been in them was gone.

"Conven?" Thor said softly.

Conven did not budge.

Thor reached out and nudged his shoulder.

"Conven?" Thor asked again.

Slowly, Conven stirred.

"Why have you come here?" Conven asked, not meeting Thor's eyes.

"Because I am your brother," Thor replied.

"We are all your brothers," Elden and O'Connor added.

Conven looked over at them, then slowly shook his head.

"You are brothers of another time," Conven said.

"Wrong," Thor replied. "We are brothers for *all* time."

Conven shook his head.

"We are your brothers when you are at your peak of glory," Thor added, "and your brothers when you're at the depths of sorrow. That's what it means to be a brother. A brother is more than a friend. Brotherhood means that when one of us is down, all of us are down."

Thor made Conven look into his eyes.

"*No man left behind,*" he said, firmly, unwavering.

Conven turned and looked down, and Thor saw a tear running down his cheek.

"I am not worth saving," Conven said. "I am happy down here. There's nothing left for me up there."

"We are left for you," Elden said. "Is that nothing?"

Conven sat there, silent.

"Your entire life is still ahead of you," O'Connor said. "You are young. You are a great warrior. You are not going to waste away down here like a common criminal."

"I am," Conven said.

"You will *not*," Thor said emphatically. "I will not allow it."

"You cannot stop me!" Conven said, defiant.

Thor thought about that, surprised at Conven's response. Finally, he sighed.

194

"You're right," Thor finally said. "I cannot stop you. Your life is yours to destroy. But keep this in mind: if you destroy your life, you destroy not only yours, but something of ours. You hurt not only yourself, but those around you. We are your brothers. You need us. But what you are forgetting is that we need you, too. Maybe not today. But there will assuredly come a day when we are low, and we will need you, and you will be there for us."

Thor paused, as he saw Conven listening, taking it all in. He could feel him thinking, debating. A long silence followed.

"The Legion must be rebuilt," Thor finally continued. "I must depart the Ring now. Elden and O'Connor will oversee it, and they need you, too. I need you. Come with us. Join us. Help rebuild the Legion. If you won't do it for yourself, then do it for others. You would be selfish to wallow here when others look to you for help."

Thor leaned over and reached out a single hand, waiting.

Conven sat there, hesitating, in a silence that seemed to last forever. Thor was beginning to wonder if Conven would not reply, if all his words were for nothing.

Finally, slowly, Conven looked up and met Thor's eyes directly. Thor saw a spark of something in them, a tiny spark, possibly of hope. Of light.

Conven slowly reached out and clasped Thor's hand. It was the clasp of the man he once knew. The clasp of a brother in arms.

CHAPTER THIRTY-ONE

Reece marched up the long, narrow wooden plank, sloped steeply from the dock, heading straight up to the deck of the massive ship before him. The wobbly plank spanned a good fifty feet, and Reece hiked quickly up, his footsteps echoing on the hollow wood, which shook with every step he took. Up above, he could see the Upper Islanders, Falus's men, all engaged in a flurry of preparation, untying ropes, raising sails, getting ready to depart the mainland for the Upper Isles. Reece, seething with rage and determination, steeled himself, forced himself to breathe deep and remain calm, to wait for the perfect moment before he wreaked havoc on them all.

Reece stepped foot onto the main deck and immediately turned looked at Falus's soldiers, gauging their reaction. None looked at him twice. Reece breathed with relief: his disguise was working. Fully dressed in the armor of an Upper Islander, from his helmet down to his spurs, they all, as he'd hoped, assumed he was one of them.

Reece had done his job well. On the way here, close to the docks, he had knocked out an unsuspecting Upper Islander soldier when no one was looking. He'd dragged him into a back alley, stripped him of his uniform, and donned it himself. He knew he would be needing it if he had any chance of pulling off his plan.

Reece had galloped through the night, had ridden here to the shore, straight from Selese's funeral, still mad with grief, his eyes still bloodshot. His fingernails still bore dirt from the fresh soil he had buried her in, and he could still feel her spirit with him, crying out for vengeance. After all, if it had not been for Falus's trickery, Reece would have found Selese alive and happy, would have married her the next day. Such a wrong could not go unpunished.

Reece had found out when and where Falus was departing the mainland and had raced here, to this lonely dock on the edge of the Empire, determined to make sure he never departed. Reece knew he would be marching onto a ship of hostile Upper Islanders, and he knew it was an act he must do alone. This disguise, at least, had bought him some time.

Reece marched quickly down the deck of the ship, pleased he had caught the ship right before it departed. He marched amidst hundreds of soldiers, all busily getting ready to depart, determined to find Falus. Selese's death could not go unanswered.

Reece saw a flurry of activity, saw more lines being thrown off the deck, and he knew the ship might depart before he could get off. He no longer cared. If he had to sail out to sea with these people, if he ended up being caught and killed by them all, it didn't matter. As long as he killed Falus first.

Reece marched and marched down the endlessly long ship, secretly clutching the dagger at his belt, tightening his palm around the grip, his heart pounding in his ears. Finally, he reached a door that he knew would descend to Falus's cabin below. His heart quickened, as he knew that Falus was behind that door. The man who had taken Selese's life.

Two of Falus's loyal soldiers stood outside it, guarding it, and as Reece approached, they stepped forward and lowered their spears.

"Where do you think you're going?" one of them asked Reece derisively, blocking his way.

Reece had anticipated this. After all, Falus had many men at his disposal, and he knew some would be standing guard.

Without missing a beat, Reece, prepared, reached down and pulled a long scroll from his waist, holding it out toward the guards.

"I bring news from the morning's falcon," Reece reported in a matter-of-fact way, hoping they would believe him.

One of them eyed Reece suspiciously, then reached out to grab the scroll.

Reece yanked it back.

"Official business," Reece said. "Do you see the seal?"

Reece turned it over and showed a wax seal.

The two guards looked at each other, unsure. Reece stood there, heart pounding, hoping they wouldn't recognize that his uniform was ill-fitting, hoping they would believe the scroll, hoping they would step aside. If not, he felt the dagger sitting at his waist, and he would kill them both. But if he did, with all the other soldiers milling about, Reece might not ever make it inside the cabin.

Reece waited and waited, his heart pounding, the longest seconds of his life.

Come on, Reece prayed. *Selese, please help. Please. Help me for you. I know I have been a terrible husband. You don't have to love me. You don't have to forgive me. Just help get vengeance, for your sake.*

Finally, to Reece's great relief, they stepped aside, raising their spears, one of them opening the door for him.

Reece hurried in, and the door slammed behind him.

Reece's eyes adjusted to the dim cabin as he took several steps down into a long room. There was only one man in the room, Reece was relieved to see. He sat at his desk, his back to Reece, penning a scroll with a quill. It was probably a message of victory, Reece realized, a message to inform the others of his success. Of Selese's death. Of his betrayal.

Reece's body flushed with anger. Here he was: his wife-to-be's murderer.

As Reece marched through the room, his spurs jingling, Falus finally turned, caught off guard.

He stood, indignant.

"Who are you?" he said. "I ordered that none of my soldiers should disturb me at this hour. Is that a scroll you bear? What news do you bring?"

He stared down at Reece, stepping toward him, scowling, and Reece continued to approach him calmly, then stopped just a foot away.

Reece raised his visor, wanting Falus to see his face.

Falus stared back, eyes opened wide in surprise, as he clearly recognized his cousin's face.

"It is a message from your cousin," Reece said.

As he spoke the words, Reece stepped forward, pulled the long dagger from his waist, and stabbed his cousin in the heart.

Falus gasped, blood pouring from his mouth as he stumbled backwards. Reece held on tight with his other hand, grabbing Falus's shirt, grimacing, as he stuck the dagger deeper and deeper into Falus's heart.

Reece, scowling, held the knife there, his face inches away from Falus's, staring into his eyes.

"Look into my eyes," Reece said. "I want you to see my face before you die."

Falus, eyes bulging, unable to move, stared back.

"You took everything from me," Reece continued. "You stole everything that I cared about in this world. And now, you will pay the price."

"You'll not get away with this," Falus gasped weakly, as his eyes rolled back in his head.

His eyes suddenly closed, and he slumped down, his body limp.

Reece let him fall to the cabin floor, his dagger still inside him. Falus lay there, frozen. Dead.

"I already have," Reece replied.

CHAPTER THIRTY-TWO

Luanda stood beside Bronson in the courtyard of McCloud's former castle, looking out in tense silence at the rows and rows of McCloud prisoners. Four hundred of the McClouds' most famed warriors stood there, facing them, arms bound behind them with cords, awaiting their punishment. These men had all been rounded up after the night of rebellion, men who'd had knowledge of the plot. They hadn't been there that night, but they were all complicit in the plot, with Koovia, to entrap and murder the MacGils.

Luanda looked out at these men, these McCloud scum, and she knew what she would do if she were ruler: she would have them all publicly executed. Make a display of it. She would solidify her power, once and for all, and teach all these McClouds the way they could expect to be ruled. Then no one would rebel, ever again.

But Luanda was no ruler, and the decision was not hers to make. Luanda stood there, seething, helpless, knowing it was a decision, instead, for her husband, Bronson, the one whom Gwendolyn had put in charge. Luanda loved Bronson more than anything—yet still, she despised his weakness. She despised that he was a loyal soldier to Gwendolyn, that he was set on implementing her policies. Her sister's policies were stupid policies, Luanda knew, policies of weakness and naïveté. Pacify the enemy. Hope for peace. The same sort of thing her father might have done.

Luanda ached to be the one in charge, to have a chance to set the outcome a different way. But she knew it was never meant to be. Ever since her return here in disgrace, back to this side of the Highlands, banished once again by her sister, Luanda had been beside herself. She had cried for days, mourning her exile, her inability to ever return to King's Court.

But Luanda had seen the look of loathing and hatred in all of her siblings' eyes, and had finally come to realize that she was an outcast in her own family, from her own people, from her own home. They had all, she felt, been so cruel. Yes, she had made some mistakes; but did she deserve such punishment? In her eyes, she was shamed once again—this time, even worse than before.

Luanda had hardened inside, since this last trip, since her return here; something inside her had snapped, and now she had no love left for her siblings; now, she hated her family—and most of all, she hated Gwendolyn. She would kill them all if she could, as punishment for making her an outcast, for humiliating her.

The only person left in the world that Luanda truly loved was standing beside her—Bronson—and it was only out of loyalty to him that she stood there and went along with whatever his decision was as ruler.

"In the name of Gwendolyn, Queen of the Western Kingdom of the Ring, I hereby grant all of you standing here today mercy," Bronson boomed out to the assembled McCloud soldiers. "Each and every one of you shall be set free. You shall be forgiven your past sins. You shall join with the MacGil army, leading joint patrols on both sides of the Highlands. All of you who would swear allegiance to Gwendolyn, who would swear to devote themselves to peace and harmony, kneel."

The hundreds of McCloud warriors all took a knee, lowering their heads.

"Do you swear allegiance to Gwendolyn?" Bronson boomed out.

"WE SWEAR!" they boomed back in unison.

"Do you swear eternal allegiance and peace and harmony between the clans?"

"WE SWEAR!"

Bronson nodded to his attendants, and dozens of his men filtered through the ranks and severed the binds of all the McCloud men. The McClouds all looked to each other in wonder and surprise.

The crowd of soldiers dispersed, and as they did, Luanda turned to Bronson.

"That was the biggest mistake of your lifetime," she said to him, in a rage. "Do you really think those men will be loyal? Will fight for Gwen's cause?"

"They have suffered enough," Bronson said. "All their leaders have been killed. Killing more men leads to nothing but more bloodshed. At a certain point, we need to trust, if we ever wish to obtain peace."

Luanda scowled.

"Those are my sister's policies. Not yours."

"I am a subject of your sister," Bronson said. "And so are you. I carry out her policies."

"Her policies will get all of us killed. You've just made our kingdom unsafe."

He shook his head.

"I disagree. I feel that we have made it safer."

Bronson turned away as advisors led him to other matters.

Luanda stood there, watching him, then turned and watched the McCloud soldiers, so happy, reveling with each other as they dispersed. She felt, without a doubt, that none of this would lead to any good.

CHAPTER THIRTY-THREE

Thor stood before the canyon, staring out at the great divide before him, embraced in a swirl of multicolored mist, and inside, his heart was breaking. He turned and saw Gwen, standing before him, holding Guwayne, and he almost could not stand to look into her eyes. He especially could not look into Guwayne's. As Gwen held him there, his son, wide awake, stared right back at Thor, alert. Thor sensed a power coming from him, one he did not understand.

Thor felt rooted to the spot, as if he could never leave this place. He had a strange foreboding, a sense of danger coming to the Ring; he knew it made no sense, with the Shield restored, with Ralibar staying behind, and with the Ring stronger than ever. Yet still, he worried again if his leaving could somehow endanger them.

Yet at the same time, Thor felt an urgency to seek out his mother, felt her summoning him. He felt that there was something momentous awaiting him in the Land of the Druids, some powers or weapons that would greatly strengthen the Ring. He also felt that was what he needed to complete his training, and to find out who he was.

Thor met Gwen's eyes, glistening, yet not crying, Gwen staying strong, especially in front of all her people, the thousands of soldiers who had gathered to see Thor off. Having already said his goodbyes to the people, to his brothers in arms, Thor now faced only Gwendolyn. At Thor's feet was Krohn, and behind him, waiting impatiently, sat Mycoples, and beside her, Ralibar, who lowered his head mournfully, rubbing it against Mycoples's neck. It was out of character; he must have known they were all leaving.

Ralibar then suddenly arched back his neck and shrieked; it was a ferocious sound, shocking them all, so out of character. Gwen had thought she'd known him, but in that moment, she realized she did not; his face was ferocious, as if anguished, and he suddenly flapped his wings, turned his back on them all, and flew off into the horizon.

Gwen watched him go with dread, wondering where he was going. Wondering if he would return.

They all watched him go, then Thor finally turned to her.

"I do not wish to leave you, my love," Thor said to Gwendolyn, doing his best to hold back his own tears. "Nor do I wish to leave Guwayne."

"You will find your mother," Gwen replied, staying strong, "and you will be back before a moon has passed. You'll come back stronger. Go. It has been foretold in all the books, this journey of yours. The Ring needs you. Your mother needs you."

"And yet," Thor replied, "you need me, too."

Gwen nodded.

"True. But most of all, I need you strong. I would not put myself before the Ring."

Thor reached out and clasped Gwen's hand.

"I'm sorry we did not marry, my love," he said.

Gwen's eyes moistened, just a bit, just enough for Thor to notice.

"The time was never right for us," she answered, "not with a funeral in the air."

"When I return," Thor said, "we shall have a lifetime together."

Gwen nodded.

"When you return," she said.

Thorgrin bent over, laid both hands on Guwayne's forehead, and kissed him. He felt a tremendous energy coursing through him, and he did not want to leave his child's side.

Thor then reached up, held Gwen's face in both his palms, and leaned in and kissed her. He held the kiss for as long as he could.

"Protect our child," Thor said. "Protect our Ring. You have Ralibar, and the Shield at its strongest, and the finest warriors known to man. And you have Krohn. I should return, I expect, before a moon has passed."

"There is nothing to fear," Gwen replied.

Despite her show of strength, Thor could see Gwen's lower lip trembling, could see that she was trying not to cry.

She quickly brushed back the formation of a tear.

"Go," she said, clearly afraid to speak anymore for fear of bursting into tears.

It broke Thor's heart. He wanted to change his mind, to stay here.

But he knew he could not. Thor turned and looked out at the horizon, at Mycoples waiting beside him, and knew his destiny was out there. The time had come for him to journey.

Krohn whined, and Thor leaned down and patted him, stroking his hair, kissing his face as Krohn licked him back.

"Watch over them," Thor exhorted.

Krohn whined, as if in response.

Without another word, Thor turned, mounted Mycoples, and took one last look at his countrymen. Thousands of them stood there, watching, waiting to see him off, among them many members of the Silver. Thor's heart filled with love for all these people who loved him so much.

"THORGRINSON!" they all yelled at once, raising their fists in a salute of respect.

Thorgrin raised his fist back.

Then Mycoples shrieked, flashed her great wings, and lifted off into the sky, turning her back on Thor's people, on the Ring, on everything Thor knew, as they flew into the mists, above the canyon, and headed for a world that Thor had never known.

CHAPTER THIRTY-FOUR

Godfrey sat in the small, foreign tavern in the McCloud city, Akorth and Fulton on either side of him, deep in drink. Godfrey needed a drink today more than usual, trying to immerse himself, to shake from his mind the images of his mother's funeral. He took a look another long swig, finished yet another mug, and immediately began on another one, determined to drown himself in drink.

It had been a rough go. First, his efforts at uniting the MacGils and McClouds had culminated in that tavern brawl, blowing up in his face, all his schemes at peace resulting in failure. Then, he had been summoned back to King's Court for his mother's funeral, and had to stand there and watch as they lowered her body into the ground. It brought up old feelings, feelings Godfrey wished had remained buried.

Godfrey's relationship with his mother had always been troubled at best, not much different, really, than his relationship with his father. Both had viewed him with disappointment, both had made it obvious that he was the opposite of the royal son they'd always dreamed of. Godfrey had thought he'd suppressed all his feelings for his mother years ago; but watching her be buried had brought it all back up again. He had never gained her approval in life, and while he had thought he didn't care, watching her buried made him realize that he did, indeed, care. He had not realized how much there was still unresolved between them. He had found himself weeping and sobbing at the funeral, like an idiot, he felt; why, he did not truly understand. Perhaps he was crying for the relationship he wished he could have had.

He did not want to analyze it further. Godfrey much preferred to lose himself in drink, to exorcise it all, his entire, awful, royal upbringing, and to make it all as distant a memory as possible.

Godfrey was jostled by a McCloud soldier, and he snapped out of it and looked around. Now that Bronson had set all those McCloud captors free, the taverns were filled with McClouds again, the mood here in this city once again jovial, restless. Godfrey had been around taverns his entire life, had been around reckless and tactless men, and none of it had phased him. Yet here, in this city, with these men, he sensed something different in the air. Something he did not trust. He felt as if at any moment any one of these men might just as likely stab him in the back as pat him on it.

His sister had decided that this gesture, releasing the McCloud men, would create goodwill and peace with the McClouds, and would get things get back to normal. And on the surface it had. But Godfrey could not help but detect something else in the air, some general sense of unease, and he could not ignore his sense of foreboding.

Godfrey knew nothing of politics, and was a poor soldier. But he knew men. He knew, most of all, the common man. And he knew resentment among the masses when he spotted it. He sensed something brewing, as much as he would wish otherwise, and he could not help but wonder if his sister had made a bad decision. Perhaps, after all, she should abandon this place and merely patrol the border, as their father had done. Let the McClouds focus on their own side of the kingdom.

Yet as long as her policy remained to make peace between them, Godfrey would stay here, trying to abet her cause in whatever way he could, as he had promised when she'd dispatched him.

There came a sudden cheer from the other side of the room, and Godfrey looked over to see several McCloud men tackle several others to the ground, and to see that half of the room erupt into a brawl.

Godfrey turned and looked back at his drink, not wanting to get involved. It was already the second one here this evening.

"Some lions can't be tamed," Akorth observed quietly to Godfrey and Fulton.

"Even strong drink can't cure everyone," Fulton added.

Godfrey shrugged.

"It is no business of ours," Akorth said. "As long as their drink is good and strong, I'll gladly drink it."

"And what of the day when their drink stops?" Fulton asked.

"Then we go someplace else!" Akorth replied with a laugh.

Godfrey tried to drown his friends out. He was tired of their endless banter, which always filled his ears, their juvenile ways. In the past he had always gone along with it; but these days, some change was stirring within Godfrey, especially since his mother's funeral. For the first time, he was starting to view his friends as juvenile, and it was actually bothering him; for the first time, despite himself, he found himself wanting to rebuke them for not being more mature. Mature. It was a scary word for Godfrey, and he did not entirely understand why he was starting to view it differently. He shuddered, hoping he was not becoming like the man he hated most—his father.

Godfrey was about to get up, walk outside, and get some fresh air, when suddenly, he recognized a familiar face—a woman—as she came up beside him.

"And what are you doing here drinking?" she asked, standing over him, disapproving.

Godfrey was shocked she had tracked him down here, and he looked away, ashamed. He had promised her not to drink, and now he was caught red-handed.

"I'm just having a quick drink," Godfrey replied, looking away.

Illepra shook her head and snatched the drink from his hand.

"You are wasting your life in here, don't you see that? Your mother was just buried. Don't you see how precious life is?"

Godfrey glowered.

"I don't need reminding of it," he retorted.

"Then why are you here?" she demanded.

"Where else would you have me be?" he asked.

"*Where else?*" she asked, puzzled. "Anywhere but here. You should be out there with your brothers and sisters, helping to rebuild the Ring. To defend our kingdom. To do any of a myriad of things except for the nothing you achieve by sitting here."

"Maybe I'm achieving great things by sitting here," Godfrey countered, sitting up straighter, defiant.

"Like what?" she asked.

"I am enjoying myself," he said. "That's great in its own way, isn't it? Look how many great men spend their whole lives building and bossing and killing—yet they never enjoy a single moment of life."

Illepra shook her head in disgust.

"I believed in you," she said. "I know you can be more than you appear to be. But you're never going to be a great man by immersing yourself in drink. Never."

She had finally gotten to him, had pushed all his buttons, and had reminded Godfrey of his father. Now, finally, he was upset, and he flushed with anger.

"And then tell me," he demanded, "what is it about killing each other that makes men so great? What is it about raising a sword and taking someone's life that makes a man someone to emulate? Yours is a narrow definition of greatness. I don't see the virtue in killing other men, and I don't see how that makes one a man. For me, virtue means enjoying life. Why is it so much greater to stab and kill a man than it is to sit back, laugh, and enjoy a drink with him?"

Illepra, hands on her hips, shook her head.

"Yours are the self-justifying words of a drunkard," she said. "Not of a King's son."

Godfrey would not give in.

"You are wrong," he said. "Do you really want to know what I think? I think that most men in this kingdom—including your precious knights—are so obsessed with killing each other that they've forgotten what it means to live. I think they kill each other for the very reason that they do not know how to live—how to *truly* live. Then they cover it up further with their grand terms and titles, chivalry, honor, glory, valor. Knights, commanders.... It is all an escape. After all, it is much easier to embrace death than it is to embrace life."

Illepra, red-faced, fumed.

"And you've figured out how to really live?" she countered. "This is life? Getting lost in drink? Drowning out life?"

Godfrey stood there, flustered, unable to come up with a good response.

She shook her head.

"You exhaust me," she said. "I'm not going to seek you out anymore. I like you. There's something special about you. But I cannot abide by this anymore. If you ever grow up and become a man, then find me. Otherwise, I wish you well."

Illepra turned, stormed out of the tavern, and slammed the door behind her.

Akorth and Fulton turned and looked at Godfrey, whistling and rolling their eyes.

"Sounds like she likes you," Akorth said.

"Maybe you should just invite her back in for a drink!" Fulton said.

They both broke into laughter, delighted with themselves.

But Godfrey sat there, frowning, mulling over her words. They had cut him deeply. Partly because she had said the same exact words he'd been mulling over himself. What, after all, was the purpose of life? Godfrey did not feel, as many others did, that the be-all and end-all of life was to kill others in the battlefield. And yet at the same time he knew his current path held no virtue in it, either. So what was it? What made one's life the most worthy?

Godfrey got up, stumbling, a little bit off-balance, realizing how much he'd drunk as it rushed to his head. He needed another drink now, and the bartender was at the far end of the bar, so Godfrey stumbled across the room.

As Godfrey found a new spot on the other side of the tavern, he overheard two voices whispering behind him. He glanced over his shoulder and saw two McCloud soldiers huddled together, talking conspiratorially.

"When do we leave?" one asked.

"Before the sun sets," the other answered. "They are assembling now."

"Who will join?"

The other one leaned in close.

"Who will not? It will be every McCloud man. The road leads but one way, and the MacGils are on their pilgrimage. We will stain the gates of King's Court red."

Godfrey felt the hairs on his arm stand up. He turned and looked straight ahead, pretending he hadn't heard a thing.

Godfrey slowly and calmly took his new drink from the bartender and walked back across the tavern as if he had heard nothing.

He walked over to Akorth and Fulton, his hands trembling. He leaned in close between them, intent on being heard amidst their laughter.

"Follow me, *now*," he said quietly and urgently, "if you want to live."

Godfrey did not wait for their reaction but kept walking straight for the door, hoping no one was watching him. Akorth and Fulton followed close behind.

They stepped outside into the cloudy afternoon, and in the fresh air, Godfrey let himself sink into a panic as he turned and faced his friends, each wearing a puzzled expression. Before they could speak, he cut them off:

"I heard something I wish I hadn't," he said. "The McClouds are preparing a rebellion. No MacGil will live."

Godfrey stood there, reeling, debating what to do, drunken, off balance. Finally, he turned and strutted toward his horse.

"Where are you going?" Akorth asked, belching.

"To do something about it," Godfrey heard himself say, then kicked his horse and took off at a gallop, having no idea what he was doing—but knowing he had to do something.

*

Godfrey dismounted at the highest point of the Highlands, Akorth and Fulton riding up behind him and dismounting, too. He had to come this high to get the lookout he needed, to see for himself if it was all true, or just more tavern talk.

Godfrey was breathing hard as he hiked to the top, out of breath, and Akorth and Fulton stumbled beside him, heaving, barely able to catch up. Godfrey knew he was out of shape, but these two were even worse off than he. As he ran, the fresh mountain air made him lightheaded, and helped him slowly come back from his drunken stupor.

"Where are you running off to now?" Akorth yelled out, heaving behind him.

"What has gotten into you?" Fulton yelled.

Godfrey ignored them, tripping and stumbling as he ran higher and higher, until finally, gasping, he reached the top.

The sight confirmed his worst fears. There, assembling on a distant ridge of the Highlands, was a sprawling and well-organized army of McCloud soldiers, all banding together, preparing for what would clearly be an organized attack. More and more men gathered by the minute, and Godfrey's heart fell as he realized that his worst fears had come true: all these men would launch an attack straight down into the Highlands, and right to the heart of King's Court.

Normally, King's Court would have nothing to fear; but given that it was Pilgrimage Day, all the knights protecting King's Court would surely be gone. The McClouds had timed this treachery well. There would be but a handful of people left to defend the city, and his sister would be endangered, along with his new nephew.

Godfrey stood there, gasping, knowing he had to do something. He had to beat these men to King's Court. He had to warn her. Godfrey was not a fighter. But he was not a coward, either.

Godfrey's first thought was to send a falcon, but he saw the falconry was empty. Clearly, the McClouds had planned this well, stripping away any means to notify King's Court. They had also been very crafty to plan it on Pilgrimage Day. It must have been a long time in the works. Godfrey wondered if they would attack Bronson, too, and had a sinking feeling they might.

"We must stop them," Godfrey said to himself.

Akorth snorted derisively.

"Are you mad? The three of us—stop *them*?"

"They will come upon King's Court unaware. My sister is there. They will kill her."

Fulton shook his head.

"You are mad," Fulton said. "There is no way for us to reach King's Court—unless we ride right now and gallop through the night and pray to god to beat these men before they murder us all."

Godfrey stood there, hands on his hips, heaving, looking out. He came to a decision inside himself.

"Then that is exactly what we must do."

They both turned to him.

"You *are* mad," Akorth said.

Godfrey knew it was crazy. And he did not understand it himself. Just a moment ago he was railing against battle, against chivalry. Yet now that he was confronted by this circumstance, he found himself reacting this way. For the first time, Godfrey was starting to understand what Illepra meant. He was thinking of others, not of himself, and it made him feel bigger than himself, as if life finally had a sense of purpose.

"Think this through," Fulton said. "You will die on this mission. You might save your sister, and a few others. But you'll be dead."

"I am not asking you to join me," Godfrey said, remounting his horse, grabbing its reins, preparing to take off.

"Godfrey, you *are* a fool," Fulton said.

Fulton and Akorth looked back at Godfrey in shock and, for the first time, with a new look—something like respect. They hung their heads in shame, and it was clear they would not follow.

Godfrey kicked his horse, turned, and galloped straight down the steep mountain slope, charging alone, ahead of the gathering McCloud army, prepared to gallop all the way to King's Court, and to save his sister's life.

CHAPTER THIRTY-FIVE

Srog sat behind the ancient oak writing desk in Tirus's former fort, trying to concentrate as he penned a missive to Gwendolyn. It was yet another gloomy afternoon here on the Upper Isles, a fog hanging thick in the sky outside his windows, the gloom ever-present. Srog could not stand to be in this place for one more day.

Srog held his head in his hand, trying to focus. He had been unable to, though, because for quite a while now, his writing had been punctuated by noises, disruptive shouts, sounding like cheers, coming from some distant place below. Srog had gone to the window several times to try to look out and see what was happening—but his view had always been obscured by the fog.

Srog tried to block it out. It was probably just another clan dispute, or another vendor dispute down in the courtyard below. Perhaps it came from one of the taverns, its rowdy patrons spilling out to the street in yet another tavern fight.

But as Srog tried to write, to put into words the depth of his misery here, the jeers of the crowd continued, escalating in strength, until finally, Srog was just too distracted to think.

He slammed his quill down in frustration, stood, and crossed the room again, going to the open-air window, sticking his head out, determined to figure out the source of it all. Clearly, something was going on below. Was it some sort of celebration? Some sort of protest? In this isle of malcontents, one never knew.

Suddenly, the huge wooden door to Srog's chamber slammed open, startling him, the first time it had ever been opened unannounced, the ancient door slamming into the stone. Srog wheeled, shocked, as he saw running toward him a messenger, one of his men, eyes wide in panic.

"My lord, you must leave here at once! They've stormed the fort! We're surrounded!"

Srog stared back at the man, confused, trying to understand what he was saying. Surrounded?

The messenger rushed forward and clutched Srog's wrist.

"Speak clearly, man," Srog exhorted. "I must leave? Why? Who has surrounded us?"

Srog heard another cheer, this one now coming from inside the fort, and he suddenly realized something was very, very wrong—and much closer than he thought.

"It is Tirus's men!" the messenger replied. "There has been a revolt on the island. Tirus is freed! They come to kill you now!"

Srog stared back, shocked.

"A revolt?" he asked. "Sparked by what? And what about our men?"

The messenger shook his head, trying to catch his breath.

"They have slaughtered all of our men! There is no one left to stand guard for you. Haven't you heard? A boat arrived with a dead body in it. Tirus's son. Falus. Killed by Reece's hand. It has sparked a revolution. The entire isle is up in arms. My lord, you must understand. You have no time—"

Suddenly, the messenger clutched Srog with both his hands on his shoulders, stared at him, wide-eyed, and leaned forward into his arms, as if to hug him.

Srog stared back, confused, until he saw blood gush from his mouth. The man slumped dead in his arms, and as he slid to the ground, Srog saw a throwing knife lodged in his back.

Srog looked up to see, charging into the room, five of Tirus's soldiers—all charging right for him.

Srog, heart pounding furiously, knew he couldn't flee. He was backed into a corner. Ambushed. Srog thought of the hidden chamber in the room, the back exit he could escape from, built into the stone wall for precisely times like this. But that was not who he was. He was a knight, and he did not flee. If he was going to meet death, he would meet it head-on, with sword in hand, facing his enemy. He would fight his way out or die.

And those were just the kind of odds he liked.

Srog let out a great battle cry, not waiting for them to reach him, and charged the men. He drew his sword and raised it high, and as the lead soldier grabbed another throwing dagger from his belt, Srog rushed forward and slashed his sword down, chopping off the man's wrist before he could throw it. The soldier dropped to the ground, screaming.

Srog did not pause, swinging his sword again and again, faster than all of them, decapitating one, stabbing another through the heart. Years of combat had made him unafraid of ambush, had taught him to never hesitate, and Srog brought down three men in the blink of an eye.

The other two men came at him from the side and from behind, and Srog wheeled and blocked their blows with his sword, sparks flying as he fended them off, fighting both at a time. Srog was doing a masterful job of fighting off two attackers at once, even as they pushed him back across the room. The clang of metal echoed off the stone walls, the men grunting, fighting for their lives.

Srog finally found an opening, lifted his foot, and kicked one in the chest. The man stumbled backwards and fell, and Srog wheeled and elbowed the other across the jaw, dropping him to his knees.

Srog was satisfied to see his five attackers all sprawled out on the floor, but before he could finish surveying the damage, he suddenly felt a sharp pain in his back.

Srog, exposed while fighting the others, had not seen the sixth soldier sneak into the room behind him, and stab him in the back. Groaning in pain, Srog nonetheless summoned some reserve of inner strength. He turned, grabbed the man, pulled him in tight, and headbutted him, breaking his nose and making him drop to the floor.

Srog then reached around behind his back with one arm, grabbed the hilt of the short sword lodged in his spine, and yanked it out.

Srog shrieked, the pain excruciating, and dropped to his knees. But at least he removed the sword, and now he gripped its hilt, his knuckles white, stood, and plunged it into the heart of his attacker.

Srog, badly wounded, dropped to one knee, coughed, and spit up blood. There was a momentary lull in the battle, yet now he realized, with this injury, that his time was short.

There came the sound of another soldier rushing into the room, and Srog forced himself to stand and face him, despite the pain. He did not know if he'd have the strength to raise his sword again.

But Srog was greatly relieved to see who it was. It was Matus, the King's youngest son, rushing toward him. Matus ran into the room, turned, and slammed shut the doors, barring them in.

"My lord," Matus said, turning and rushing toward him. "You are wounded."

Srog nodded, dropping to one knee again, the pain excruciating, feeling weak.

Matus ran over and grabbed his arm.

"You're lucky to be alive," Matus said in a rush. "Everyone else in the castle is dead. I'm alive only because I'm an Upper Islander. They will kill you. You must get to safety!"

"What are you doing here, Matus?" Srog said, weak. "They will murder you if they find you helping me. Go. Save yourself."

Matus shook his head.

"No," he said. "I will not leave you."

Suddenly, there came a thumping at the door, the sound of men trying to break in.

Matus turned and looked at Srog, fear in his eyes.

"We have no time. We must get out! Now!"

"I will stand and fight," Srog said.

Matus shook his head.

"There are too many outside that door. You will be a dead man. Live, and fight another day. Follow me."

Srog finally conceded, for Matus's sake, wanting the boy to live and knowing he could not fight himself.

They ran across the room to the secret passage hidden in the stone wall, Matus feeling the wall with his hands. He finally found one stone slightly looser than the others, pulled at it, and as he did, a narrow opening appeared in the stone, just wide enough for the men to enter.

The banging grew louder on the door, and Matus grabbed Srog, as Srog hesitated.

"You'll do no good to Gwendolyn dead," Matus said.

Srog relented and allowed Matus to drag him inside, both of them concealed in the blackness, as the stone wall closed behind them. As it did, there came a crash behind them, the sound of the door bursting open, of dozens of men rushing into the room. They continued on, deeper into the passageway, Matus leading them to safety, Srog limping along, not knowing how much longer he would live—and knowing that the Upper Islands, and the Ring, would never be the same again.

CHAPTER THIRTY-SIX

Gwendolyn sat in her father's former study, scrolling through yet another pile of scrolls, wading her way through kingdom business. Gwen loved to spend her time here in her father's study, where she felt connected to him. She would spend countless days in here as a young girl, its dark walls lined with ancient, precious books he had gathered from all corners of the kingdom, as if keeping her company. Indeed, when she'd rebuilt King's Court, she had made sure to make this study a focal point, and had it restored to its former splendor. It was more beautiful now than it had ever been, and Gwen would have loved to see her father's face after she had restored it. She knew he would have been thrilled.

Gwen looked back at the scrolls, and she tried to get back to the work of running her kingdom, tried to force things back to normal. Yet she knew that things were nowhere near normal. She could hardly concentrate, she felt shaky inside and overwhelmed with grief, images of Thor's departure, or Selese's death, flashing through her mind.

Gwen finally set the scrolls down. She rubbed her eyes and massaged her temples, sighing, eyes blurred from so much reading. The business of the Ring was endless, and no matter how many scrolls she waded through, there were always more yet to come. It was late in the day, she had been up all night with Guwayne, and she felt more alone than ever with Thor gone. She was not thinking clearly these days, and she needed a break.

Gwen rose from her father's desk and walked through the tall, open-air arched doorway leading out onto the stone balcony. It was a beautiful summer day, and it felt great to be outdoors as a gentle breeze wafted through, and she breathed deep. She looked down over King's Court, at all the people milling contentedly below. On the surface, all looked well; but inside, Gwen was trembling.

Gwen looked at the huge banners flapping lightly in the wind, which she had ordered to be hung at half-mast in honor of Selese. The funeral still hung heavily in Gwen's mind—as did the cancellation of her own wedding. She felt so shaken from her new friend's death, from her day of joy, which she had been preparing for for moons, being transformed so suddenly into one of grief. Gwen was starting to wonder if anyone would ever stay in her life permanently. She also wondered if she and Thor would ever get married; a part of her wondered if they should just run off and get married alone, somewhere in seclusion, away from the eyes of everyone. She didn't care about the pomp and circumstance; all she wanted was to be married to him.

Gwen herself did not feel like celebrating. She felt sick, hollowed out, from what had happened to Selese. From her brother's grief. From the whole tragic misunderstanding. She could already tell that Reece would never be the same, and that frightened her. A part of her felt that she had lost a brother. She had been close to Reece her whole life, had always appreciated his happy, joyous, carefree manner—and she had never seen him so happy as he had been with Selese.

And yet now, she could see in Reece's eyes that he would never be the same. He blamed himself.

Gwen could not help but feel as if, one by one, people she was close to were being stripped away. She looked into the skies and thought of Thor. She wondered where he was right now. When he would come back for her. *If* he would ever come back.

Thankfully, at least, Gwen had Guwayne. She spent nearly every waking hour with him, holding him close, valuing so much the precious gift of life. She found herself crying for no reason, feeling how fragile life was. She prayed to every god she knew that nothing bad should ever come to him.

For the first time in a while, Gwen felt shaky, vulnerable, unsure what to do next. Her whole life, these past moons, had revolved around her wedding, and now, without warning, it had all changed. Gwen could not help but feel as if the tragedy with Selese was just the beginning, was foreboding awful things to come.

Gwen flinched as there came a sudden pounding on her father's study door, the iron knocker slamming into it and sending a jolt through her body, as if confirming her awful thoughts.

Gwen turned and walked back into the study—yet without waiting for her, the door flew open by itself. In rushed Aberthol, joined by Steffen and several other attendants, their faces stark, urgent, Aberthol clutching a scroll as he raced across her father's study, right for her. Gwen, upon seeing them, felt a pit in her stomach; she knew that whatever it was, it had to be very, very serious. None of these men would enter her father's study uninvited unless it were a matter of life and death.

"My lady," Aberthol said, bowing with the others as he came close, an urgency to his voice. "Forgive my interruption, but I bring news that bears the most urgent haste."

He paused, and Gwen could see that he was hesitating, and she steeled herself for whatever it might be.

"Out with it," she said.

Aberthol swallowed. He held out a scroll with a shaky hand, and Gwen took it.

"It appears that Tirus's eldest son, Falus, has been murdered. He was found dead on his ship this morning. And all facts attest to his murder being by your brother's hand: Reece."

Gwen felt her blood run cold as she heard the news. She clutched the scroll and stared back at Aberthol, not needing to open it, not wanting to read one more scroll. Slowly, his words sank in, as did the ramifications.

"Reece?" Gwen asked, trying to process it all.

Aberthol nodded.

She should have known better. Reece was mad with grief, desperate for vengeance. How stupid of her not to rein him in.

Gwen's mind spun with the implications. Tirus's eldest son dead. She knew that his sons were beloved by the Upper Islanders. She realized that word had probably already spread to them. Who knew what actions they would take? She knew it would not be good, and that whatever followed, it would ruin her efforts to unite the two MacGils.

"There's more, my lady," Aberthol said. "We have received reports that revolts have erupted on the Upper Isles. They have destroyed half of your fleet, my lady. And Tirus has been freed."

"Freed?!" Gwen asked, horrified.

Aberthol nodded.

"It's worse, my lady. They have ambushed Srog's castle, and Srog has been gravely wounded. As we speak he is being held captive. They have sent word that they will kill Srog and destroy the remainder of your fleet, if we do not make amends for the death of Falus."

Gwen's heart was pounding; it was like a nightmare unfolding before her.

"What amends?" she asked.

Aberthol cleared his throat.

"They want Reece to come to the Upper Isles, and to apologize to Tirus personally for the death of Falus. Only then will they release Srog, and make peace."

Gwen involuntarily slammed her fist on her father's table, the same gesture her father used to make when he was upset. She was burning with frustration; all her carefully laid plans were now laid to waste by her brother's impulsive murder of Falus. Now Srog, her trusted emissary, was wounded, captive. Half her fleet destroyed. They were her responsibility, and she felt the guilt weighing on her.

And yet, at the same time, Gwen recalled Argon's prophecy of the invasion of the Ring, and she knew she could not abandon the Upper Isles. She needed a place of refuge, now more than ever. What Reece had unleashed was the worst thing to happen at the worst possible time.

Gwen could not abandon Srog, either. Or her fleet. She had to do whatever it took to make amends, to bring peace to her kingdom. Especially if it only required an apology.

"I want to see my brother," Gwen said coldly, hardening.

Aberthol nodded.

"I knew you would, my lady. He waits outside."

"Bring him in," she ordered. "And the rest of you, leave us."

Aberthol and the others bowed and hurried from the room.

As they walked out, Reece came in, alone, his eyes bloodshot, looking cold and hard and mad with grief, looking nothing like the brother Gwen had known her whole life.

"Close the door behind you," Gwen commanded, the voice of a Queen, not of a sister, as cold and hard as Reece's features.

Reece reached out and slammed the arched oak door to their father's study, and Gwen walked forward as he walked over to greet her.

As they neared each other, Gwen, furious with Reece for getting her kingdom into this mess, reached up and smacked Reece hard across the face. It was the first time in her life she had done so, and the sound echoed in the room.

Reece stared back, shocked.

"How dare you defy me!" Gwen said to him, fury in her voice.

Reece stared back, and his shock morphed to anger, his cheeks turning red.

"I never defied you!"

"No?!" she cried out. "Do you think that killing our cousin—a royal MacGil, Tirus's son, one of the de facto leaders of the Upper Isles—was something that you were at liberty to do freely, without my command?"

"He deserved it—and more!"

"I don't care if he deserved it!" Gwen yelled, her face burning with anger. "I have a kingdom to rule! There are many men who deserve to die each day whom I don't kill. You have that luxury—I don't."

"Will you then sacrifice what is just for what is political?" he asked.

"Do not speak to me of justice," Gwen said. "Many of our men—good men—died on the Upper Isles today because of your actions. Was that justice for them?"

"Then we shall kill the people who killed them, too."

Gwen shook her head, frustrated beyond belief.

"You may be a good warrior," she said, "but you do not know how to rule a kingdom."

"You should be taking my side," Reece protested. "You are my sister—"

"I am your *Queen*," Gwen corrected.

Reece's face fell in surprise.

They stood there, facing off in the silence, Gwen breathing hard, feeling sleep-deprived, feeling overwhelmed with conflicting emotions.

"What you have done affects the state, affects the Ring, affects the security of us all," she continued. "Srog is wounded.

He is held now at the point of death. Half of my fleet has been destroyed. That means hundreds more of our men have been killed. All for your hasty actions."

Reece reddened, too.

"I did not start this war," he said, "*they* did. Falus had it coming. He betrayed me; he betrayed us all."

"*You* betrayed you," Gwen corrected. "Falus did not murder her. He merely brought her news. News which contained a partial truth, due to your actions. It may have been duplicitous, and deserving of punishment, or even death, but you must acknowledge your role in this. And you must realize that punishment is not yours to mete out—certainly not without checking with me."

Gwendolyn turned and stormed across the room, needing to clear her mind.

She reached her father's desk, leaned over, and threw off all the books, sending them down to the floor with a great crash, a cloud of dust rising up. She shouted in frustration.

In the tense silence that lingered, Reece not moving, watching her, Gwen sighed and marched to the window, looking out, taking a deep breath, trying to remain calm. A part of her knew that Reece was right. She hated the MacGils, too. And she loved Selese. In fact, a part of her admired what her brother had done. She was glad Falus was dead.

But as Queen, what she wanted or admired did not matter; she had to balance the lives of many.

"I don't understand you," Reece said finally, breaking the silence. "You loved Selese as much as I. Didn't you, too, crave vengeance for her death?"

"I loved her as a friend," Gwen replied, calmer. "And as a sister-in-law."

She sighed.

"But as a Queen, I must balance vengeance with judgment. I do not kill one man to have hundreds of other men killed. Nor can I allow you to do so—brother or not."

She stood there, leaning over, lowering her head, her mind swarming.

"You have put me in an impossible position," she said. "I cannot allow Srog to be killed—or any of my other men. What's more, the rest of my fleet are valuable, and I cannot abandon the Upper Isles, which I need now, more than ever, for reasons you do not know."

She sighed, thinking it all over.

"I am left with only one solution," she said, turning to her brother. "You will travel to the Upper Isles at once and apologize to Tirus."

Reece gasped.

"I will NEVER!" he exclaimed.

Gwen hardened.

"YES YOU WILL!" Gwen shouted back, twice as loud, her face bright red. It was a shout that terrified even her, the voice of a hardened Queen, a powerful woman. It was the voice of her father coursing through her.

Yet Reece, her brother, carried the voice of her father, too. They stood there in their father's study, each facing off with the strength of their parents, each equally strong-willed.

"If you do not," she said, "I will have you imprisoned for your illegal actions."

Reece looked at her, and his face fell in disbelief.

"Imprison me? Your brother? For executing justice?"

He stared back at her with a look that pained her, a look that said that she had betrayed him.

"You are my brother," she said, "but you are my subject first. You will do as I say. Leave my sight. And do not return to me until you have apologized."

Reece, mouth open in shock, pain and anguish etched across his face, stared back, speechless. She wished she could summon compassion for him, but she had too little of it left to go around.

Slowly, Reece turned, walked to the door as if in a trance, opened it, and slammed it behind him.

Gwen stood there in that echoing silence, wishing she were anywhere in the world but here, and wishing she were anyone else in the world, anyone, but Queen.

CHAPTER THIRTY-SEVEN

Erec galloped on his fine white horse, Alistair on the back of it behind him, her hands clasped around his waist, and never feeling as content as he did at this moment. Here he was, journeying south, toward his homeland, Alistair with him, and finally, after all these years, about to return to his homeland, to be reunited with his family. Erec could not wait to introduce Alistair to his family, his people, and to become wed to her. Meeting Alistair had been the greatest thing that ever happened to him, and he couldn't imagine being apart from her, even for a minute. He was overjoyed that she had decided to come with him.

As they rode further and further south as they had been doing for days, Erec could feel the air getting heavy with moisture, could smell the ocean air, and he knew they were getting closer to the southern shore. His heart quickened. He knew that just around the bend would be the cliffs, the ocean, the ship waiting for him, to take them to his homeland. Erec hadn't been there since he was a boy, and he was brimming with excitement. He missed his family dearly, and most of all, he ached to see his father before he died. He hoped they arrived in time.

As Erec rode, he felt mixed emotions about the Ring. After all, the Ring had become his home. He had been taken in here as a young boy, had risen to become the greatest knight of the realm, and King MacGil had been like a second father to him. He had been taken in and raised in King's Court as if it were his own home. He had been raised with the brotherhood of the Silver, and behind him, Erec could hear the clang of their spurs, a dozen of them accompanying him even now as a gesture of respect. They were true brothers to him. A part of him felt guilty to leave their side, to leave the Ring unprotected.

Yet at the same time, Erec knew he was leaving the Ring in fine hands, with Kendrick and all the others still here to protect it. He also knew the Ring was stronger than it had ever been, with all its forts and castles repaired, the canyon protected, the Shield up, bridges and keeps strengthened. And most of all, Ralibar to watch over it. Leaving was painful, but at least Erec could be confident the Ring was impregnable—and if there was ever a time to return to his homeland, now, with his father dying, and his vow to marry Alistair among his people, the time had come.

Finally, they crested a ridge, and they all stopped and looked out at the vista before them. Erec looked out and saw the dramatic rolling waves of the Southern Ocean, and looked straight down and saw, way down the cliffs below, huge clouds of foam spraying into the air, as waves crashed against the shore. The Southern Ocean.

Erec scanned the shores, expecting to see, waiting for him on the shore below, the huge ship with the towering white sails that would take him home.

Yet, as all the knights stopped beside him, Erec looked down, perplexed.

His ship was missing from the shoreline.

Erec, stumped, scanned the shoreline up and down.

"It cannot be," he said to himself.

"What is it, my lord?" one of the knights asked.

"Our ship," he said. "It is not here."

Erec sat on his horse, wondering what had happened, how this could be. There was no way home without it. Would they have to turn around?

He knew there was only one way to find out: they'd have to ride down below and see for themselves.

Erec kicked his horse, and they galloped down the steep cliffs, taking winding pathways cut into the rock, weaving around and around until finally they reached the shore line below.

They rode on the sand all the way to the water's edge, and Erec looked left and right, searching for any sign of them. In the distance, to his left, he did see another ship. But it flew different color sails, black and green, which he did not recognize. It was not his.

"I don't understand," Erec said. "It was the ship my father sent. They were supposed to meet us here. I don't know what could have happened."

"Gone!" boomed out a voice.

Erec turned to see a large man with a stubbly chin and a receding hairline, who looked like he was once a warrior, but was now past his prime. He marched out from behind a cliff, flanked by several men in ragged clothes, sailors, and they all headed right toward Erec.

"They left three days ago!" the man boomed again, as he got closer. "They waited, then must have decided you weren't coming. They went back to wherever it was they came from. Apparently, you're late."

"Because we took a different route," one of the knights said to Erec. "Back at that fork."

Erec shook his head.

"We are only three days late," he said. "They should have waited."

"Another group arrived yesterday," the man said, "and they paid more. They had a customer. And they took it."

Erec reddened.

"They gave my father their word. Is there no honor anymore?" he asked aloud, to himself.

"Where are you going?" the man asked, walking closer, lighting a pipe. "That is my ship," he added, gesturing over his shoulder to the other ship on the shore. "Maybe I can take you there."

Erec looked the man up and down suspiciously. He did not get a good feeling. He then looked out to the man's ship. It was clearly past its prime. It looked dirty, worn out, and even from here, seemed to be peopled with crude types.

"I depart for the Southern Isles," Erec said. "My homeland, my father, the King, awaits us."

"For the right price, I'll take you," the man said.

"For the right price?" one of Erec's knights said, stepping forward on his horse. "Do you not know to whom you speak? This is Erec, the champion of the Silver. You will speak to him with the greatest respect."

The man looked back, expressionless, unfazed, as he sucked calmly on his pipe.

"Silver or not, everyone has a price," the man said calmly. "I am a businessman. And chivalry earns me nothing."

Erec looked back out at the ship, wondering. He sighed, realizing his options were few. He had to see his dying father.

"Money is not an issue," Erec said. "What I care about is the safety of your ship. I will not endanger my wife upon a leaky ship."

The man grinned and gave Alistair a look which Erec did not like.

"My ship is the safest at sea. Don't let its appearance fool you. One sack of gold, and the voyage is yours. If not," he said, tipping his hat, "a pleasure doing business with you."

"An entire sack!" one of Erec's knights called out. "That is exorbitant!"

Erec looked the man up and down, and thought hard. This was not what he wanted. But there was no other option. He had to see his father before he died.

Erec reached into his waist, grabbed a sack of gold, and threw it to the man. It hit the man in the chest, and he caught it, opened it, and grinned.

"There is your fee, and more," Erec said. "Get us there quickly. And safely."

The man bowed low, grinning wide.

Erec turned, dismounted, helped Alistair down, and embraced his brothers.

"Protect the Ring," Erec said.

They embraced him back.

"We shall see you again soon, my lord," they answered.

"Yes, you shall."

Erec took Alistair's hand, and together they walked off down the shore, following the raggedy group of men. Deep in his gut, Erec knew that something was awry, but he could not figure out what. As he walked to the ship, holding Alistair's hand firmly, he turned and looked back and saw his men had already ridden off. He looked back up to the huge ship before them, looming ever closer, and wondered if he had just made the biggest mistake of his life.

CHAPTER THIRTY-EIGHT

Luanda immersed herself in the cold spring, alone, high up in the mountains of the Highlands, as was her habit every morning. She ran the cold water through her hair, now grown back fully, and the icy feel on her scalp made her feel alive, awake. It reminded her of where she was. She was not home; she was in a foreign land. On the wrong side of the Highlands. An exile. And she would never return home. The cold water reminded her, as it did every morning, and in some ways, she had come to enjoy it. It was her way of reminding herself of what her life had become.

It was empty up here in these mountain springs, surrounded by thick summer woods and leaves, and covered in a morning mist. And despite hating everything about this side of the Highlands, Luanda had to admit that she'd actually grown to like it here, in this spot that no one else knew about. She had discovered it accidentally one day, on one of her long hikes, and had come here every day since.

As Luanda slowly emerged from the water, she dried herself with the thin wool towel she had brought, and then, as was her habit every morning, she took the long branch of herbs the apothecary had given her, and relieved herself on it. She placed the herbs on a rock in the sunlight, beside the water, and waited. She closely watched their green color, as she had every day for moons, waiting and hoping they would turn white. If they did, the apothecary told her, it meant she was with child.

Every morning Luanda had stood there, drying off, and had watched the long, curved leaves—and every morning she had been disappointed. She had now given up hope; now, it was just a matter of routine.

Luanda was beginning to realize that she would never get pregnant. Her sister would beat her in this, too. Life would be cruel to her in this way, too, as it had in every other way.

Luanda leaned over the water and stared at her reflection. The perfectly still waters reflected the summer sky, the clouds, the two suns, and Luanda reflected on the twists and turns life had thrown her. Had anyone ever really loved her in her life? She wasn't certain anymore. She knew she loved Bronson, though, and that he loved her back. Perhaps that should be enough, with or without child.

Luanda gathered her things and prepared to leave, and as an afterthought, she glanced at the branch lying on the rock.

She stopped cold as she did, holding her breath.

She could not believe it: there, in the sun, the branch had turned white.

Luanda gasped. She raised her hand to her mouth, afraid to reach out for it. She lifted it with shaking hands, examined it every which way. It was white. Snow white. As it had never been before.

Luanda, despite herself, started crying. She gushed with tears, overwhelmed with emotion. She reached down and held her stomach, and felt reborn, felt overwhelmed with joy and happiness. Finally, life had taken a turn in her favor. Finally, she would have everything that Gwendolyn had.

Luanda turned and raced from the spring, through the forest, back down the ridge. In the distance she could already see the fort that held her husband. She ran at full speed, tears streaming down her face, tears of joy. She could hardly wait to tell him the news. For the first time she could remember, she was happy.

She was truly happy.

*

Luanda burst into the castle hall, raced past the guards, took the spiral stone stairs three at a time. Out of breath, she ran and ran, dying to see Bronson. She couldn't wait to see his reaction. He, Bronson, the man she had come to love more than anything in the world, who had himself come to want a child so badly.

Finally, their dreams had come true. Finally, they would be a family. A family of their own.

Luanda burst down the hall and hurried through the tall arched doors, not even noticing that there were no guards there, that the door was already ajar, not perceiving anything she normally did. She hurried into the room and stopped short.

She was confused. Something was wrong.

The world started to move in slow motion around Luanda as she looked about the room, and there, on the cold stone floor, beside the door, she noticed two bodies. They were Bronson's guards. Both dead.

Before she could register the horror of it, Luanda noticed, lying there, toward the back of the room, another body. She recognized his clothing immediately: Bronson. Lying still, on his back. Not moving. His eyes opened wide, staring at the ceiling.

Luanda felt her entire body shake violently, as if someone had split her in two. She stumbled forward, her knees going weak, and collapsed to the floor, landing on top of her husband's body.

She clutched Bronson's cold hands and looked down at his blue face, at the stab wounds all over his body. And slowly, but surely, it all sank in.

Her husband. The one thing she still loved in the world. The father of her child. Dead.

Assassinated.

"NO!" Luanda wailed, again and again, shaking Bronson, as if somehow that would bring him back. She wept and wept, clutching him, her body convulsing, wracked with tears.

Luanda needed someone, something, to blame. There were the McClouds, of course, who had done this, and who she wanted to murder. If only Bronson had listened to her, if only he had not set them free.

But that wasn't enough. She needed to blame someone else. The person behind all this.

In her mind, Luanda settled on one person: her sister.

Gwendolyn.

It was her fault. Her policies; her stupid naïveté; it had all led to her husband's death. She had ruined everything. She had not only taken away her life, but the life of the one person she loved in the world.

Luanda shrieked, beside herself, determined. Now, with Bronson's death, there was nothing left for her in the world. All that remained was for her to instill in everyone else the same suffering they had instilled in her.

She would do it.

Luanda stood, cold and hard, resolved. She turned and marched from the hall, her heart quickening. She had an idea. Something that would ruin Gwendolyn, once and for all.

And it was time to put it into motion.

CHAPTER THIRTY-NINE

Kendrick, devastated since his encounter with his mother, tried to clear his mind and ease his thoughts on this holy day, as he walked slowly up the mountain face, following the path in smooth, broad circles, hiking with hundreds of Silver and soldiers as they wound their way up the holy mountain, each with a rock in hand. Pilgrimage Day had arrived, one of the holiest days of the year, and as Kendrick did every year, he joined his brothers in arms in the trek to this place. They'd spent the morning immersing in the river, collecting the choicest rocks, then spent the afternoon on the long hike up the mountain, walking slowly, circling its way up, higher and higher.

When they reached the top, the tradition was to place a rock, to kneel, and to pray. To purge themselves of the year's past sins, and to prepare for the year to come. It was a sacred day for all those defending the kingdom. It was considered especially auspicious for a knight to trek with a woman whom he loved. Kendrick had asked Sandara, and she had agreed to come with him. She walked now, by his side, also immersed in silence.

Try as he did, it was hard for Kendrick to shake thoughts of his encounter with his mother. Although hundreds of miles had passed since the encounter, it still hung heavy on his heart. He wished he had never met her; he wished he had never sought her out. Kendrick wished, instead, that he had lived with the mystery his entire life, lived with the fantasy that his mother was someone else. Sometimes, he realized, fantasy was more precious than reality. Fantasy could sustain you, whereas real life could crush you.

"Are you okay, my lord?" Sandara asked.

Kendrick turned and looked at her, interrupted from his thoughts. As always, the sight of her lifted his worries. He loved Sandara more than he could say. So beautiful, so tall, with broad shoulders, dark skin, dark eyes, and the look of the Empire race, so exotic, so different from anyone he'd ever known. He reached out and took her hand as they walked.

"I will be fine," he said.

"I think, my lord, you are still upset from your encounter with your mother," she said.

Kendrick bit his tongue, knowing she was right, but not feeling ready to talk about it.

Sandara sighed.

"My mother was a cold, cruel merciless woman," she said. "She hated me. My father was a great warrior, and kind to everyone. I am not cruel or mean like my mother was. I chose to take on the traits of my father."

He looked at her and saw her staring at him, intensely.

"Don't you see?" she said. "Who your mother, or father, was, does not affect you. You look for yourself in them. But you are yourself. To understand who you are, look to yourself. Be the person you *choose* to be. You choose who you are, you mold yourself every moment of every day."

Kendrick thought of her words as they walked, circling the mountain, and realized she bore great wisdom. It was hard to do, but he had to let go of his parents. He had to discover who he was, himself.

Kendrick felt better already, and he turned and studied her.

"My parents never married," he said. "They didn't spend their life together. I myself do not wish to live this life alone. I wish to be married. To have children who know me. Children who are legitimate. Sandara," Kendrick said, clearing his throat, "I wish to marry you. I know I've asked you before. But I truly want you to think about it. Please."

Sandara looked down to the ground, and her eyes welled with tears.

"I love you, my lord," she replied. "I truly do. But my home is far away. If there were not an ocean between us, yes, I would marry you. But I must return home. To my people. To the Empire. To those I know and love."

"But you are not there," Kendrick said. "You are here now. And your family is enslaved there."

Sandara shrugged.

"True. But I'd rather live a slave in my home than be free and away from my people."

Kendrick could not really understand, but he knew he would have to accept her wishes.

"At least I'm with you now, my lord," she said. "I will not be departing for several days."

Kendrick held Sandara's hand tighter, and he wondered why all the women he cared about in the world had to disappear from him. He knew he should just cherish the time he had with her now. But thinking of her leaving made it hard.

They walked, silently, with hundreds of others, until finally they reached the peak of the mountain. It was solemn up here, quiet, and a sacred feeling hung in the air. Kendrick felt immediately at peace.

Kendrick knelt on the grass of the wide plateau, and along with other knights, placed his rock on the growing mound of rocks. As he did, he bowed his head low.

Please, God, he prayed silently, *do not take this beautiful woman away from me. Allow us to be together. Find some way. I do not wish to part from her.*

Kendrick opened his eyes and slowly stood, surprised at the prayer he chose. He had not been planning it. He usually prayed for the year to come, usually prayed for strength against his enemies, for courage, for valor. But this was the prayer that entered Kendrick's mind, and he did not stop it.

He turned to Sandara, and she smiled back.

"I prayed for you, my lord," she said. "That you find wisdom and peace."

Kendrick smiled back.

"I said a very special prayer, too."

As Kendrick looked over Sandara's shoulder, he detected movement off in the horizon, and suddenly, his smile collapsed. He was confused by what he saw; it made no sense.

Kendrick pushed Sandara aside and studied the horizon with a professional warrior's eye. As he did, his heart beat quicker in his chest.

It couldn't be. There, on the horizon, was a dust cloud, black smoke, and thousands of warriors in armor, charging, heading down the road toward the unguarded King's Court. This was the only day of the year, Pilgrimage Day, when the gates were left open. Of course, Kendrick never thought it would need to be protected. Who on earth could be attacking them when the Ring was so safe and secure?

As Kendrick looked closely, his face flushed red as he recognized the armor of the McClouds. He fumed, mad at himself for not leaving more protection behind. He was a good half day's ride away, and those McClouds were already so close, too close, already overriding the gates.

In moments, Kendrick realized with a shock that his sister, unprotected, would be dead.

Kendrick let out a great battle cry, and all his men turned and saw what he saw, then they all followed suit as Kendrick quickly raced down the mountain, sprinting for his horse, eager to join the fight—but realizing, with a sinking feeling, that it was already too late.

Within moments, everyone he knew and loved would be dead.

CHAPTER FORTY

Godfrey galloped down the endless road, as he had been doing all night, alone, gasping for breath, glancing back over his shoulder for any sign of the McCloud army. He spotted them, as he had throughout his whole ride, raising up a huge cloud of dust on the horizon, no more than a half-hour's ride behind him. Godfrey swallowed hard and kicked his horse harder.

Godfrey knew he had no room for error as he galloped, more exhausted than he'd been in his life, his drunken stupor entirely worn off, and feeling as if he might keel over at any moment. He was sweating, too out of shape for this, the sweat dripping into his eyes, stinging him. A ridge lay before him, and he prayed to all the gods he knew that when he crested it, King's Court would be in sight.

His prayers came true. Finally, in the distance, Godfrey was relieved to see the rebuilt gates of King's Court. As he suspected, they sat wide open, with only but a handful of soldiers standing guard. Of course. It was Pilgrimage Day, and the hundreds of knights who usually stood guard would be away, up on the mountain, and would not return until evening. But by then, Godfrey knew, it would be too late. Everyone would be killed, the entire city ransacked.

Godfrey kicked his horse with fresh determination as he charged at breakneck speed, barely breathing, his heart slamming in his chest.

Finally, as he neared the gates of the city, the few guards before it, young, novice soldiers, stared back at him in surprise, not understanding.

"BAR THE GATES!" Godfrey shouted.

"What?!" one of them called back.

The soldiers looked to each other, puzzled, as if assuming Godfrey were mad. Indeed, Godfrey realized, he probably looked mad, given his appearance, slovenly, sweating, unshaven, hungover, hair in his eyes and having ridden all night.

Godfrey reddened, determined.

"AN ARMY COMES!" he shouted. "CLOSE THOSE GATES OR I'LL KILL YOU MYSELF!"

The soldiers finally looked over Godfrey's shoulder, watching the horizon; at first, they were expressionless, distrusting.

But then, Godfrey watched their eyes open wide in panic, and he realized the McClouds must have crested the ridge.

The soldiers, suddenly frantic, rushed to lower the gate.

"SOUND THE HORNS!" Godfrey shouted, as he rode through the open gates, right before the men lowered them.

The sound of horns filled the city, echoing each other in a chorus. They sounded out in a pattern of threes, the sound for an evacuation of the city, a sound that Godfrey had never heard in his life.

Thousands of civilians emerged quickly from their dwellings, well-disciplined, prepared, hurrying through the city streets, heading in an orderly way for evacuation route throughout the back of the city. Gwendolyn had thought of everything, and had prepared her people well. Godfrey was pleased to see that it was working, and felt an odd feeling, one he'd never felt: it was a feeling of purpose. A feeling of having contributed, of having made a difference. Of being fearless. Of being wanted and needed.

It was a feeling of responsibility. It was foreign to him. And he liked it.

Godfrey, emboldened, charged right for the castle where he knew his sister would be, and as he ran, the attendants threw the doors for him, recognizing him as the Queen's brother.

He did not take the time to dismount, but rather galloped right through the entrance, into the grand hall, and all the way down the corridor until he reached the staircase.

He leapt off his horse, tumbling to the ground, gasping for air, and stumbled for the stairs, taking them three and four at a time, heaving.

Finally, he made it to the upper floor, raced down the corridor, and reached the ancient doors to the Queen's council chamber, the room where their father had sat with his council.

Godfrey did not even pause as the guards tried to block his way; he ran into them with his shoulder, bumping them out of the way, then put a shoulder into the door and crashed it open.

Godfrey stumbled into the room, startling everyone. His sister, on her throne, holding Guwayne, stood, as did the dozens of council members, all staring at him, shocked. Clearly he'd interrupted an important meeting.

"Godfrey," Gwendolyn said, "why are you here? What is the meaning of this—"

"Evacuate now!" Godfrey gasped, breathless. "Have you not heard the horns? We are under attack!"

The room broke into chaos as Gwen and all the councilmen ran to the windows, Gwen clutching her baby, and threw open the newly installed stained glass window panes. As they did, the sound of the horns rushed into the room, as did the sound of commotion and chaos below.

Godfrey joined them, and as they all looked out, their faces fell in a horrified expression. Godfrey, standing beside his sister, could see the McCloud army racing right for their gates.

While panic and fear spread throughout the room, even amongst all these hardened soldiers, Gwen remained calm. She had become a tough leader, Godfrey realized, tougher even than all these men.

"Evacuate at once!" Gwendolyn commanded her men. "Do as my brother says. All of you. Now!"

The councilmen rushed into action, racing from the room. Steffen, though, refused to leave her side, coming up and standing beside her.

Gwen stood holding Guwayne, Steffen the only one left in the room with her, aside from Godfrey.

"You must go with them," Gwen said to Godfrey.

"And what about you?" Godfrey asked, amazed at her calm, at her fearlessness.

Gwen shook her head.

"I will be fine," she said.

Yet Godfrey suspected that she was just being strong; as he looked back, he was inspired by her.

"No," he said, something within him shifting. "I cannot leave. The men will need help guarding the gates."

Gwen shook her head.

"You will die," she said.

"Then I will," Godfrey said. And for the first time, he was unafraid. Truly unafraid.

Gwen must have sensed the change in him, because for the first time in her life, she looked at him differently.

She reached out and laid an approving hand on his shoulder and looked him firmly in the eye.

"Father would be proud of what you've done today," she said.

Godfrey felt himself warming with appreciation and love. It was the first time anyone in his family had ever approved of him, had ever viewed him as anything other than a drunkard.

Godfrey nodded back, his eyes glistening, and gave her one long, last look, hoping he would see his sister again one day. He feared he would not.

"Be well, my sister."

Godfrey turned and sprinted down from the hall, determined, racing down the stairs and out the castle door, and right for the huge front gates of the city. He did not pause as he jumped in and helped a dozen soldiers struggling to close it. He came and put a shoulder into it, and it made a difference; due to him, the groaning iron gate finally closed all the way. As soon as it did, Godfrey helped the men hoist a thick iron bar and wedge it before the bars.

It was not a moment too soon. A few seconds later, the McCloud army reached the gates and slammed into them. They stopped short, unable to crash them.

Godfrey followed the other soldier, rushing up the stairs to the upper level of the fort and grabbing a bow with the others. He knelt and took a place amongst the ramparts with the others. He took aim and fired his first arrow, and it felt good.

He would defend this city. He would not win; in fact, he knew he would die on this day. But that no longer mattered to him; all that he cared about was that he go down in one great act of honor.

CHAPTER FORTY-ONE

Gwendolyn stood on the upper ramparts of her castle, Guwayne in her arms, crying, Steffen beside her, and looked out at the horizon, facing east. Her heart ripped in two as she saw, filling the horizon, rows and rows of black banners, born by McCloud warriors, thousands and thousands of them on horseback, all charging right for King's Court. In the distant horizon behind them, black plumes of smoke rose to the sky, clearly from villages they had already plundered.

It was a river of devastation—and it was heading right for her.

Horns sounded again and again, up and down the castle walls, and below, Gwendolyn's people raced to evacuate King's Court, as she had rehearsed all these moons. The evacuation was more orderly than she had imagined, no doubt because she had planned and rehearsed it so well, and as she looked below, she was satisfied to see that King's Court was now nearly empty, all of her people flocking out through the back gates, onto the endless array of horses and carts that awaited them, to take them, as she had planned, toward the shore, toward a fleet of ships that would take them far away from here, to the Upper Isles. To safety.

There came the sounds of the McClouds slamming into her iron gates, again and again, and as the iron began to give, she looked down and realized the McClouds would destroy her city, everything that she had worked so hard to rebuild.

But they would not kill her people. While Gwen cried inside for what would happen to her city, she at least took satisfaction in knowing her people would not be harmed. The McClouds could have the city and all its riches; but her people would live another day.

"My lady, we haven't much time," Steffen said, beside her.

Gwendolyn scanned the skies, her stomach in knots, and wished now, more than ever, that Thor could be here, by her side, could arrive with Mycoples, and save them all.

But her husband-to-be was long gone, in some land far away, and who knew if he would ever return.

Thor, she prayed. *Return to me. I need you.*

Gwen closed her eyes, and silently, she willed for him to return. She also willed for Ralibar to appear. Deep down, though, she sensed he would not. Mycoples's departure had done something to him, and she had not seen him since. It was as if he had fallen into some sort of depression; every morning he used to come to her, but now he did not come. She could not help but wonder if maybe he had abandoned her for good.

Gwen opened her eyes, hopeful—but the skies remained empty, filled only with the cries of men engaged in battle below. No Thor. No Ralibar.

She was on her own, once again. She knew, as she had always known, that she would have to rely on herself, and no one else.

"My lady?" Steffen prodded, his voice mounting with alarm.

"I commanded you to go," she said to him.

Steffen shook his head.

"I am sorry, my lady," he said, "but that is one command of yours which I must defy. I will not leave without you."

Guwayne squirmed and cried in her arms, and Gwen looked down and felt all the love she possibly could for her child. She could not stand to leave her city—and yet she knew there wasn't much time to get him to safety.

"This is my home," Gwen said, clinging to this place, hanging on. "My father's home."

Gwen stood watching it all, and she could not stand to leave her city, this place where she was born. After all she had done to rebuild it, it would be at the mercy of these barbarians.

"It is time to find another home," Steffen said.

Gwen searched the skies one last time, hoping for any sign of Thor or Ralibar. She searched the roads, hoping for any sign of the Silver. But the roads, too, were empty. She knew they could not come. They were all far away, deep into their Pilgrimage. The McClouds had timed it well.

Gwen breathed deep, and slowly let it out.

"Let's go," she said.

Gwen turned and, clutching Guwayne, who was now screaming, hurried with Steffen across the ramparts, down the spiral staircase. They soon reached the ground floor of the castle, hurried out the back, and they joined in with the rest of the stream of humanity, all heading out the back gates of King's Court, toward the horses and the carts.

As Gwen and Steffen reached the rear gate of King's Court, Gwen was touched to see that several attendants stood before it, keeping them open, waiting for her. In fact, all of her people were waiting for her, all sitting in their carts, none of them leaving until she appeared.

Gwen was the last person to pass through the gates. As she did, the attendants pulled back the heavy iron gates, slamming them shut with an echoing bang.

Gwen climbed into a waiting carriage with Guwayne, the last carriage to leave King's Court. The driver whipped the horse, and she, and all her people, took off at a gallop.

Gwen turned and looked back over her shoulder as they went, and she watched as King's Court disappeared from view. The sound of those closing gates, of the reverberating metal, echoed through her mind as she watched the city she loved get smaller and smaller, soon, she knew, doomed to become a pile of rubble and ashes. Everything she loved was about to be destroyed.

They were heading for the Upper Isles, for another hostile place, and who knew what sort of life would await them there.

Life, she knew, would never be the same again.

CHAPTER FORTY-TWO

Romulus marched, leading his army through the smoldering forests of the Wilds, the sounds of thousands of boots crunching leaves behind him, the skies filled with the sound of dragons cries above, and he smiled in triumph. Here he was, invincible, having crossed the ocean with a fleet of ships, leading his army, and the dragons, on the last leg of their march, just moments away from reaching the canyon and being able to destroy the Shield. His time for vengeance, for complete control of the world, had come.

As they went, the dragons dove down and rained fire on the Wilds, destroying miles of forest, decimating the creatures that lived on this side of the canyon. The dragons flushed the creatures out of the woods, and hordes of them, shrieking, charged right for Romulus and his men.

Romulus rushed forward, sword held high, and chopped off the head of one wild beast after the next, as all of his men joined in. It was a bloodbath, the men destroying everything in their path like a plague of locusts, killing whatever the dragons had left over. Romulus had not had this much fun since he was a boy.

Romulus marched and marched, feeling victorious, triumphant, prepared for the greatest victory of his life. In moments, he would destroy the Shield, invade the Ring, take King's Court, and murder Gwendolyn. He would have what his predecessors, even Andronicus, never had: complete dominion of the world. He would enslave and torture everyone in sight.

Romulus smiled and breathed deep at the thought. He could almost taste the bloodshed now.

The sorcerer had prophesied that Romulus would destroy the Shield—but he had not specified exactly how. Romulus could only assume that, with all these dragons in his power, their joined force would ram it, destroy it, and lead the way for him to cross the canyon, into the Ring. After all, how could the strength of the Shield stand up to these dragons?

Romulus finally rounded a bend, and as he did, he breathed deep, in awe at the sight which never got old: there, before him, was the vast canyon, its mists rising up, luring him to approach. There was his destiny.

Romulus marched right up to the edge of the canyon crossing, the vast bridge spanning the two worlds, and as he did, he looked up to the skies and waited. He closed his eyes and commanded his host of dragons to race forward, right for the invisible Shield.

He opened his eyes and watched as they all flew overhead, right for the gaping canyon, his heart pounding with excitement. He braced himself for the destruction. For his moment.

But as Romulus watched, he was shocked to see all the dragons slam into the invisible wall and bounce back. The dragons shrieked in fury, circled around, and bounced into it again and again and again.

But they could not get past the Shield.

Romulus stood there, baffled, crushed with disappointment. How could the Shield possibly withstand the power of all these dragons? He was meant to enter the Ring. It had been prophesied. What had gone wrong?

Romulus, burning with frustration, knew he had to test the Shield another way. He reached over, grabbed one of his men, and hurled him into the invisible Shield.

The man flew into it face first and as he did, he shrieked as he was eviscerated, burning up, landing in a pile of ashes at their feet.

Romulus fumed. It couldn't be. What had gone wrong? Had he been led astray? Would he have to turn back, in humiliation, once again? The thought was too much for him to bear.

It made no sense. He was lord of the dragons. There was nothing on this planet—nothing—that should be able to stop him.

Romulus stood and stared, the mainland of the Ring looking so far away. As he stared, all of his hopes and dreams began to melt. For the first time, his sense of unstoppable power began to feel shaken. What was he missing?

As Romulus stood waiting, watching, realizing with humiliation he would have to turn around, abandon his plans once and for all, suddenly, slowly, something appeared in the distance. It was a woman. She walked slowly, on the far side of the canyon, and stepped foot onto the bridge.

She moved tentatively at first, one step at a time. She held her arms out to her side, and with each step she took, she came a little bit closer. Romulus recognized her.

Could it be? Were his eyes playing tricks on him?

It made no sense. A woman was voluntarily crossing the bridge, toward his side of the Ring. A woman he recognized. The one and only woman he needed most in the world:

Luanda.

CHAPTER FORTY-THREE

Luanda stood before the vast bridge spanning the canyon, and with a cold, hardened heart, numb to the world, she looked out at the sight before her. On the far side of the canyon, in the land of the Wilds, there were thousands of Empire soldiers, led by Romulus, standing there, hoping to cross. Above them hovered a host of dragons, screaming, flapping their wings against the invisible Shield that held them out. Romulus himself stood before the far end of the bridge, hands on his hips, watching.

Luanda felt ready to end it all as she took her first step onto the bridge, all alone, with nothing left to live for. A gust of wind met her in the face, icy despite the summer day, matching her mood. With Bronson dead, Luanda was cold, embittered, her heart dead inside. She knew there was a baby in her stomach, but now it was a cruel joke, a baby without a father, a baby doomed by fate. What other cruel tricks would life have for her? Would it take her baby from her, too?

It was time, she felt, to leave this world. To leave this Ring. To leave this planet.

But before she did, she first, more than anything, felt a burning desire for vengeance on Gwendolyn. She felt a need to wreak destruction on Gwendolyn and the MacGils, on her former family, on King's Court, and everything good left in the Ring. She wanted them all to suffer, to know what suffering felt like, as she had. She wanted them to know what it felt like to be an outcast, an exile.

Luanda, numb, took another step onto the bridge. Then another.

She knew that Romulus wanted her to cross. She knew she was the key. She knew that when she crossed to the other side, the Shield would lower. Romulus would enter the Ring with his men and his dragons, and he would crush it forever. And that was exactly what she wanted. It was the only thing left that she wanted.

Luanda took another step, then another. Halfway across the bridge, she closed her eyes and held her arms out wide, held her palms out to her side. She continued to walk, eyes closed, leaning her head back, up to the heavens.

Luanda thought of her dead father, her dead mother. Her dead husband. She thought of all that she had once loved, and how far away all of it was for her now.

She felt the world move beneath her feet, heard the cry of the dragons, smelled the cool moisture of the swirling mists, and she knew that in just moments, she would be across, in Romulus's arms. Surely, he would kill her. But that no longer mattered.

All that mattered was that she had not been there in time to spare her husband from death.

Please, Bronson, she prayed. *Forgive me.*

Forgive me.

CHAPTER FORTY-FOUR

Reece, on the Upper Isles, in Tirus's castle, walked slowly down the long, red carpeted aisle leading to a massive throne—atop which sat Tirus. Inside, Reece was burning up with emotion, hardly able to believe he was here. The vast chamber was packed with hundreds of Tirus's loyal subjects, his men in arms lined up on either side of the room, along with hundreds of Upper Islanders, all packed into the hall to witness the moment. To witness Reece's apology.

Reece walked slowly, feeling hundreds of eyes on him, taking each step deliberately. He looked in the distance and saw Tirus staring down at him triumphantly, clearly relishing the moment. The tension was so thick it could be cut with a knife. With each step Reece took, his spurs jingled, the only sound in a room completely frozen in silence.

Gwendolyn had sent Reece here on this humiliating mission, to bring a truce between the two MacGils, to unite the Upper Isles, to fulfill her greater agenda, whatever that was. He loved and respected his sister more than anything, and he knew that she needed this. She needed this for her whole kingdom, for the Ring, for her loyal subject, Srog, who was injured, and whom Reece could see even now, bound beside Tirus, along with his cousin, Matus. Reece's apology would free them both. It would bring a truce between the kingdoms. It would help Gwendolyn's greater plan, would unite the Upper Isles. And it would free the other half of Gwendolyn's fleet held hostage in the rocks below, and the thousands of sailors aboard, surrounded by Tirus's men. Reece knew what had to be done, however much his pride told him otherwise.

With every step Reece took, he thought of Selese. He thought of the vengeance he had carried out on Falus. It was satisfying. But it would never bring Selese back to him. It would never change what had happened to her. For Reece, it was just the beginning. He wanted to kill them all, every single Upper Islander in this room. And Tirus, most of all. The very man he was being forced to apologize to.

Reece came closer, ever closer, to Tirus, still seated on his throne. Reece began to mount the ivory steps leading up to it, one at a time, ascending higher and higher, closer to him. He felt everyone watching, all the arrogant and smug Upper Islanders relishing this historic moment, the moment that a true and honest warrior would be forced to kneel and apologize to a traitorous, lying pig.

Reece burned at the thought of how politics forced one to act; to betray one's morals; to betray one's sense of right. It forced one to compromise principles, even integrity, for the sake of the greater good. But weren't principles and integrity in and of themselves the greater good? What did one have without them?

Reece understood Gwen's decisions. They were the decisions of a wise and tempered ruler. But being a ruler, if that's what it meant, was something Reece wanted nothing to do with. He would rather be a warrior than a ruler any day. He would rather have limited power and live his life to the highest integrity, than have the greatest power and have to compromise who he was.

Reece finished ascending, taking the final step and standing before Tirus, staring back defiantly as Tirus stared at him.

The tension was so thick in the room, so palpable in the air, Reece could almost feel it.

"You have taken one of my sons from me," Tirus said, his voice cold, hard. "Murdered him in cold blood."

"And he had taken my wife from me," Reece countered, equally somber.

261

Tirus frowned.

"She was not your wife," he replied. "Not yet, anyway. And he did not murder her. She killed herself."

Reece scowled.

"She took her own life because of the false reports your son gave her. It was he who murdered her."

"He did not wield the blade," Tirus said.

"He wielded a message," Reece countered, "which is stronger than a blade."

Tirus reddened, clearly fed up.

"Your act is deserving of death," he concluded. "But as an act of mercy to Gwendolyn, I have chosen to allow you to live. All you need do is apologize. Kneel, and apologize for taking my son's life."

Reece felt himself burning with every conflicting emotion, everything inside of him screaming out that it was wrong. *All* of this was wrong. It might be good politics, but it went against a knight's code of honor. Tirus's son deserved to die. Tirus himself deserved to die, this pig who had betrayed the Ring, who had partnered with Andronicus and had tried to murder them all.

Yet, despite every ounce of his body protesting, Reece slowly, painfully, forced himself to take a knee before Tirus.

Tirus smiled, relishing the moment.

"Very good," he said. "Now—apologize. And make it good."

"I apologize…" Reece began, then trailed off, the words catching in his throat.

Tirus glared down, impatient.

"For what?" Tirus demanded.

Reece felt himself overpowered with emotion, with passion, unable to contain it. The whole world became a blur, his mind swirling. He felt as if his entire life had led him to this one moment in time. As if all destiny had converged, right here. The moment in his life where all paths met, the intersection between what was wise and what was *right*.

Reece raised his head, looked up, and stared Tirus right in the eye.

"I apologize…" he continued, "…for not taking your life, too."

As he spoke the words, Reece reached down, grabbed a dagger from his belt, lunged forward, and, before Tirus or anyone else could react, he plunged it into Tirus's heart.

Tirus let out an awful shriek as Reece leaned in close, scowling, holding the dagger still. Reece knew he had just signed his death sentence; he knew he was utterly surrounded, and was about to be killed by everyone in that room. He knew he had just set the Ring into a tailspin, a civil war, that countless thousands of men would meet their deaths.

But he no longer cared. He had done what was *right*. His beloved Selese was avenged. Honor was restored. Chivalry was alive. No matter what happened, he would die with honor.

"Greetings," Reece said, "from Selese."

NOW AVAILABLE!

A REIGN OF STEEL
(BOOK #11 IN THE SORCERER'S RING)

"A breathtaking new epic fantasy series. Morgan Rice does it again! This magical sorcery saga reminds me of the best of J.K. Rowling, George R.R. Martin, Rick Riordan, Christopher Paolini and J.R.R. Tolkien. I couldn't put it down!"
--Allegra Skye, Bestselling author of SAVED

In A REIGN OF STEEL, Gwendolyn must protect her people as she finds King's Court under siege. She strives to evacuate them from the Ring—but there is one problem: her people refuse to leave. As a power struggle ensues, Gwen finds her queenship under challenge for the first time—while the greatest threat to the Ring looms.

Behind the McClouds lie the threat of Romulus and his dragons, who, with the Shield destroyed, embark on a catastrophic invasion, nothing left to stand between them and the complete annihilation of the Ring. Romulus, with Luanda at his side, is unstoppable while the moon lasts, and Gwen must fight for survival—for herself, for her baby, and for her people—amidst an epic battle of dragons, and of men. Kendrick leads the Silver in a valiant battle, and he is joined by Elden and the new Legion recruits, along with his brother Godfrey, who surprises everyone, including himself, with his acts of valor. But even so, it may not all be enough.

Thor, meanwhile, embarks on the quest of his life in the Land of the Druids, trekking across a fearsome and magical land, a land unlike any other, with magical rules out of its own. Crossing this land will require every ounce of strength and training he has, will force him to dig deeper within, to become the great warrior—and Druid—he was meant to be. As he encounters monsters and challenges unlike ever before, he will have to lay down his life to try to reach his mother.

Erec and Alistair journey to the Southern Isles, where they are greeted by all of his people, including his competitive brother and envious sister. Erec has a dramatic final meeting with his father, as the island prepares for him to ascend the throne as King. But in the Southern Isles, one must fight for the right to be King, and in an epic battle, Erec will be tested as never before. In a dramatic twist, we learn that treachery hides even here, in this place of noble and great warriors.

Reece, embattled and surrounded on the Upper Isles, must fight for his life after his vengeance on Tirus. Desperate, he finds himself united with Stara, each wary of the other, yet untied in a quest to survive—one that will culminate in an epic battle at sea and will threaten the entire island.

Will Gwen cross the sea to safety? Will Romulus destroy the Ring? Will Reece and Stara be together? Will Erec rise as King? Will Thor find his mother? What will become of Guwayne? Will anyone be left alive?

With its sophisticated world-building and characterization, A REIGN OF STEEL is an epic tale of friends and lovers, of rivals and suitors, of knights and dragons, of intrigues and political machinations, of coming of age, of broken hearts, of deception, ambition and betrayal. It is a tale of honor and courage, of fate and destiny, of sorcery. It is a fantasy that brings us into a world we will never forget, and which will appeal to all ages and genders.

About Morgan Rice

Morgan is author of the #1 Bestselling THE SORCERER'S RING, a new epic fantasy series, currently comprising eleven books and counting, which has been translated into five languages. The newest title, A REIGN OF STEEL (#11) is now available!

Morgan Rice is also author of the #1 Bestselling series THE VAMPIRE JOURNALS, comprising ten books (and counting), which has been translated into six languages. Book #1 in the series, TURNED, is now available as a FREE download!

Morgan is also author of the #1 Bestselling ARENA ONE and ARENA TWO, the first two books in THE SURVIVAL TRILOGY, a post-apocalyptic action thriller set in the future.

Among Morgan's many influences are Suzanne Collins, Anne Rice and Stephenie Meyer, along with classics like Shakespeare and the Bible. Morgan lives in New York City.

Please visit www.morganricebooks.com to get exclusive news, get a free book, contact Morgan, and find links to stay in touch with Morgan via Facebook, Twitter, Goodreads, the blog, and a whole bunch of other places. Morgan loves to hear from you, so don't be shy and check back often!